AN INCONVENIENT DEATH

A JOE BOYD SUSPENSE NOVEL - BOOK 2

DAN WALSH

BAINBRIDGE PRESS

PRAISE FOR DAN'S JACK TURNER
SUSPENSE NOVELS

When Night Comes (Book 1)

"Though Walsh steps into a different genre, fans will not be disappointed. He continues to infuse historical facts into his books, bringing history to life in this character-driven tale. The pace quickens as events unfold, making it challenging for the reader to predict the twists and turns." – *RT Book Reviews, 4.5 Stars*

"Dan Walsh surprises with his new novel, *When Night Comes.* This engrossing mystery/thriller is a break from his normal superb Christian fiction and proves Walsh is more than one-dimensional." – *New York Journal of Books*

Remembering Dresden (Book 2)

"Few authors can straddle multiple genres successfully but Dan Walsh is proving he is in that elite group as he releases his second suspense novel...Remembering Dresden gripped me from start to finish. Once again, Walsh weaves together historical and contemporary events, resulting in a compelling tale...He fills the book with believable personalities well-suited to the story, as well as a plethora of heart-wrenching and heart-pounding moments, making it impossible to set aside." *– Mocha with Linda Blog*

"Walsh has another suspense-filled hit, proving that his flair for an engaging tome spans genres. History buffs will love his latest, which could be read as a standalone, though it is second in the series. The past and present scenes seamlessly blend together to create a fast-paced, intriguing story which will leave readers anticipating the third book."
  – RT Book Reviews Magazine, 4.5 Stars/Top Pick!

(Also Available, Books 3 and 4 of the Jack Turner Suspense Series, and Book 1 of the Joe Boyd Suspense Series)

For a look at these and more of Dan's books, go to Amazon and type "Dan Walsh Books," or visit his website at:

http://danwalshbooks.com/books/

COPYRIGHT INFO

An Inconvenient Death
  Joe Boyd Suspense Series – Book 2
  Bainbridge Press
  Editor - Cindi Walsh
  ISBN: 978-1-7341417-3-3
  Copyright © 2020 Dan Walsh

1

Lt. Joe Boyd really needed this trip.

"This looks like as good a spot as any," Joe said, although on this excursion he was going more by *Hon* or *Dad*.

"Nice and flat," Kate said. "And I like all the shady trees. You need my help backing the pop-up into place?"

"No, think I'm finally getting the hang of this." Seemed like it took him forever to get his mind around backing this camper up. He kept wanting to turn it the way you would a car, but to get it to go the direction you wanted you had to turn the steering wheel in the opposite direction.

"Don't want you backing into a tree," Kate said.

"I'll be fine. You and the kids can start setting up lunch on that picnic table over there."

From the back seat of their SUV, Joe Jr. said, "Maybe I should take Chance for a walk. He's acting like he's gotta go." Chance was the latest addition to the Boyd family, a mostly-

Beagle pup they picked up at the Humane Society a few weeks back.

"Mom, it's my turn to walk him," Kristen said.

"You can do it twice in a row next time," Kate said. "I need your help getting lunch set up."

"Remember that, Joey," said Kristin. "Twice in a row next time."

"Know where Jack and Rachel are?" Kate said.

Joe looked toward the woods in the direction they came. "Thought they were right behind us. Must-a got stuck at a light. I'm sure they'll turn up soon. He knows where we are."

He put the SUV in park. Everyone but him got out, including the dog. Kate and Kristin muscled the red cooler over to the picnic table. Joe waited till he saw Joe, Jr. off to the right by the edge of the woods walking Chance, before he started backing up. Took him a few tries to get the pop-up squared away, but he got there. At this point, he had the rest of the set-up routine down pat. He could get the pop-up ready to use in just under twenty minutes.

As he worked, he kept his eye on Joe Jr. "Hey Joey, don't you go wandering off."

"I won't."

Chance's little nose was hugging the ground, tail straight up in the air. "And you keep a firm hand on that leash. That little guy likes us, but he gets hold of the scent of some nearby animal, and off he goes."

"I know," Joey said. "I got 'im."

Joe kept on working, getting the thing balanced then he cranked up the top and pushed out the sides, lowered the front stairs, set up the front door. Right then, he heard the sound of Jack's new Dodge 1500 Ram pickup crunching through the dirt path, towing their new travel trailer, a virtual house-on-wheels.

"Here they come," Kate said. "This is their first time using it, right?"

"Yep, first time."

"I haven't been in it yet."

Joe had.

"Can't wait to see what it looks like inside."

"You're not allowed in there," Joe said.

"Joe..."

"I ain't kidding. You go in there, it'll ruin you for our pop-up."

"I love our little pop-up," Kate said.

"As of this minute you do. You go in that thing, you watch, ten minutes later you'll stick your head out the door and tell me to bring your pillow over."

Kate laughed. "I will not."

"I might," Kristin said.

"Neither one of us will," Kate said. "You're forgetting baby Jack still gets up every couple of hours during the night."

Jack's shiny black pickup came into the clearing followed by their camper. Jack's face all smiles. He lowered the window and waved. "Finally made it. Didn't make it through that last traffic light then got stuck behind a slow-moving tractor."

Joe could see Rachel through the windshield, looking all around. "Saved you the bigger spot over there." He pointed to his right beyond the picnic table. "You see the slab there? Just pull in between it and the electrical hookups and you should be all set. You need any help backing her up?"

"Don't think so," Jack said. "Used to have a boat some years ago, got pretty good backing things up."

Why was Joe not surprised?

Pulling up, Jack leaned his head out the window. "Love all the trees around the edges here."

"I know," Kate said. "There's kind of a nice breeze blowing through here, too. Got lunch all set to go. Hoagies and chips. Made enough for you guys."

"Sounds great," Jack said. "Baby Jack's already had his lunch just before we left. He's out cold."

"Could you talk a little quieter," Rachel said softly. "I'd like him to stay that way."

"Sorry," Jack said. "Why don't you get him out and sit with Kate while I get the trailer set in place?"

"Okay." She came around to the back door. Fortunately, they had one of those car seats where you could just unclick a few buttons and lift it out of place.

Joe headed back to the pop-up and finished the last few set-up items on his checklist. By the time he'd finished, Jack was heading over to meet them. His trailer looked all set up already. The jacks were all in place, awning extended, front stairs lowered. Joe could even hear the A/C humming on the roof.

"All electric," Jack said, as he walked up to the table.

Joe sat down. "Okay, let's just get this out right up front. I'm not jealous of you guys. No matter what my face looks like, nor the tone of my voice. I'm really happy you guys got such a nice rig."

"I believe you, Joe," Jack said, smiling. "But you remember, I didn't really have to pay for this thing. Remember I got that inheritance a few years back from my old professor? We used the money from the sale of the cabin to pay for it and the truck."

Joe lifted his hoagie off the platter. "That's supposed to make me feel better?"

IN LESS TIME than it took Joe to set up his pop-up camper, Jack had his camper-trailer all set and ready to go. The baby was inside napping, a little monitor was sitting next to Rachel on the picnic table. Everyone had pretty much finished their lunch. Joe Jr. got up to bring his paper plate and crunched up napkin to the trashcan, set on a pole in between their two campsites.

"That's nice," Rachel said, "he's already trained to clean up after himself."

"Yeah," Kate said, "he's good that way. Now, if I could only get him to sit at the table more than thirty seconds after he finishes eating."

Rachel laughed.

"Hey, Joey," Joe said, "don't forget to close that trashcan lid down tight. They got raccoons around here."

"I will," Joe Jr. said, as he lifted the lid.

"Say, Dad," Kristin said, getting up from the table. "Okay if Joey and I take Chance for a walk? I saw a trail heading off in the woods a few yards up the road from where we turned in here."

"Yeah, Dad. Can we?" said Joe Jr.

"I don't want you guys going off getting lost on us," Kate said. "That'd just about spoil the trip for me."

Jack and Rachel both laughed.

"You'll be all right, Kate," Joe said. "This ain't like when you and I were kids. Remember that app on their phones? All they gotta do is mark this spot as home plate, and they'll have no problem finding their way back. Besides, there's lots of other campsites spread throughout these woods. They can't go too far without bumping into one."

"Well, I still want them staying on the path," she said.

"We will," the kids said in unison.

"My turn to hold Chance's leash," Kristin said.

"I get to do it on the way back," said Joe Jr.

"No, I get to do it twice in a row, remember?"

The kids got Chance and headed off toward the trail.

FOR THE NEXT FIFTEEN MINUTES, everything got nice and quiet. Jack's camper had a nice outdoor kitchen component, so everyone fixed themselves a nice cup of Keurig coffee. Kate and Rachel were drinking theirs inside, sitting in the cozy living area, which had great big windows with a nice view of the lake and the woods. Joe and Jack were drinking theirs under the shade of Jack's big awning.

"You brought your detector, right? Joe said.

"Oh yeah," Jack said. "And my fishing gear. Which one you want to do first?"

"Thought maybe we'd do some metal detecting first, then grab the poles and head down to the lake, see if we can reel in some dinner. Wished I had thought of it sooner, could've had the kids go with us."

Just then, the men were startled by loud voices in the distance. It was the kids yelling something. Joe shot to his feet, started running toward the sound. Jack right behind him. As they got to the dirt road, Joe saw Kristin running out of the woods... by herself, her face frantic.

"What's the matter?" Joe said. "Where's Joey, and the dog?"

"Joey's running after Chance. I told him not to, but he went anyway."

"What do you mean?"

"Everything was going fine, Chance was just sniffing the ground. All of a sudden, he must've got hold some scent, or maybe it was an animal. I don't know. But he just took off after it, about yanked my arm out of its socket. I tried to hold on but Chance got away, Joey ran after him, and I ran back to get you."

Joe and Jack led Kristin back into the woods. "Let's go," Joe said. "Take us to where you last saw him."

They ran through the woods for a few moments, everyone yelling out Joey's name.

It didn't take long before Joey yelled back in reply. "I'm here. I'm over here. And I got Chance."

"Keep talking," Joe said, "till we see you." About a hundred yards in from that point, everyone saw Joe Jr. standing there through the trees. As they got nearer, Joe saw him holding onto the dog's leash. Chance was pawing at the ground furiously, digging up a storm.

"I don't know what he's going after," Joe Jr. said. "But he's digging like it's buried treasure."

Joe walked up to him, said, "Here, give me his leash." He put his other hand on Joe Jr.'s shoulder. "You all right?"

"Yeah, I'm fine. I was just worried about him. He ran after some animal at first. A rabbit I think. It got away, but then he picked up the scent of something else, and I kept chasing him until he stopped here. Look at him dig."

Joe bent down toward Chance. "What you got there, boy?"

They all watched him dig a few moments more.

Suddenly, Joe saw a very disturbing shape emerge through the dirt.

"Say, Joe," Jack said. "Are you seeing this?"

"Dad..." Kristin said, "is that...?"

Joe stood, started pulling back on Chance's leash. "Okay, boy. That's enough now." He took a couple steps back. "That's a good boy." Chance was still straining at the leash, trying to get back to his prize.

All four of them stood there, dumbfounded, staring down at the thing that had so completely captivated Chance's attention. It was still partially covered by dirt, but enough had been uncovered to remove any doubt about what it was.

The skeletal remains of a human hand.

"Oh, crap," Joe said.

2

Joe and Jack quickly moved his kids and the dog away from this grim discovery, down the trail toward the dirt road. Of course, Chance was the only one resisting this decision.

"Was that really a dead body?" Joe Jr. asked. "Is that what we just saw?"

"Yeah, Joey. It was," Joe said. "Well, I don't know if there's a whole body buried there, not yet anyway." He released a deep sigh.

"I can't even believe this," Jack said, as they reached the dirt road. "How am I going to explain this to Rachel?"

Joe stopped walking when they reached the road, so everyone else did, too. "I know, right? This is like the last thing in the world I want to see right now."

"But Dad," Joe Jr. said, all excited, "you just got another murder to solve. You're going to be on the news again. Maybe, they'll even want to interview me and Chance."

His son thought what Joe did for a living was the coolest

thing and whenever Joe was in the news, his son's friends at school made a big deal out of it.

"Joey," Kristin said, "this isn't a good thing. Don't you get what this means? Our vacation is over."

Joe Jr.'s joy quickly deflated. "No, it's not. It's not, Dad, right? Tell her she's wrong."

Joe shook his head, looked down a moment. Sighed again. "I don't know, Joey. It could be. We'll just have to see how this plays out. The Captain might let Hank run this one without me, I don't know. We'll just have to see. But listen, either way, even if I get sucked into this, doesn't mean you guys can't have fun. We're all set up for a five-day camping trip. No reason that has to end. I'll just be coming home to the camper instead of the house."

"But it won't be the same without you," Joe Jr. said.

"Not even close," Kristin said.

"Look guys, don't get all worked up over this. Let's just wait and see what happens." He looked at Jack. "Can you take them back to the campsite? I better call this one in."

"I could," Jack said. "But I think it might go over better with the ladies if we're both there to explain what happened. It's not as if that... *discovery* is going to go anywhere in the next thirty minutes. Looks like it's been there for several years, don't you think?"

Joe thought a moment. "Yeah, you're right. First things first."

They started walking back to the campsite. "Listen kids," Joe said as they walked. "You can talk about this with me and your mom and the Turners. But that's it. You got me? Not a word to your friends. Not a word on social media."

"But Dad —" Kristin said.

"No, but Dad. Not a word to anyone. You hear me? Not until I give you the okay."

"When will that be?" Joe Jr. said.

"I don't know. Probably not until the investigation gets underway. I'll let you know."

When they got to the campsite, Kate and Rachel were sitting at the picnic table. The baby was rocking gently in a swing. The ladies got up as soon as they saw the group returning. "Is everyone all right?" Kate said. "We saw you and Jack take off toward the woods."

"We've been worried sick," Rachel said.

"We're fine, Mom," Joe Jr. said. "No one got hurt. Chance just found a dead body in the woods, that's all."

"WHAT?" Kate yelled. "Chance found *what*?"

"A dead body," Joe Jr. repeated. "He dug it up in the woods."

Geez, Joe muttered. "Joey, that's enough. You let me and Mr. Turner do the talking from here."

When they reached the ladies, Kate hugged the kids. She looked up at Joe. "Please tell me our boy is joking and that our dog did not dig up a dead body in the woods. Tell me he's pulling a prank."

Joe looked over at Jack, then at Kate. "I wish I was, Hon. You don't know how much."

"Oh, Jack..." Rachel said. "You guys found a dead body? In the woods?"

"We didn't find it. It's the dog's fault. Anyway, we don't know if it's a whole body yet."

"You found *part* of a body?" Kate said. "That would be better?"

"Like Jack said, we don't know yet," Joe said. "Joey you

explain what happened. Stop at the part when Jack and I show up."

So, he did and ended with, "Chance got hold of this other scent and stopped chasing the rabbit. He starts digging in the dirt like a maniac. Then I hear everyone yelling out for me."

"So, we get there," Joe said, "and see he's fine. We see the dog again, like he says. Then we see the bones of this hand emerge, and I thought I saw part of a sleeve. But I'm not thinking like a cop yet, I'm thinking like a dad who's got to get his kids out of there."

"Thank God for small mercies," Kate said.

"So, how far away is this... body?" Rachel said.

"I don't know," Jack said. "Maybe three hundred yards."

"Sounds about right," Joe said. "Hey, I could use a bottle of water. We got some ice-cold ones in the cooler. Anyone else want any?" Jack and the kids all did. Joe told Joe Jr. to get some water in the bowl for Chance.

"Now, wait a minute here," Kate said. "We're not just shifting gears back to normal here. You guys just came in from the woods saying we got a dead body about a football field away from here?"

"Nobody's shifting gears, Kate," Joe said. "I'm just thirsty. And it's about three football fields away from here."

"Well, that's so much better."

Joe took a refreshing swig. "I know this stinks, Hon. Believe me, I'm hating this. But it is, what it is. As crazy as it sounds. It really happened. Somehow, someway, some bunch of years ago, some bad guy killed somebody and buried their body in the woods. Probably thinking no one would ever find it. They had no idea that on *this* day a mixed-beagle pup would chase a rabbit who, apparently, ran right by his shallow grave. And our little guy's nose, firing on all eight cylinders, would smell those remains--even after all these years--right where he left it, and start digging after it like nobody's business."

Kate looked over at Jack and Rachel. "That's one of the reasons I married him. It's like a gift, the way he puts things."

They laughed. Then Rachel said, "But seriously, what happens next? This pretty much ends our little trip, doesn't it? Three football fields away is not like three miles. I'm not gonna be able to sleep in this lovely spot, knowing there's a dead body just over yonder."

"It'd make a great campfire story," Jack said.

Rachel slugged Jack in the arm. "That's not even funny."

Joe Jr. laughed. "That's a good one, Mr. Turner. I like it when you tell stories."

"Well, he's not telling this one, Joey," Kate said. "But really, Joe. What happens next? I know you're going to have to call this in."

"You're right, I am. And it's probably gonna change everything, at least in terms of our immediate plans. But I think we might still be able to salvage a good bit of this trip. We'll have to move our campers to another spot."

"Like, as far away from here as possible," Rachel said.

"Right," Jack said. "But that won't be a problem. They've got campsites spread out all over these woods. And since school's in session, I'm sure we'll find one just as nice as this one."

"I know we can," Joe said. "When I booked this one, there were still tons of openings for other spots. Why don't you get hold of the management folks, Jack, set that all up, while I call Hank and let him know what's going on. And you kids, start helping your mom pack everything back up into the camper."

"We're leaving?" whined Joe Jr.

"Not leaving, changing spots," Joe said. "If you get on it right now, we can be in our new spot in no time." Joe took out his cell phone started walking toward some privacy.

Kate followed. "What do you think, Joe? Are you as optimistic as you just sounded with the kids? Or should I prepare myself to finish this trip without you?"

Joe looked at her, hesitated. "I don't know, Kate. All I can say is, I'm gonna try and get them to give this to Hank. But you know how the Captain is."

3

J ust over an hour had passed. The camp had been relocated on the far side of the lake, almost a three-mile drive from the site they had originally set up. Far enough away that Joe knew they wouldn't hear any sirens or see any of the flashing lights from the various police and emergency vehicles that would soon arrive.

Major crimes were a rarity in the Culpepper area, so when they did occur—or like in this case, were discovered—it was a very big deal and everyone wanted in on it. Joe was heading back to the site now after leaving Kate, the kids, and the Turners at the new campsite getting dinner together. Joe wasn't sure what they were fixing, but he knew one thing that wouldn't be on the menu...fresh trout he and Jack had caught out on the lake.

Oh well, maybe tomorrow.

He still hadn't been able to reach the Captain, so Joe didn't know how much of his vacation would remain intact. Right now, according to his GPS, he should almost be back at that spot on the dirt road where he and Hank were supposed to meet. Close to that trail in the woods where his kids and Chance had found the dead body. Hank agreed it might be a good idea for the two of them to meet at the crime scene before calling in the cavalry.

One or two S-turns later, and Hank's car came into view, pulled off to the side of the road. Hank was leaning on the fender looking down at his phone. He looked up and smiled, as Joe's SUV approached. "You can't catch a break, can you?" he said, walking up.

Joe got out of the car. "I know, right?" They shook hands. "Gotta be honest, I was half-tempted just to leave it alone for the next five days, call it in when our camping trip was over. It's not like that dead body's going anywhere. But that would've freaked out my kids, not to mention Kate or the Turners."

"That's right. You guys were camping with Jack and Rachel. Guess they can't catch a break, either."

"No, but Jack doesn't have to call anybody when something like this happens or cut his vacation short."

"You think that's gonna happen here? I'm willing to take this, Joe. Completely, if you trust me with it."

"It's not you, Hank. I totally trust you. It's Pendleton. You know how he gets with these murder cases. Especially these cold cases, which this one's certainly gonna turn out to be."

"Positive publicity," Hank added.

"Right. Those last two we solved left him a little... shall we say, less than satisfied on that score."

In the last nine months, Joe and Hank had been able to clear two of the unsolved murder cases from the 1980s. They were part of a series of murders the Captain wanted Joe and

Hank to work on, the reason he created the Cold Case squad in the first place. Unfortunately, from a publicity standpoint, those two yielded almost none. It turned out, he and Hank had been able to run some DNA tests on a few pieces of evidence that directly tied both murders to a known serial killer, one who'd been traveling through their part of the state that year. He'd been caught a few years later for murders committed in another state and had already died in the gas chamber back in 1998.

"Well, let me walk you back there," Joe said, "let you see what we're dealing with here." They started heading down the trail through the trees.

"How long you figure this body's been back here? You said it was just a skeleton, right?"

"Yeah. Even after all the homicides I've been on, only a handful have been in this condition. I'm talking about, just bones. Dry bones. I didn't want to say much with my kids there. All the dog had uncovered was the right hand. But when I stood up, I could pretty much see the outline of a shallow grave. I'm thinking we got the whole body here, and it's been here a good long while. Many years." They walked down a slight hill and around a large fallen oak. "It shouldn't be too much further."

"Look at you," Hank said. "Who'd a-thunk it? Joe Boyd, the big city cop, following a trail of footprints through the woods like an Indian tracker."

Joe laughed. "Yeah, look at me." About fifteen yards later, Joe stopped. "Here's the place where Chance went off the trail, guess the rabbit he was chasing tore off through here. I made a few mental notes, using some of these trees as landmarks."

"Keep going. I'm just following," Hank said. "Hope we don't get any ticks."

They kept walking for two or three more minutes. "It's right over this little hill." Joe got to the top of it and looked down. He could see the dozens of footprints and the obvious place where Chance had been digging.

Hank came up behind him and stood by his side, surveyed the scene. "Yeah, that's a dead hand... I mean, well, you know what I mean. And I can see what you're saying about the shallow grave. We definitely got a whole body here." He grabbed a stick, squatted down and used it to lift the skeletal hand. As he did, part of the forearm became exposed. "It's pretty tattered, but I'd say that's part of a sleeve, don't you think?"

"Yep." Joe squatted down, too. "Hard to say for sure, considering all the years it may have been sitting here in the elements, but doesn't that look like green to you?"

"It does. And I guess since he or she wasn't wearing a coat, kinda rules out the murder taking place in the winter months."

"Maybe," Joe said. "Or maybe, since whoever did this is likely not the most caring person, they could've just dragged our vic' out here in the cold without a coat. Or maybe, they liked their coat so much, they stole it after killing them."

Hank looked over at Joe, smiled. "Maybe." He stood back up, looked around at the immediate scene. "Well, I guess the CSI guys aren't going to be able to get any footprint evidence."

"No, but they weren't gonna anyways. A body been out here this long with dozens of animals traipsing about and hundreds of weather events, all that's been washed away long ago. But they'll still want to scour the area, bag anything that Mother Nature didn't drop on the ground."

Hank looked off in the direction they had come from. "How far away was this from where you guys were camping?"

"Maybe three hundred yards."

"How far do you think it is to the next camping area?" He pointed in the other direction.

"I'm guessing about the same," Joe said. "That's one of the things I liked about this place. They've got clusters of sites grouped together with electric hookups and nice slabs, but enough distance and woods between them to make it seem like you got the whole place to yourself."

"I'm wondering," Hank said, "if maybe this vic' was somebody camping at either your site or the next one over, and he and a buddy got into it. The buddy kills him and drags him deep into the woods, buries him here and takes off. You know, never looking back."

"It could be, Hank. We'll have to see when these campsites were developed. Then wait and see when the Doc places the time of his death." Joe looked down at the bony hand. "But this guy, or gal, could've been down there even years before that, for all we know."

Hank noticed something, grabbed his stick and squatted down again. He brushed away some dirt and leaves just to the right of the skeletal hand, exposing some material. A very dull red. "You see this?"

Joe did. "Lift it up a little, see if you can see what it is."

Hank did. "It's kind of puffy and smooth."

Joe gasped. "I know what that is. I had one of those as a kid."

"What is it?"

"It's Marty McFly's vest."

"It's what?"

"Marty McFly. You know, Back to the Future? The movie."

"They made those movies in the 80s, didn't they?"

"Yeah," Joe said. "The first two anyway."

"You think then this could be one of the cold cases from the 1980s?" Hank said. "The ones from our list?"

"Could be," Joe said. "And if it is, it's not going to be one of those two-or-three-day media stories, like those DNA cases we solved. It's gonna be a big deal."

"A very big deal," Hank said. "The kind Captain Pendleton goes ape over,"

Joe sighed. Yeah. The kinda case Cap wouldn't let Joe turn over to Hank in a million years.

4

Thirty minutes later, the gang had all arrived.

Four uniform patrolmen, the CSI guys, and even Dr. Hargrove, the Medical Examiner. Joe had called them all using his cell phone to avoid the press hearing about it over the in-house radio. They'd hear about it soon enough, but he wanted a little time to keep a lid on things before it got too crazy. He'd let Hank brief them all, hoping they'd get used to taking their cues from him on this case. He still held out little hope Captain Pendleton would let Hank run the show.

As Hank talked, Joe held up his cell phone signaling he was going to try and reach Pendleton again. Hank nodded and kept talking to the crew. Once Joe was out of earshot, he hit the dial button on his phone. To his surprise, Pendleton picked up after two rings.

"Hey, Joe, what's up? I saw your earlier calls and was going to call you back, but I'm out with the wife. You know how that goes. Figured it couldn't be anything too important since you're on vacation. But maybe I'm wrong, seeing as this is the third phone call in less than an hour."

"Yeah Cap, hate calling you on your time off. Hate even more calling you when I'm supposed to be on vacation, but it had to be done." Joe spent the next ten minutes filling him in on this crazy situation, only leaving out the details he thought might ring any alarm bells in Pendleton's head that this case might be something Hank couldn't handle. He ended with the part about Hank briefing the team right now.

The problem was, Pendleton had been a pretty solid detective back in the day, and his first set of questions immediately began to dig at the part of the story Joe had been avoiding.

"I know it's early on," Pendleton said, "but did you guys see anything that might indicate how long the corpse had been out there? Any clues that might give us an approximate date? I know you said it was reduced to bones, but that could mean it's been there anywhere from several months to several hundred years."

Joe sighed. "I'd say we can probably rule out anything recent, or anything too ancient."

"How so?"

Joe couldn't lie. "Remember that movie, Back to the Future? Talking about the first one."

"Yeah, loved that movie. Why?"

"Remember that puffy red vest Marty wore?"

"I do."

"Well," Joe said, "pretty sure our vic' was wearing one. It was pretty deteriorated, and I could only see a part of it. But I'm ninety percent sure that's what it was."

"Didn't that movie come out in the eighties?"

"1985, I think," said Joe. "But those vests stayed popular for quite a few years after that."

"Yeah, Joe, they did. But I think we gotta assume it's more likely this is one of those 80s cases you and Hank have been working on. Don't you think?"

"Could be, sir."

"Could be? I'd say, it most likely is. Can't be more than half a dozen or so left, right? And if you got something that specific on what the vic' was wearing, shouldn't be too hard to figure out who it is. That is, assuming it's one of the murders in our files. Since it happened out in the woods, might be something we don't even have on our radar. Either way, this isn't going to be one of those quickie DNA cases like the others. We got a bonafide cold case murder mystery here, my friend. And this one's all ours.

Joe hated hearing him talk like this.

"And you know what that means," Pendleton continued. "Some serious good publicity for this department, cause I know you and Hank will nail this sucker like you do every case."

"Speaking of me and Hank," Joe said, "remember how we started off this conversation?"

"I...I think so. What are you getting at?"

"The part about being surprised to get a phone call from me when I'm supposed to be on vacation."

"Oh, yeah. I remember."

"Well, I'm still supposed to be on it. As we speak, three miles from this very spot where I'm talking to you, my wife and kids, as well as Jack Turner and his wife and baby son, are at our new camping site fixing dinner. They're probably waiting on me to show back up, so we could eat it. Later on tonight, we were thinking of having a campfire, doing the whole bit, you know?"

"I hear you, Joe. I know where you're coming from. But Joe, this is kind of a big deal, this body you guys found out there. Not the kind of thing that happens every day. Or even every year in a town like Culpepper."

Seemed to Joe like it did pretty much happen every year. At least every year since he'd moved here. "I know that, Cap. But Hank's worked very closely with me on these cases. He's a sharp guy. He knows what he's doing. Did I mention he's managing the crime scene activity right now?"

"You did. And I think Hank's got a lot going on for a young man his age. That's why I put him on your team, gave him that raise. But he's not you, Joe. He doesn't have your instincts. Not all of them yet anyway. He can't handle the media like you can. And people in this town trust you, Joe. Heck, most of them like you way more than they like me. I don't know how that happened, but it did.

That last part of Pendleton's argument made no sense to Joe. You'd think people were asking him for autographs. "What's people liking me have anything to do with it? Last I checked, public relations wasn't on my job description. The only people I care about liking me is my wife and kids. You pull me off this vacation to work on this case, and my stock is gonna go way down with them."

Pendleton didn't say anything for a few moments. "I hear you, Joe. I really do." He released a sigh. "But you know what I'm saying about Hank is true. He's not ready to handle a major case all by himself."

"He won't be by himself. I'm not saying leave me

completely alone till my vacation's over. I'm just saying, can't we make some kind of compromise?"

"What do you have in mind?"

"I stay on vacation, but I keep my phone on. But Hank will be running point, at least till this camping trip's done. But only he calls me, nobody else. Everybody else calls him first. I'll give him guidelines, and I know he won't abuse them. Right now, the press is not involved. Maybe we'll get lucky, and it'll stay that way a few more days. Maybe for a few after that, he can stall them a bit. But if somebody has to deal with them, I'll take care of it. How's that sound?"

Again, no reply for a few moments. "I'm willing to try that, Joe. See if it works. But since we're working out a compromise, are you willing to jump back in, full on, if I start getting a bunch of complaints that Hank's losing his grip on things?"

"Totally okay with that," Joe said. Because he knew nothing was going to happen over the next week that Hank couldn't handle. This dead person had been dead for decades. Nobody was even looking for them anymore. It might take the CSI guys the better part of a week to even come up with preliminary findings. The only variable in this whole thing was the press and social media.

At that, Joe quickly made his way back to the crime scene. Everyone was already doing their thing. The CSI team was working the gravesite. The uniformed officers had fanned out and were starting a grid of the surrounding area, looking for anything relevant left on the ground. Joe stood atop the little mound overlooking the scene. "Hey everybody," he yelled, "listen up. Let me grab your ear a few seconds."

Joe waited until they gathered around. Hank looked over at him. Joe held up his cell phone, nodded and smiled. Wasn't sure Hank understood, but he would in a few moments. "Okay, I'm about to bug out of here. Hank is in charge. I don't just mean now. I mean for the next several days. Most of you probably know I'm supposed to be on vacation. Well, I just confirmed with the captain that he's okay with Hank taking point till my vacation's over." Joe enjoyed the surprised look on Hank's face. You got any reason to come to me, you go to Hank. He decides if I get a call. And Hank knows how much I don't want any calls. About us much as any of you'd want to get a call when you're spending time with your kids. The only thing I can see screwing this up for me are these."

Joe held up his smartphone. "Social media. Look around, notice who you don't see messing up our crime scene. No press and no curious onlookers. I know at some point the news on this vic' will break, but don't let any of you be the cause. Hank and I will decide when to go public with this, and we ain't in no hurry. So, don't you be. Word on this gets out--and I find one of you were the reason--I'll ring your neck."

Half of them laughed.

"Those of you who laughed? Look at the guys who didn't. They know I'm serious. C'mon guys, I really need this time with my family. Are we good on this?"

Everyone told Joe in one way or another that they got it, and that they were fine without him. A few even said they'd be better off if he'd just go away for good.

He was pretty sure they were joking.

5

Joe dismissed the guys, so they could get back to what they were doing. Hank walked Joe out to his SUV.

"I can't believe you got Pendleton to go along with this," Hank said.

"What, you taking point?"

"Yeah, what'd you have to do, threaten to quit?"

"Nah, nothing so drastic. He's not really concerned you can't handle the behind-the-scenes stuff. He's just nervous you won't handle the PR stuff as good as me."

"He's got a right to be concerned about that," Hank said. "I hate that stuff."

"Well, you keep making sure the guys keep a lid on this, and neither one of us will have to deal with that part of it. You were right, though. He jumped right on the idea that this is likely gonna be a major case that could generate some good publicity for the department."

"Seems like that's all he cares about when cases like this turn up."

"I don't think that's it," Joe said. "He cares way more about it than you or me, but he's the guy who's gotta deal directly with the powers-that-be to get the budget approved every year. And since most of those guys are elected, they're all about the public's perception of things. When you and I solve big cases, it generates the perception that we're doing our job, that their money's well spent. Which makes Pendleton look good."

"Sounds like you're proving my point," Hank said.

Joe laughed. "Kinda does, I guess. The point is, it's not his only focus, but it's part of his job to pay attention to that. You and me? We get to do way more interesting stuff. But part of the agreement with Pendleton letting you take point is...if and when we have to interact with the media, he wants me to do it, not you."

"I've got no problem with that."

"Me either...as long it doesn't happen while I'm on this camping trip with the family."

"I'll do my best to make sure that doesn't happen. But how involved you want to be?"

"As little as possible. Seriously. I trust your instincts, even if Pendleton doesn't yet. Call me if you get stuck on something that matters. Other than that, how about I call you mid-afternoon each day for an update? You can run the smaller stuff by me then. We're only talking about the next five days, Hank. It'll be over before you know it."

"Sounds good."

Joe opened the car door.

"Say, Joe. Before you go, you don't have that metal detector in the back of your SUV, do you?"

"Actually, I do. Why?"

"I don't know," Hank said, "I've been thinking, hearing you talk about how good it works, that we should get one for the department. You know, for times like these. We got the guys walking a grid around the body searching for clues. But they're just using their eyeballs. Might be nice to run a detector, at least around the immediate area, see if it picks up anything they miss."

"It's a good idea, Hank. See? I never thought of that. Only problem is, I brought the one in the back to play with. Me and Jack are going to do some detecting probably tomorrow morning."

"That's not a problem. Still got a couple of daylight hours left. What if we just use it between now and then? When we're done, I'll drive over and get it back to you."

"Sure Hank, that'll work." Joe walked around to the back, opened the lid, then spent the next five minutes showing Hank the basics of working the detector.

When Joe got back to their campsite, he found everyone moving toward the big picnic table, which appeared all set for dinner. They all turned and smiled as he pulled in behind the pop-up.

"We were just about to give up on you," Kate said.

"We're starving, Dad," Joe Jr. said.

Joe got out of the car, headed their way. "I'm surprised you waited this long. What did you wind up fixing?"

"Rachel's chili," Jack said. He sat at the picnic table. "You're gonna love it, I promise. She could win an award for the stuff."

"And my award-winning cornbread," Kate said, "from the Walmart bakery."

"Looks great. I really am hungry." Joe sat down. When everyone was ready, he said the blessing and Kate started dishing out the chili into everyone's bowl.

"So, I guess they let you go?" Jack said.

"Mostly," Joe replied. "Got my captain to let Hank take the lead. He's going to do his best to handle everything he can and only involve me when absolutely necessary."

"How'd you manage that?" Kate said.

"Took a little...creative verbiage, but we got there."

"So, is the dead body still over there?" Joe Jr. said.

"Joey," Kate said, "how about we don't talk anymore about dead bodies during dinner?"

"But, Mom..."

"How about this, Kate?" Joe set his spoon back in the bowl of chili. "I give everyone a quick update, then we don't talk about that very unpleasant episode we experienced earlier for the rest of the trip? I know everyone's curious. They gotta be."

"I guess that's fine," she said. "But remember, a quick update. And...be as vague as you can possibly be."

So, that's just what Joe did. After he finished, Kate smiled, indicating his summary had met her approval. He ended reminding his kids if they slipped and told any of their friends about this while on this trip, the trip would probably be over within hours after that. They seemed to get the message.

The conversation at the table was pleasant and relaxing, and Jack hadn't hyped his wife's chili too much. Everyone asked for seconds, including Joe Jr. who barely tolerated

Kate's chili. Kate took special note of that and told Joey, "There will be consequences."

When everyone finished, the kids took Chance for a walk down by the lake. "Don't go too far," Kate warned. "If you can't see our campsite, that's too far. And keep a strong hold on that leash."

"Okay, Mom," Kristin said.

Jack and Joe helped the wives clear up the dinner mess, then Kate put some coffee on. Rachel went inside to change the baby's diaper. Jack and Joe went over to start a fire to roast marshmallows for the s'mores later on. Joe thanked Jack for the nice big stack of wood he'd made.

"Me and the kids kept busy while you were meeting with Hank," Jack said. "How's the case looking, so far I mean? You don't have to answer that if you don't want to."

"No, I don't mind talking about it with you. Just not around the kids, and even with Kate. It's really too early to tell very much. Hank's going to give me an update tomorrow afternoon. Not expecting much from it right now. The forensics guys will bring everything back to the lab. That'll take a while. Same with the M.E. and the body. What's left of it. So, we might just make something out of this trip after all. Hank and I did see one interesting thing before the gang showed up."

"What's that?" Jack said.

Joe told him about finding the red Marty McFly vest on the body. "Makes us think this kid might've been laying there since the late 1980s."

"And," Jack added, "could make identifying the body a lot easier, wearing such a specific piece of clothing. Can't be too many unaccounted for missing persons from the Culpepper area wearing something like that when they were last seen, from that time period."

"No, you're right. Same thing my boss said. We might not even have to wait for the forensics tests to come back."

Just then, two things happened. Kate came walking up with two mugs of coffee and Hank pulled into their campsite.

Kate's face fell. "Well, that didn't take long."

"No, it's not like that. He's just here dropping off my metal detector." Joe stood, started walking toward Hank. "I'll explain why when I come back."

By the time Joe made it to Hank's car, he already had the back door open and was pulling out the detector.

"Find anything useful?" Joe said.

"Actually, we did."

"Let me guess...was it a Civil War coin or musket ball?"

"Neither," Hank said, handing the detector to Joe. He pulled an evidence bag out of his pocket, held it up. "How about a Culpepper High School senior class ring? Found in the brush not ten feet away from the body."

Joe looked at it. "Well, I'll be. Any initials engraved on it?"

"Doesn't look like it. But can you see the year engraved on the front?" He handed it to Joe.

Joe spun the ring around, pressed it up against the clear plastic bag. "1989. Well, would you look at that? Guess that makes sense, considering the Marty McFly vest." He handed it back to Hank.

"Guess the captain's going to get his wish," Hank said. "A full-fledged cold case murder to solve from the 1980s."

"Anyone else know about this?"

"Just you and me. I did the detecting myself. Took a

couple photos of it to show how close it was to the body before bagging it."

"That's great work, Hank. Put it in with anything else the guys may have found, but don't make a fuss over it yet. But I'd say take out the rest of the files from the 1980s, see if any of them line up with this ring and our red vest."

"My thoughts exactly. I'll let you get back to your campfire."

Joe turned to find Jack already had the fire going nicely. "Talk to you tomorrow afternoon."

6

6:55 pm Fellowship Hall
Culpepper Evangelical Church

Melissa Hendricks stepped carefully from the parking lot onto the sidewalk. It was almost dark, and she was still getting used to her new bifocals. Three other ladies, all friends by now, were up ahead just walking through the glass front doors into the church hall, where their monthly Word Weavers writing group had met for the past five months.

Melissa wasn't sure if she was more nervous or excited about sharing the paper-clipped stack of pages she'd brought to the group. It was the first chapter of a new book, her first foray into fiction. She'd only brought devotionals to the group so far. Being a former English teacher, she rarely had to endure any criticism about things like punctuation or sentence structure. When criticism came — and it always came — it centered mainly on things like being overly descriptive and wordy sentences.

She knew receiving criticism was a normal part of the writing experience, but she wished she wasn't so thin-skinned. It still stung way too much, even though she'd never let it show. She tried to focus on the encouraging things said, and there were always plenty of them, too. But for some reason, she always latched onto the things wrong with her writing, not the good parts. As she reached the front door, Melissa prayed silently: *Please, Lord, let them like it.*

"Here, let me get that for you."

Melissa was startled by the deep male voice coming from behind. She turned to see Andrew Tubbs reaching around her to grab the other front door handle. Before she could say, "I've got it, thank you," he already had it opened and held it for her.

"Ladies first," he said. "That's how I was raised."

She quickly stepped through. "Thank you, Andrew."

"Call me, Andy, remember? Just like folks did back in high school." He followed behind her as they walked to the front table to sign in.

Why did he have to come back? He had missed the last two months, and Melissa had secretly hoped Andrew had dropped out of the group for good. It was wrong to be that way, but he...well, to put it plainly...he creeped her out. She signed in.

"Didn't you used to call me Andy back in high school?" Tubbs said, standing behind her.

"To be honest Andrew, I mean Andy, I don't remember if we even knew each other back in high school. Did we ever even talk? Maybe we did, but it was just so long ago." She set the pen down and stepped aside.

Tubbs picked it up and signed in on the clipboard. "I don't know. I thought we did. I remember we had the same algebra class in eleventh grade. And then the same speech class in our senior year."

Melissa had no recollection of that. She did remember seeing him in school back in the day and remembered he pretty much creeped her out back then, too.

"I remember fairly well, cause I had a pretty good crush on you then."

Melissa hurried toward the tables where everyone else was sitting. She had the sinking feeling Tubbs might still be holding onto that crush. A couple of the women turned to greet her, and she quickly engaged them in conversation, relieved for the distraction. Out of the corner of her eye, she watched to see where he sat, so she could sit at a distant table. Thankfully, he sat between two of the four guys who regularly came to the group and quickly struck up a conversation with one. A nice, safe gentleman named Brian.

Melissa sat in the next available seat next to her friend Lisa, who also wrote fiction. She glanced over at Tubbs, who was now looking over the submission he'd brought to be critiqued. Maybe she was wrong about him still having that crush on her. She hoped so. But that wasn't the only thing about him that creeped her out. Actually, it was the pages in his hands just now. His manuscript. The last time he'd been here, she'd been put in his group and wound up having to be the one who read aloud what he'd written.

Tubbs had described it as a murder mystery.

Normally, they started meetings as one big group. The

chapter president would open things up, greet any first-time guests and explain a little about what they could expect. They'd have one of the members share a little writing-related devotional, see if anyone had any success stories to share about their writing, maybe go over a few announcements. Then they'd be divided up into their critique groups, usually with four to six people per group. Each member who'd brought something to be critiqued, would pass it out and they'd take turns having it read aloud by the group member on the right. The rest of the group would listen then take several minutes to write down the things they liked and any concerns or suggestions they might have.

The last time Andrew Tubbs had attended, he'd been put in Melissa's group. She'd made the unfortunate decision to sit on his right, which is why she had to read his submission aloud to the group. As was customary before most submissions were read, the author would take a few moments to set the context providing a brief background on what they'd written.

When Tubbs shared his little summary, he said he'd been thinking about writing a novel for many years. Specifically, a murder mystery. That in itself wasn't strange. Word Weavers is a Christian group, and while Christians certainly don't condone murder, hundreds of murder mystery novels have been written by Christian authors. They're like most murder mysteries but told from a Christian perspective. The problem with what Andrew Tubbs had written, for Melissa — apart from all the normal beginner mistakes — was how dark the entire tone of the story sounded. And there didn't seem to be anything remotely Christian about it.

After one of the other critique members brought this up,

Tubbs had simply said in his deep, dark voice: "That'll come out in later chapters."

Another problem Melissa had was that, even though Andrew had said this was a fictional story, everything about it sounded vaguely familiar. She just couldn't put her finger on the reason why.

FIFTEEN MINUTES LATER, the critique groups were announced. Melissa groaned when she heard Andrew's name read as the last person added in Group Two. Her group. As they got up and relocated to different parts of the hall to form their groups, she said a little prayer asking God to help her be more compassionate toward Andrew or at least be a little less creeped out. This time, however, she waited until he sat down first and chose a seat at the far end of the table.

Since they had no guests, the group leader didn't need to explain the ground rules on how to give Word Weaver critiques. She announced who would go first. It was Tubbs. Lisa sat on his right, so she would get the privilege to read what he was now passing out to each member of the group.

Melissa looked down at the first page and noticed right off, the title centered at the top:

An Inconvenient Death

Lisa did also. "You didn't have a title for this the last time, did you Andrew?"

"Very observant Lisa. No, I didn't. I just came up with that a few days ago. Considering the location where my murder takes place, I thought it might be seen as a clever play on words."

"Have you told us yet where the murder takes place?"

"Not yet. But that'll come out in later chapters. I also thought people might recognize the title, cause it sounds a little bit like that Al Gore documentary, *An Inconvenient Truth*."

"That's the first thing I thought," Ralph Albertson said from across the table. "Never saw the movie, but I do remember the title."

"Okay," the group leader said, "anything else you want to tell us, Andrew, before we start to read?"

"No. I think the writing will speak for itself. You go ahead, Lisa. I'm curious to hear what everyone else thinks."

See, Melissa thought. It was stuff like that. Who talks like that? By the look on his face, he thinks his writing's up there with Grisham or James Patterson.

"Okay," Lisa said, "here goes."

She read for the next ten minutes, stumbling numerous times on missing, misspelled or misused words. A couple of sentences didn't make a lick of sense, though Lisa patiently read them as if they had. At Word Weavers, when giving critiques, you're supposed to work hard at encouraging other members' submissions, not just point out what might be wrong with it. Melissa found this an almost impossible task with Tubbs. As Lisa read on, that same overly dark tone permeated the tale. And even more disturbing to Melissa was...the story continued to chime familiar bells in her mind. As if this was *not* something Andrew had made up from his imagination. Like it wasn't a fiction story at all but something that really happened.

Just before Lisa reached the end, Ralph blurted out, "This sounds more like a horror novel than a murder mystery. You sure you picked the right genre?"

Tubbs just smiled and said, "Music to my ears."

See, Melissa thought. She wasn't the only one being creeped out by Mr. Andrew Tubbs.

7

The next morning, Hank got out of his car in the Culpepper PD parking lot aware of the better mood he'd been in since he'd gotten out of bed two hours ago.

Elaine, his wife, noticed it too. "Who do I have to thank for your smiling face?" she had asked.

"I guess you can thank Joe for going to bat for me with the captain," was Hank's reply. He'd explained to her how—for the next five days anyway—he was running the show on this case. It wasn't going to change everything, but it might improve the ratio on this two-man Cold Case Squad, in Pendleton's eyes, by the time it was through. Right now, it was probably 80-20, with the 80 going to Joe. Hank told Elaine he had a chance to close the gap a little, maybe get it to at least 70-30. Maybe even 60-40.

She'd kissed him as he'd headed for the front door, saying: "I'm not sure I understand that completely. Joe doesn't seem to be aware this is a competition. But I'm glad for anything that makes you happy."

He opened one of the glass front doors to the station and walked in, still smiling. He passed by the cubicle where his desk used to be and greeted three or four coworkers on his way to the hallway leading to his new office, which was actually Joe's old office up until a month ago. As a perk for Joe solving those last two DNA cases from the eighties, the captain had remodeled a former conference room, finally giving his lead detective a proper office space. Even had a window.

Hank didn't mind that his office didn't have a window, or that it was half the size of Joe's. It was twice the size of his old cubicle and enclosed by walls that separated him from everyone else. For some reason, that mattered. He also loved it when some of the newer cops called him Detective instead of Hank, like everyone else who'd worked there for years. For a little while, he'd actually entertained the idea of asking everyone to start calling him Henry, his real first name. Sounded more professional.

Hank sounded like a hick name.

He ran it by Elaine. She'd quickly shot it down. She'd fallen in love with a handsome young guy in high school named Hank, and he wasn't a hick. She didn't marry anyone named Henry, didn't even know anyone named Henry. Hank reminded her that his parents had named him after Hank Williams, the country music singer. She reminded him that Hank Williams was no hick; he was a country music legend, and he'd better get rid of this silly notion right away, because she had no intention of ever calling him anything but Hank.

"Hank!"

Hank looked up from his desk into the face of Captain Pendleton, standing in the doorway.

"Just wanted you to know, Joe called me yesterday, briefed me on the dead body found out by that campground west of town. And about you taking point on the case till his vacation's over. I'm okay with it. But I know it's your first, so if you need any help on anything, don't be afraid to ask."

"Thanks, Captain. I will. But Joe and I ran over some things yesterday, so I should be okay for a bit."

"Great. Anything big develops, keep me in the loop."

"I will, sir."

Pendleton headed down the hall toward his office.

Hank got up briefly to close his door. He slid the box of cold case files he'd set on the corner of his desk last night to the center, then sat down. Last night, he'd come in for a few minutes to secure the class ring he'd put in the evidence locker. Pulling out the files, one by one, he'd spent the next hour reading through them, searching only for information pertaining to what the victim had been wearing when last seen.

Most of the victims were young girls who'd been wearing dresses or blue jeans and various blouses or T-shirts. One had been wearing an official Culpepper University sweatshirt. No mention of anyone wearing a long-sleeve green shirt and puffy red vest. Seemed to Hank more like something a guy would wear.

He tipped the box toward him to see if there were any files he'd missed, found one lying on the bottom. It was thinner than the rest. He pulled it out, set it on the desk and opened it. Read aloud the name of the victim at the top of the first page: *Myron Simpson*. This looked promising. Myron was 17 years of age at the time he'd gone missing. Hank quickly eyed the date he was last seen: *December 8, 1988.*

Hmmm. Not 1989, like the ring. He was sure the ring had to be connected somehow. Hank scanned the form until he found what the young Mr. Simpson had been wearing. Bingo. Long-sleeve green shirt, red vest and khaki-colored pants.

"Think we've found our vic," Hank muttered. Had to be him. No way this was a coincidence. He reached for his phone, looked up the number for Dr. Hargrove, the county medical examiner. Two minutes later, after Hargrove's assistant patched him through, Hank was talking with the M.E. "Hey Doc, it's Hank Jensen here at the Culpepper PD. We met yesterday at the crime scene out at the campground."

"I remember you, Hank. You work with Lieutenant Boyd. I was there when he said you'd be running the show while he's on vacation."

"That's it. Thanks for taking my call. Had a couple quick questions about the body we dug up."

"Well, you know I really haven't had very much time to begin my analysis of the situation."

"I realize that," Hank said. "I'm not looking for anything deep. It's just, I wasn't there when the victim was zipped up in the bag. I didn't get a chance to see the kind of pants he was wearing. Joe and I already saw the green shirt and red vest. But that's all I saw. Any chance he was wearing khaki-colored pants?"

"I noticed you are referring to our victim as *he*," Dr. Hargrove said. "Not sure if you're just guessing on that point, but that's one preliminary finding I can confirm. Our victim was definitely a male. But if I recall, you might be right about the pants, too. Give me a second to check."

Hank waited a moment until Hargrove got back on the phone.

"They're completely in tatters, but I can tell the pants do appear to be khaki in color. How did you know if you didn't see the body before we closed up the bag?"

"Doc, I know you still have to run your tests and dental records, and so forth. But I think we could almost certainly ID our victim at this point. I'm looking at—" Hank caught himself, decided not to say anymore just yet. He realized if he went too far with Hargrove, Hargrove might inadvertently let the victim's ID slip out, and that might get the press involved prematurely. "Let's just say," Hank continued, "with you confirming the khaki-colored pants, we're well on our way to identifying our vic. Joe and I will eagerly await your final report."

"Glad I could be of help," Dr. Hargrove said.

"One other quick question, Doc. Totally off the subject. I never bought a class ring, but I'm wondering if maybe you did."

"I did in fact. For both high school and college. I'm not wearing either one at the moment."

"That doesn't matter. But here's my question. If I found a class ring dated 1989, does that mean it would've been bought in 1989? Do kids ever buy them early, you know like the year before they graduate?"

"I know I did, as did many of my friends. I bought my high school senior class ring when I was a sophomore and my college class ring as a junior. Why do you ask?"

"Just crossing some T's and dotting some I's," Hank said.
"Thanks Doc, you've been a great help."

Hank hung up, took a look back at the file. He scanned
the report but couldn't find any mention of Myron Simpson
wearing a class ring. To Hank, this could only mean one
thing. He'd have to run it by Joe this afternoon to make sure,
but he was all but certain they wouldn't need to wait on
dental records to prove the ID of their victim. His name was
Myron Simpson. Hank was holding his file in his hand. He
was sure of it.

And he might have already nailed down the first piece of
evidence linking his killer to the crime scene.

8

I t was about 3:30 in the afternoon. Joe and Jack were fishing for trout out on the dock just a few minutes' walk from their campers. Joe Jr. had been with them up until ten minutes ago when he accepted an invitation from Kate to take a walk with her, Rachel, Kristin and the baby. At first, he'd said no thanks, then Kate sweetened the offer by saying he could walk Chance the whole time.

"He really likes that dog," Jack said.

"Yeah, he does," Joe said. "He's been asking for one every Christmas and birthday for years. I'd have given in, but Kate said he had to wait until he was old enough to take care of it by himself. He'd always tell her he was already old enough. She'd take him for a walk carrying a plastic Walmart bag, wait till they passed a pile of dog poop and hand him the bag. She'd point to the mess in the grass and say, pick it up. He'd recoil in horror, of course, and say *With my hand?* She'd show him how to put his hand through the bag and do it, but he never would. That would pretty much end the discussion for a while."

"So," Jack said, "I take it he recently passed the poop test?"

"Yes, he did."

Just then, Jack's line got a hit and his pole arched right over. Jack instantly set the hook and started wrestling with his catch.

A moment after that, Joe's phone rang. He looked at it, saw it was Hank and noticed the time. That's right, their afternoon update. He reeled in his line, set his pole down and answered the phone, as he walked off the dock toward the shoreline.

"Hey Hank, how's it going?"

"Going pretty good over here. Making some good progress."

"Already?"

"Yeah, I'd say so. Definitely. I think you'll think so, too, after you hear it. How's the vacation going? Were you able to get back into things last night, shut the mind machine down a while?"

"I was. Still am, in fact. Guess I needed this break more than I realized. I haven't hardly thought about what happened yesterday, ever since I got off the phone with you. It was a little challenging last night around the campfire. Joey kept wanting to talk about it."

"Well," Hank said, "can't fault him for that, right? Kid that age finds a dead body out in the woods? That's all I'd want to talk about. Heck, that's why I'm calling you now, at this age."

Joe laughed. "Yeah, I know. But Kate put her foot down. She reminded Joey how I'm no fun to be with when my body's with the family but my mind's on a case. Joey knew exactly what she meant. She told him unless he wanted me to be like that the rest of our trip, he needed to let it go. He hasn't brought it up since."

"A wise lady you've got there. Kids don't need zombie dads."

"No, they don't. So, what you got for me?"

"Well, it's a decent update. But it can wait. Don't want to get your mind back on the wrong thing."

"No, I'll be all right. Right now, I'm watching Jack yanking the hook out of a nice keeper-size trout. I've got plenty of positive distractions here. So, go ahead."

"Okay, where do I start? We pretty much finished working the crime scene a couple hours after we talked. The ME's got the body, what's left of it, in his lab. Starting the preliminary stuff. All the evidence collected at the scene has all been bagged, tagged and locked in the evidence locker."

"Find anything else significant?"

"Nothing as good as that class ring."

"Well," Joe said, "we'll have to wait to hear what the ME says about the body's actual age, but I think this is pretty conclusive."

"I'm not so sure, Joe."

"Sure about what?"

"That we have to wait for the ME's report to ID this body. I took a look at the files, like you said. Then confirmed with Dr. Hargrove about the pants the vic was wearing, to compare it with something I read in one of these files. Turns out, it was spot on. I think we got our Vic identified, Joe. In fact, I know we have."

"Tell me more."

"His name is Myron Simpson, last seen on December 8th, 1988, wearing a long-sleeve green shirt, khaki pants, and a padded red vest."

"But I thought you said the ring you found was from 1989."

"It is, but I confirmed it could easily have been dropped there in 1988. Kids buy those rings a year or two before they graduate all the time."

"Really? That's great, Hank. You have made significant progress. Did you share these findings with Hargrove?"

"Almost did, but decided to keep it to myself a few days. He's got plenty to do on his end. I doubt anything he finds will contradict anything I found. It'll just add some more layers. And he certainly doesn't need my info."

"Good thinking. We can sit on this a few more days. Not like anyone's waiting on this information to come out."

"Give you a chance to catch some more trout, make some more memories."

"That's great, Hank. Really appreciate it. Got anything more before we sign off? Like, we know what this kid was wearing when he was last seen. How about the location? He's been missing all these years. Where did he go missing from?"

"Got that, too. He was working evenings out on the edge of town, at that convenience store just passed 270."

9

"You talking about that 7-Eleven," Joe said.

"Well, it's a 7-Eleven now, but according to what's written in this report, it was some Mom-and-Pop store back then, called Hampton's Quick-Stop. That's the owner's last name."

"Guessing it wasn't listed as a homicide."

"No," Hank said. "This was a Missing Person's report, since no body was ever found. I'm guessing our counterparts in the eighties weren't big fans of writing reports. Only a few pages on this case in here to go on. Foul play was suspected, at least by some. There were a few drops of blood found on the floor, but not enough to conclude a murder had been committed. A customer came in, found the store empty. Noticed the cash register drawer was open, but all the cash was gone. Called the cops. They called the owner, who said it had to be a robbery. Should have been at least a couple of hundred dollars in that drawer around then."

"The only question is," Joe said, "who took it?"

"Right," said Hank. "We know now it was probably taken by the killer, but the report says at least some people thought our vic might've taken the money himself, staged things to look like a robbery."

"And then ran away?" Joe said.

"Guess that was the idea. But it says both the owners and the kid's parents insist he would've never run away, and he certainly wouldn't have stolen that money. Of course, no one could explain — if there was a robbery and a murder — where was the body? Why would someone robbing a convenience store shoot the cashier, then take the body with them? One other angle was that it was a robbery-kidnapping, not a murder. Which would explain why there was no body. But we're talking about a seventeen-year-old boy here, not a pretty girl gone missing. But that's pretty much all there is about the incident in the paperwork. There's something of a concluding summary dated a few months after the kid went missing. It says, essentially, given there was no conclusive evidence of a murder, and the kid's age, they concluded it was likely the kid took the money and split. I'm heading over to the library tomorrow morning, since we have the date nailed down, look up whatever the newspapers said at the time. Figured I could do something like that without attracting too much attention. Might give me some more to go on."

"Well, you already uncovered a lot," Joe said. "Good job, Hank."

"Thanks."

"Tell you one thing, whoever the killer was, and whatever their reason was for taking the body, the place where they buried it tells me the culprit is someone local."

"Right," Hank said. "Only a local would be able to find a spot like that in the dark. Well, that's all I have for now. You go on back to your fishing adventure with Jack, and I'll get back to work."

"Great, Hank. Talk to you tomorrow."

DRIVING in his car the next morning, Hank loved the freedom he had in his new position. He used to have to show up on time at the department to clock in. But now, being salaried, he was free to make executive decisions like driving straight from home to a 7-Eleven out by 270 on the edge of town. It was more than a coffee and breakfast sandwich stop. This was the same location where the young Myron Simpson was abducted back on December 8th, 1988.

As he pulled into the parking lot of the now fairly modern-looking 7-Eleven, he stopped off to the side and pulled out his tablet. Last night, he did some checking. Found out, the property had been purchased by the 7-Eleven folks in 1998, ten years after the murder. Of course, they'd demolished the original building to put up one more in keeping with their franchise expectations. But on Google, Hank was able to find some photos of the original convenience store when it was still owned by Mr. and Mrs. Hampton.

Amazing the oddball things you can find on Google these days.

Hank had parked close to the same location as the person who'd taken the old picture of the store. Holding his tablet up, he compared the two buildings and the surrounding area. The 7-Eleven was significantly bigger and included gas pumps, which were not there in the original.

But it clearly lacked the quaintness and hominess of Hamptons. Gone was the newspaper machine by the front door. And the picnic table on the right. There was no big ICE-COLD–COCA-COLA or BEER signs at the 7-Eleven. Or the proud handwritten sign: "We Sell Boiled Peanuts Inside."

Surprisingly, except for those differences the surrounding area looked very similar. A lot of trees on either side of both buildings, and behind, and not much else. Upon closer inspection, Hank could see one glaring difference outside. In the old picture, there weren't any streetlights. He could just imagine how dark the property would have been back in the day. Actually, there were no streetlights on either side of the road coming in from town, back then or now. And hardly any commercial properties out here to keep this one company.

Seemed to him like a scary place for a high school kid to be working all by himself at night. And the population back in the eighties was half what it is now. Yes sir, could be a very lonely spot. Someone with dark intentions might find a place like this easy pickings, especially at night.

He closed the lid on his tablet and pulled into a parking place. He walked inside to grab that cup of coffee and sandwich, which formed half his reason for coming here, tried to get some kind of vibe about what it might have been like that night, but it was just no use.

The whole place was just too modern. The layout probably bore no resemblance to the way it looked back then. He paid for his purchases, smiled at the middle-aged lady cashier and headed back out the door. As he got to his car, he saw a black man riding slowly up to the sidewalk. Had to be as old as Moses. Deep lines etched on his face, solid white hair. Hank opened his car door, put his things inside then got a hunch. He walked over to the old man and greeted him. "Hello, sir. How are you doing this fine morning?"

The man dropped the kickstand and turned to face Hank. "I be doing just fine, young man. Be doing a bit better once I get inside, get me some nice, hot coffee."

"Tell you what," Hank said, "how about I buy that coffee for you in exchange for a few minutes of your time?"

"No need, young fella. Marjorie in there always gives me my coffee on the house, on account-a me being her oldest customer. That's how she puts it, anyway." He took a few steps down the sidewalk. "So, what you selling? Not that I'm looking for anything much beyond my coffee at the moment."

"I'm sorry. I'm not a salesman." Hank took out his ID badge. "I'm Detective Hank Jensen from the Culpepper PD." He extended his hand.

The old man shook it. "A detective? What you doing out here? Investigating some kind of crime? I ain't heard about any crimes happening 'round here lately."

"You live around this area very long?"

"Ages. I've lived 'round here since about the sixties. Got me a little cabin a short bike ride from here. Not on the lake but close enough to where I can walk there and back. Was out there fishing just this morning."

"Then you must remember the store that was here before the 7-Eleven?"

"Certainly do. Run by the Hamptons. Irma and John.

Nice people, the Hamptons. Treated me like everyone else, even way back then."

"That's great. I don't mean how they treated you, which was a good thing. I'm talking about the fact that you were *here* back then. I'm actually investigating something that took place in 1988."

The old man paused, then said, "Only bad thing I recall from that year was way toward the end, a few weeks before Christmas. When that poor white boy went missing. Don't remember his name at the moment. Used to know it, guess I've forgotten it."

"Myron Simpson?" Hank said.

"Myron," the man repeated. "That's it. Myron. Nice boy. You could tell he was raised right. Always called me sir. I didn't know him as well as Irma and

John, on account-a I didn't come to the store at night too often. That's when he worked, you see. Nighttime."

"That's right," Hank said. "And that's when he went missing, at night. It was December the 8th, 1988. You member anything about that night? The night he went missing?"

The man's face became very sad. "Afraid I do. I was the one who came in the store that night, needed a can of dog food for Boomer...what a great dog he was. Found the store empty. Walked each aisle, even the back room, but couldn't find Myron. That's when I called the police."

10

December 6th, 1988
Culpepper, Georgia

Ray Dodson pulled into Tony's Pizza Parlor in his parents' white Ford Tempo — the ugliest car known to man. He hated bringing it to a place like Tony's, where so many kids from the high school hung out. But he had no choice. Tony's was too far from his house to ride a bike. He'd begged his parents to at least let him tint the windows, so no one would see him driving it, even vowed to pay for it himself. Of course, he'd have to pay them back. He'd never save up enough from his $3.35 an hour, part-time dishwashing job.

The first twenty parking places Ray drove by were full. He recognized most of the cars – all far superior to his — as belonging to kids from school. Wealthier kids. Kids whose parents bought them nice cars to drive and nice clothes to wear out in public. Kids who received hefty allowances to cover all their expenses and even fund their desires.

Kids like Glenn Burton.

Glenn drove an almost-new, shiny black Monte Carlo SS. Ray just drove past it. This car was amazing, inside and out and under the hood. Ray knew this firsthand. He'd ridden in Glenn's Monte Carlo at least thirty times since the school year began, fighting Chip Masters — the third member of their trio — for the privilege of riding shotgun whenever the three of them drove together.

Ray had come to Tony's to share a pizza with Glenn and Chip. Typically, a guy like Glenn would never hang around guys like him and Chip. Chip's family was just barely better off than Ray's. He and Chip had been friends since seventh grade. Glenn came into the picture by accident.

Or maybe it was fate.

It happened during the first week of school. Ray and Chip had just left for the day and decided to head out a side door, closer to where Ray's car was parked. They came around the corner just in time to catch three crackheads pummeling Glenn behind a dumpster. Well, two were beating him while the third was snatching the cash from his wallet. Ray and Chip didn't hesitate. Ray went for the guy with the wallet, while Chip tackled the two guys punching Glenn. He used to play football and made quick work of them both. Ray had at least fifteen pounds on the kid with the wallet plus the element of surprise.

After sending the crackheads running for the hills, they had helped Glenn to his feet. Ray gave him his wallet, not a dollar missing from it. The three of them had been friends ever since.

And because of that one unselfish act, Ray now knew what it felt like to drive around in a shiny black Monte Carlo with plush red interior. He saw the car beside it backing out in his rearview mirror. As soon as it was clear, Ray put his Tempo in reverse and claimed the spot next to Glenn's. As he walked toward the front door, Chip's red Honda Prelude pulled into the parking lot.

Chip stopped when he saw Ray, rolled down his window. "Glenn here yet?"

"Yeah, I just parked next to his Monte Carlo. Was here when I got here."

"Great," Chip said. "I'll pick a spot and find you guys. If Glenn hasn't ordered the—"

"Of course, he's ordered the pizza. First guy in always orders."

"Okay, see you in a minute. Got some exciting stuff to share with you guys." Chip drove off, rolling his window back up.

Ray walked into Tony's, got blasted by the music and all the delicious smells. The place was packed, as usual. He looked around over all the heads in the booths and tables until he found Glenn, chatting with a cute brunette who was trying too hard to keep his attention. He was sitting. She stood next to the table bending over with her elbows on it. Judging by Glenn's body language, her face was a little too close to his.

That was the thing Ray never got. This girl was pretty cute. Certainly somebody Ray would be happy to call his own. But she'd never give him the time of day. It wasn't his looks. Ray knew he wasn't bad looking. As best as he could judge such things, he was above average. Certainly better looking than Glenn. But Glenn just had something that most guys don't have. Ray didn't know what it was, but he could see it, plain as day. He just exuded a level of confidence and charisma that made people want to be around him. Girls especially.

He wasn't ugly. Not by a longshot. Dressed really well. Hair always perfect. Hi-end cologne. Definitely had the gift of gab. The kind of guy who could sell flip-flops to Eskimos. Ray was pretty sure his own IQ was considerably higher than Glenn's, but you'd never know it at school. Glenn talked like someone who knew an awful lot about everything, but somehow never came off sounding like a know-it-all.

Glenn saw Ray approach the table. Turned to the brunette, smiled and said, "Christie my love, it has been a joy chatting with you. It really has. But my man Ray has arrived, which means my man Chip can't be far behind."

"He's parking his car," Ray said.

"See? So, we'll have to chat some more later. Me and my boys have some big plans to discuss."

Christie stood up straight, still smiling, still batting her eyes at Glenn as she backed away. "I'll go, but you're going to call me, right?"

"Got your number." Glenn refocused his gaze on Ray, sending a signal to Christie to keep on walking. "Have a seat, my friend."

She seemed to get the message.

Ray slid all the way into the booth, leaving room for Chip. As usual, Glenn sat in the middle on the other side of the table, all spread out. Didn't matter that because of Chip's size, the two of them always sat uncomfortably close together. This was how things were done. Glenn was top dog. The one running the show, even when no show was playing.

"Do we?" Ray said.

"Do we...what?" Glenn replied.

"Do we have big plans to discuss?"

"What? No, I just said that to let Christie down easy. I'm sure we'll talk about something with the weekend coming up."

"Well, how about next time, instead of sending someone like Christie away, you introduce me to her, tell her what an amazing guy I am."

"I could. Maybe I'll try that next time, see if it works."

They both knew, it wouldn't. "Speaking of plans," Ray said, "Chip said he did have something big he wanted to talk about."

"You know anything about it?" Glenn said.

"No, but here he comes through the front door. Guess we'll find out together. When's the pizza gonna get here?"

"Should be any second."

Ray waved at Chip who headed their way, walking behind the gal carrying their pizza. The waitress set the pizza down, confirmed it had the right toppings. Pepperoni and Italian sausage, as always. She headed back to the kitchen. Per their standard arrangement, Glenn took the first and biggest slice. Then Ray and Chip each grabbed a slice simultaneously. Another unspoken rule was: *everyone could talk with their mouth full.*

No one said anything for three or four bites. Then Glenn said, "So Chip, Ray says you got something exciting to share with us."

Chip was temporarily distracted by Amy Collins walking

by. A blonde cheerleader. It was kind of a disgusting sight. Chip's head turned to follow her as a big glob of gooey cheese stretched with him, still attached to the slice. She turned and smiled at Glenn. Saw Chip, made a face and kept walking.

"You really know how to woo the ladies," Glenn said.

Ray laughed.

"I think she smiled at me," Chip said, still chewing.

"You think?" Ray said. "Maybe you should invite her over, offer her a bite."

"Naw, I could never do that."

"So, Chip," Glenn continued, "like I was saying...what's this exciting news you got for us?"

"Oh, yeah. That's right. I heard about it on the radio driving over here. You guys hear about the Aerosmith concert?"

All three of them loved Aerosmith. Listened to their CDs all the time. Cassettes if listening in Ray's Tempo.

"No," Glenn said, "where?"

"In Savannah, this Saturday night."

"You're kidding," Glenn said.

"No way a group as big as them are playing in Savannah," Ray said. "You mean Atlanta?"

"No, they repeated it two times. They're playing in Savannah, at the Civic Center. I swear it."

"That's crazy," Glenn said. Both cities were a good distance from Culpepper, but Savannah was an hour less of a drive. "How much are the tickets?"

"That's the problem," Chip said. "Thirty-five smackers apiece."

"Might as well have said thirty-five-hundred," Ray said.

"I've got like ten dollars to my name, and I don't get paid again till the weekend after the concert."

"I've probably got maybe fifteen bucks," Chip said. "That might just cover the gas there and back. But we've got to go to this thing. We may never get another chance to see them this close."

Both he and Ray looked at Glenn. Good old Glenn. With the shiny black Monte Carlo and the generous, weekly allowance.

"Guys, don't look at me," he said. "Not this time. I got put on financial restriction a couple weeks back. Don't you remember? When I got caught swiping those CDs from the record store? My Dad almost killed me. There's no way he'd give me a dime for at least another two weeks."

The three of them sat there in the booth chewing pizza, totally deflated.

Finally, Chip spoke up. "There's just got to be a way to get the money. We need just over a hundred bucks."

After a few seconds, Glenn chimed in. "Maybe there is a way...if you guys are up for an adventure."

"What is it?" Ray said.

Glenn looked around. "Can't tell you here. Finish your pizza, and I'll tell you in the car."

11

Present Day
Culpepper Library

Hank pulled into the library parking lot still thinking over the earlier conversation he had with Mr. Eldred Chambers, the old black man on the bike he'd met at the 7-Eleven. It was almost a God thing, bumping into him like that. Mr. Chambers hadn't been able to share a ton of new factual information, but his recollection of that night was still quite vivid. He was able to set the scene on how things looked inside the store in a way the old photograph could not. And since there was no video footage to watch — the store didn't have a security camera — Mr. Chambers' really helped Hank get a better feel for things.

Mr. Chambers had stayed at the store until the police arrived and so was able to share with Hank a little about their initial activity, at least as much as he understood. One of the officers did question him, but that didn't last long since he really hadn't been a witness to what took place. Apparently, no one had. As he was about to leave, he'd heard another officer say something that really bothered him, though. Enough to cause Eldred to stop and respectfully disagree. The officer had suggested the possibility that Myron may not really be missing. Maybe he had taken the money himself and fixed the scene to look like a robbery.

Eldred had told Hank, "Ain't no way that boy took no money. He just not that kind of fella." He was certain of it, then and still. Hank told him his assessment matched what the store owners and the boy's parents had said about Myron. But beyond that, Eldred really didn't have any more relevant details to offer.

Hank got out of the car. Maybe he'd find out something more here. He walked into the library. Joe had talked with Hank about this unique resource—reading old newspaper accounts—something that could really provide decent background info on cold cases. Maybe even spark some new leads. Hank walked over to the desk area, greeted one of the volunteers, identified himself. "Know where Mrs. Hopkins is?" She was the head librarian.

"I do. You can find her over in the fiction section. She's finding homes for some new books we just got in."

"And where might that be? The fiction section?"

She pointed the way. Hank headed across the library, mindful to be as quiet as he used to be in church as a kid. He found Mrs. Hopkins in the third aisle. As he got close to her cart, she straightened up, a little startled by his sudden appearance.

"Oh, hello there," she whispered. "Were you standing there long?"

Matching her volume, Hank said, "No, I just walked up. Don't know if you remember me."

"You look somewhat familiar."

"I'm Detective Hank Jensen, work with Lieutenant Joe Boyd."

"Oh, yes. I know Joe. We go to the same church, and he comes in here every now and then. Usually when he's working on a case."

"Well, that's why I'm here. Kinda filling in for Joe. He, Kate and the kids still have a few days left on their vacation. But this case came up, so I'm seeing how much progress I can make till he gets back."

"You want to look up some old newspapers from our microfilm collection?"

"That's right, unless you have the dates I'm interested in converted to the computer."

"What year are you looking for?"

"December 1988."

"Nope. We're not there yet. Slowly making our way, though. Think we've gotten back to 1993 so far." She set one of the new books on her cart, pushed it to the side. "I'll take you over there, help you get situated."

"I don't want to bother you. I think I can figure it out."

"No bother. I need to stretch my legs a little anyway. Hurts my knees to be bending down for too long." She walked past him then turned right at the end of the aisle. "Follow me."

When they got to the microfilm area, it was pretty much as Hank remembered. He'd never used it before but had been here a couple of times with Joe, mainly to fetch him because he'd turned the volume off on his cell phone. Which reminded Hank to do the same now. Mrs. Hopkins showed him all the drawers containing the microfilm containers and how the date system worked. She brought him over to the microfilm reader, briefly explained how to run it, even though the instructions were clearly spelled out and posted on a laminated sheet of paper beside it.

"If you have any questions at all, Detective, don't hesitate to ask. You said the date you're interested in is 1989?"

"88," Hank said. "December."

"I was here for most of that decade," she said. "I came in the first half to go to the university. Then I met my husband, who was from here, so after I graduated, we stayed. I do remember we had an unusually high number of murders here during that period, for such a small town. It was actually kind of scary. I paid pretty close attention to the stories, so after you're through, feel free to ask me about the case you're working on. I'll be happy to share anything I remember. That is, if you're at liberty to talk about it."

"Well, actually Mrs. Hopkins, I'm not free to talk about this specific case just yet. But I will probably be in a few days. If you don't mind, I'd like to come back and talk to you then."

"Anything I can do to help." She nodded and headed back toward her project in the fiction area.

Hank found the container for the specific week of 1988 he was interested in, and in a few minutes had the microfilm loaded and was slowly making his way through the days leading up to the murder. He kept getting distracted by all the interesting news stories of the time, and even the ads.

The day before Myron Simpson's murder, it had been announced that USSR General Secretary Mikhail Gorbachev would be making an official visit to the United States the following week. "Little did you know, Mikhail," Hank muttered aloud, "in just a few years the Soviet Union will completely disintegrate." He read an article about the new President-elect George Herbert Walker Bush preparing for his upcoming inauguration next month. Wow. Little did he know that he'd only be a one-termer and that his eldest son--affectionately nicknamed "Dubya"--would become president twelve years later...and serve two terms.

Even more fascinating were the price of pork chops: only 40 cents a pound. Movie tickets averaged $3.50 each. A gallon of gas was 91 cents. He found brand-new, decent-looking houses in Culpepper selling in the mid-to-low fifties. It was crazy. He could have bought five houses back then for what it cost to buy the house he and Elaine lived in today. Rents for really nice two-bedroom apartments went for $425 a month.

"Man, I lived at the wrong time," he whispered. Then he scolded himself for getting so far off track, forced himself to stop indulging his curiosity and get back to work.

He finally scrolled to the reprint of Page One of the local section for "December, 9th, 1988," the day after the incident at the Quick-Stop on 270. Of course, the headline didn't talk about a murder. At this point, only he, Joe and a select handful of people in Culpepper knew what became of the victim.

The Headline read:

Local Teen Disappears from Convenience Store

12

The article was pretty substantial.

It wasn't the main story on the front page of the local section but certainly ran a close second. Hank read it through twice. It included quotes from the owners, Irma and John Hampton and even old Mr. Chambers. It mentioned photographs would be forthcoming in the evening edition. Back in the pre-internet days, the Culpepper Gazette published morning and evening editions. Hank would have to check out the evening edition next, see what these folks looked like.

It even mentioned Myron's name, which surprised Hank seeing he was a minor. But then the reason became obvious in the next paragraph with a quote from the boy's mother, pleading for Myron's safe return. There was no mention of the possibility that Myron took the money, or that he had possibly run away. That was purely speculation on the police report. The article simply said, "at this point the young man's whereabouts are unknown."

Unfortunately, Hank thought, that part of the mystery wasn't a mystery anymore. Soon, he or Joe would have to break the news to the parents. Preferably, Joe. Although this one might not be such a heartbreaking task, since so much time had passed. His folks might even be relieved to finally know what really happened. Of course, so far all they knew was that he had definitely been killed; he was not a runaway or kidnapped.

The quote from Irma Hampton mentioned the robbery. "Whoever it was, they cleaned out the cash drawer completely," she'd said. "Don't know yet if anything else was taken." It ended with a request from the police, asking anyone who'd driven by the store between nightfall and closing to please contact them if they'd seen anything unusual or suspicious.

Hank was just about to scroll to the right, looking for the evening edition when Mrs. Hopkins came up.

"How's your research going, Detective?" she said softly.

He turned to see her standing behind her cart. "Pretty well. Found the first article on the incident we're investigating already. Just about to read the second."

She leaned forward and whispered, "Would it have anything to do with the missing Simpson boy?"

So much for secrecy, thought Hank. He leaned in her direction, to convey the idea that this really was confidential information. "Actually, it is. But I wonder if you could do me a big favor and keep this between us for now?"

"I'm very good at keeping secrets. But I'm curious...why all the cloak and dagger? Joe never seemed to care about keeping his research under wraps the last few times he's been in here working on cold cases."

How could Hank explain that Joe was the only reason he

was keeping things under wraps, to buy him a couple more days' vacation time with his family? "This one has some extenuating circumstances. For one thing, we haven't notified the boy's family, and we wouldn't want them to find out anything until they hear from us first."

"That makes sense," she said. "Does that mean you found his body? Assuming that he's dead. I think pretty much everyone who was around at the time knows that he must have been killed. Myron's family wasn't well-off, but he was a good boy, and his folks were good people. He wouldn't have just run off like that, leave them without a word. And even if he did run away for some crazy teenage reason, he'd have never stayed away all those years."

"Well," Hank said, "I can't really discuss the details of the investigation just yet. But guess I can say, he definitely didn't run away. So, you knew his family? You remember this case pretty well?"

She looked around to make sure no one was near. "Oh yes, it was a big story for quite a few weeks. Had search parties out and everything. But then a week before Christmas, a big cold front blew in, dumped about a foot of snow. People stopped searching. The Christmas holiday came front and center, and before long no one was talking about what happened to Myron anymore."

"That's sad," Hank said. "But I know that's how these things go. Everyone else moves on...except the family."

"I'm sure that's true, and it is sad. But speaking of moving on, I don't know where, but his folks did move out of Culpepper. I remember reading about it. Think it was maybe the second anniversary of his disappearance. Had an article in the paper about it, where they talked to his parents, and they were in some other city or town. Somewhere in Georgia, but I don't recall where."

"Thanks, I'll make a note of that." Just then Hank's phone started to vibrate. Hank quickly grabbed it, mouthed the words, "So sorry."

She made a face, feigning annoyance. Then whispered back, "Happens all the time in here."

He looked at the screen. It was the Medical Examiner's office. "I've got to take this. I'll step outside. Can I leave this here, like this, for a few minutes?"

"I'm sure that'll be fine. Hardly anyone ever uses it."

Hank hurried toward a side exit, answered the call. "Hi, this is Hank. Give me just a sec. I'm leaving the library."

"That's fine, Detective. This is Dr. Hargrove's assistant."

Moments later, Hank stepped outside walked to a bench under a shady tree. "Okay, I can talk now." There was no reply. "Hello? Anyone there?" Again no reply. He looked at his phone. The call was still active. Then he heard a male voice, saying, "Hello, Detective Jensen?" Hank put the phone back to his ear. "I'm here."

"Sorry, this is Dr. Hargrove. My assistant got me on the line when she confirmed she had reached you."

"You have something for us already?"

"I do. Nothing like a positive ID yet. Still awaiting the results of several more tests. But I came across something very significant this morning as I examined the victim's abdominal cavity."

"I thought he was pretty much just a skeleton at this point," Hank said.

"He was, or is. But perhaps what I found was lodged in his rib cage or spine and came loose while the body was being transported. I found it as I was removing what was left of his shirt, in the material that would have covered his back."

"What was it?" Hank said.

"Very likely the bullet that killed this young man."

"Really?"

"That is correct," Hargrove said. "When the body is this decomposed, it can often be tricky coming up with a precise cause of death. Unless there is something obvious inter-acting with the remaining bones. Like a hole penetrating the skull, or significant cuts in the bone, say in the case of a violent stabbing. But there wasn't anything like that on these remains, so finding this bullet was quite unexpected."

"That's great, Doc. Joe will be excited to hear this news. So, you think we can say with some certainty, he was killed by a gun? That would narrow down the field of possible murder weapons."

"Yes, I'd say he was killed by a gun. And I can say further, the murder weapon will be some kind of pistol or revolver, not a rifle."

"Great. We can do a ballistics test on it, figure out exactly what kind of gun was used."

"I can actually be of some help with that also," Hargrove said. "I'm not a ballistics expert, but I am something of a gun connoisseur. I've built quite a collection over the years. I can't put my finger on it just yet, but this bullet is not your normal run-of-the-mill ammunition. I'm well aware of what a spent 45, or 9 mm, or thirty-eight caliber bullet looks like. This is none of those."

"That's interesting," Hank said. "Any idea what it is?"

"Not yet. But I'm going to do some checking and get back

with you. An unusual bullet often comes from an unusual gun. I must say, seeing this has piqued my curiosity."

"Wow, Doc. We obviously don't have a murder weapon yet, but that kind of unique info might really come in handy down the road."

"I thought you'd find it interesting," Hargrove said. "I'll let you know if I nail down anything more specific, then get the bullet back to you."

Hank put his phone in his pocket and headed back toward the library. Man, he'd have some good stuff to tell Joe when he called that afternoon.

13

J oe was really enjoying this.

Being out here in the woods camping with the family. Well, sort of camping. At least, their pop-up included some tent material. Jack and Rachel were out in the woods with them, but you couldn't really call their situation camping. The insides of their trailer were several notches up the ladder from his and Kate's first two apartments in Pittsburgh. But hey, they were great people and super-easy to be with.

It was mid-afternoon. He, Jack and Joe Jr. were metal detecting just off the trail a ways. First time out for Joe Jr., and he was loving it. They'd already found a rusty old spoon. Jack thought it could honestly be from the Civil War era. If true, that meant Civil War soldiers had to be either camping or walking through this neck of the woods. Which meant there was likely a bunch more Civil War stuff to find buried in the dirt. That got Joe Jr. really excited. He'd said after finding the spoon, "There's gotta be more, right Dad? Ain't like a Civil War soldier's gonna be walking out here by himself with a spoon."

Joe had said, "Think you're right, Joey. And stop saying ain't." Kate was a stickler for things like that. She never corrected Joe when he talked that way, but held out at least a glimmer of hope Joe Jr. might learn how to talk right. Joe was pretty sure there was an insult in there somewhere.

His phone rang. Pulling it out of his pocket, he saw it was Hank. Right on time. "Okay Joey, I gotta get this. Remember I said Hank was gonna call?"

"I'm fine, Dad. I got this. You go ahead."

Joe looked at Jack, who looked back at him, gave Joe a nod letting him know he'd keep an eye on Joey. Joe walked several yards away, so he could talk freely. "Hey Hank, how's it going?"

"Moving right along, Joe. In fact, making such good progress you could probably take a few more days off if you want."

"So, you like being king, eh?"

"Seems to suit me."

Joe laughed. "Okay, King Hank. Gimme the update. You're interrupting my playtime."

"Well, started off the day grabbing a cup of coffee at that convenience store where our vic' went missing. Bumped into an old black gentleman who's been going there for his coffee since back in the days when it was owned by the Hamptons."

"Really? He remember when the kid went missing?"

"Better than that. He was the guy who came to the store that night, found it empty. He knew the kid who worked there and knew something was wrong. Found the cash drawer opened and cleaned out, so he called the police."

"Did he have anything significant to offer? Anything to add we don't already know?"

"Not really," Hank said. "But he was able to give me a good feel for things, the way they were that night. And he agreed with the owners and the kid's parents that there was no way the kid stole the money or ran away. Speaking of the kid's parents, found out an interesting detail about them."

"What's that?"

"Well, I went to the library next. Met with Mrs. Hopkins, like you suggested."

"She get you set up on the microfilm?"

"She did. Easy as pie, like you said. Found the article in the Gazette, written the day after. Read it several times. Didn't learn anything too much from it. Just reaffirming things we already know mostly. Direct quotes from the owners and the kid's parents. The owners were sure it was a robbery. Everyone bewildered by the boy's disappearance. Nothing even hinted about him possibly being murdered. Read the next installment in the evening edition. Pretty much the same story, except the second one included pictures of the kid, the store and the owners. Kept on reading follow-up articles over the next week or so. The search for the kid seemed to be a pretty big deal. I mean, that seemed to become the story after the first day. Where was he? Where could he be? Pictures of people searching the woods and empty lots all over town. Of course, they never made it out as far as where you found his body. But they were definitely looking."

"And then what?" Joe said. "People just lost interest after a while, stopped looking?"

"That was part of it, I'm sure. Also had a major snow-storm blow through. That ended the search completely, and I guess they just stopped looking after that."

"So, what was the detail about the parents you found out? You led off with that but never got back to it?"

"Oh, yeah. Found out from Mrs. Hopkins that they don't live in town anymore. Moved out a year or two later. So, won't have to be flipping coins to see who has to drive to their place and break the news."

"Well, we still gotta hunt them down, call the law enforcement agency closest to where they live."

"On my checklist," Hank said. "But hey, listen, I haven't gotten to the best part."

"There's more?"

"Just one. Saved the best for last."

"What is it?"

"How about the cause of death for our vic? And possibly a lead on the murder weapon itself?"

"What?" Joe said. "Hargrove got back to you already? Usually takes him days. Must've been something obvious."

"It wasn't. Well, in a way it was." Hank told him what the M.E. had said about how tricky it was to nail down the cause of death unless it was obvious, and that there were no visible signs on these remains.

"So, how could he be so sure about the cause of death? Hargrove doesn't call unless he has something real."

Hank told him about Hargrove finding the bullet in what was left of the kid's shirt. "He said it must've lodged in his spine or rib cage and came loose when we were moving the body. But here's the best part... I guess Hargrove is some kind of big gun collector."

"Yeah, he's talked to me about that a few times."

"Well, he recognized this bullet as something unique. He didn't know what it was just yet, but knew it likely came from some kind of rare gun. At least, that's how he made it sound."

"Wow, Hank. You got all this in a day? Maybe I don't need to come back so soon."

"I know, right?" Just then, there was a knock at Hank's office door. He looked up, saw the head and shoulders of Captain Pendleton poking through. His face didn't look too happy. He saw that Hank was on the phone, walked the rest of the way in, closed the door behind him.

"I'm just giving Joe the afternoon update."

"That's Joe on the phone?" Pendleton said.

Hank nodded.

"Good. Tell him he needs to get his butt back in here. Pronto."

"What?"

Joe heard him, too, through the phone.

"Joe needs to come back," Pendleton said. "Just got off the phone with Tom Hazelton over at the Gazette. Calling to ask if I could confirm the rumors that we're reopening the case of Myron Simpson, the convenience store worker who disappeared back in '88."

14

"Hank, put me on speaker," Joe said. He heard a click then Hank's voice.

"Joe can hear you now, Cap."

"Joe? You hear what I just told Hank?" Pendleton said.

"I did. You said two things. Hazelton at the Gazette called about this case, and you want me back in the office ASAP. But I'm not sure how those two things go together."

"What are you talking about, Joe? That was our deal, remember? I was okay with you staying on vacation as long this thing stayed out of the news. Hank's doing a good job, but I want you handling the media side of this, once it starts up. Looks like it has."

"Mind me asking what you told Hazelton so far?"

"I said no comment."

"Did he say he's running with the story?"

"No," Pendleton said. "I think he's fishing for info at the moment."

"Right. So, it's still not in the news."

"C'mon, Joe, you know he's not gonna go away. He's a reporter in a small town where nothing happens. You think he's gonna drop a chance to break a story like this?"

"No, I don't, Captain. But from reading the stuff he writes, he seems like old-school journalism to me. Kinda guy that'll wait till he gets the facts straight. It's not like he's got serious competition to worry about. The only other paper in town is the one the college puts out. And they only cover stuff that goes on at the school." Pendleton didn't say anything to that. Joe knew he was making a dent in his case.

"How do you think he got wind of this?" Pendleton said.

"I don't know," Hank interjected. "I've been quiet as a mouse."

"But you're talking to people, right?" Pendleton said. "People surrounding the case?"

"Just a handful so far, sir. Really, just two. But I don't think either one of them would have blabbed to anyone."

"Well, somebody did. And it's just a matter of time before this thing breaks loose."

"I agree, Captain," Joe said. "We don't have that much more time before it does. But with all due respect, sir...we're not there just yet. I only need a couple more days, and then our little family trip is over. How about I call Hazelton myself? I've worked with him before. He seems like a fairly reasonable guy. I'll explain the situation to him, without going into any detail. Tell him we'll talk to him first as soon as we can talk about the case."

"I guess I'm okay with that. But Joe, if this starts showing up on social media, I want you back here to manage it. I remember this case from back when I was in high school. It was a big deal. There's still a lot of people in this town who were around back then. If the story breaks, there'll be a lot of interest in every aspect of it. Especially now that we know it's a murder."

"Wait, Captain," Hank said. "I forgot you were here back then. Okay if I ask you some questions once Joe hangs up?"

"Yeah, I suppose. Not sure I can be of any help."

"So, we good?" Joe said.

"Yeah, Joe. Go back to your fishing or whatever else you were doing. But keep your phone on."

Joe hung up and immediately checked to see if he had that reporter, Hazelton, in his phone. He did, so he took a chance he might reach him and called.

"Hello, this is Tom Hazelton at the Gazette. Who am I speaking to?"

"Hey Tom, this is Lt. Joe Boyd at the Culpepper PD. Just got off the phone with Captain Pendleton."

"Really? That was quick. So, what? The chief wanting to put a fire out before it spreads too far?"

"Something like that," Joe said.

"Guess that kinda confirms the rumors are true. Or why else would he call you and tell you to call me?"

"Well, actually, it was my idea to call you. I told him I thought you were a pretty reasonable guy... or a journalist. You know what I mean."

"If I had a soul, I might have taken that as an insult."

"Good thing you don't have a soul then," Joe said.

Hazelton laughed. "So, what is it you want to tell me, Lieutenant? Want to add a few comments to your captain's no comment reply?"

"Not exactly. Not yet anyway. What I'd like to do is make a deal with you...you being a reasonable guy and all."

"Okay, I'm listening."

"We're not talking to anyone yet about anything, and I don't know how you found out about this, but it is true. For reasons I can't explain yet, we are looking into that convenience store case back in the late 80s."

"We're talking about the case of Myron Simpson, right?" Hazelton said.

"Correct. But I'm asking you, as a personal favor, not to go public with this just yet. For at least a couple more days."

"Can I ask why?"

Joe knew he'd ask this and didn't think Hazelton would appreciate Joe's need to spend a few more days with his kids. "Well, for one thing, we're going to need a few days to locate the kid's folks. We've learned they moved out of town a couple of years after he went missing. We have no idea where they are. Now, I know the Gazette is a local paper, but you guys put your stuff online like everybody else these days. We don't want this kid's parents hearing the first update about his case in decades from some news story someone posted on their Facebook page."

"I can appreciate that," Hazelton said. "Even without a soul."

Joe laughed.

"But I guess something fairly significant must've happened," Hazelton said, "as you said, for a case with no updates for over a decade, to suddenly become a thing you're actively working on."

"That's correct. Something significant has happened. And I promise you, as soon as I can talk freely about this, me or Hank will talk directly to you and no one else. I mean in the press. Do we have a deal?"

"How much time are we talking about here?" Hazelton said.

"Couple of days, tops."

"Well, I guess I can sit on it, if that's all we're talking about."

"Really appreciate it, Tom. Which brings me to another related issue. Who did you hear this rumor from?"

"Well, I don't like to reveal my sources if I don't have to."

"I understand. But it kind of blows up our effort to put a temporary lid on this thing if you're the only one cooperating. What if the person who told you this starts spreading that rumor on social media?"

"I see your point. But I don't think that's going to happen. In fact, I know it's not."

"How can you be so sure?"

"Because it's my wife," Hazelton said. "She volunteers down at the library three days a week. She saw your partner —Hank I think his name is—at the library working in the microfilm area. She had to put some books away in a nearby aisle, saw him and Mrs. Hopkins talking. Then Hank got a call and stepped outside a few minutes. She walked by, saw the article he was reading on the microfilm machine, all about the missing boy from the convenience store."

"I see. Any chance you could give her a call, explain things a bit?"

"I'll call her soon as we hang up."

"Thanks, Tom. Really appreciate it."

"No problem. But I can expect to hear from you in a couple of days, right?"

"Definitely," Joe said. "Me or Hank will let you know

when the light turns green. And if you want, you can interview me then, too."

"Then we have a deal, sir. Thanks for the call."

Joe hung up, looked around in the woods for Jack and Joe Jr. Saw them through the trees about a hundred yards away, still metal detecting. He glanced up at the sun, figured there was still enough daylight left to get in some good father-son time before dinner.

15

Hank was just about to get into something else when Captain Pendleton came back into his office. A few minutes ago, he had asked the captain if he could interview him about the convenience store case from the 80s, once Joe got off the phone. Pendleton had said yes but then said, "I better go use the bathroom first." He'd been gone long enough for Hank to wonder if he might be having some trouble, but Hank would never ask Pendleton such a thing. Not out of any sense of respect, but because Pendleton was the kind of guy who would not only answer such a question, but go into way too much detail.

"Sorry for being gone so long." Pendleton sat in one of Hank's two office chairs. "Fire away, but get right to it. Can only give you a few minutes. But I'm guessing you might not even need that long. Like I said, not sure I can be of any help."

"That's all right, Cap. You never know unless you try,

right? So, you were in high school with this kid? The one who got killed?"

"Yeah, I was. But I didn't really know Myron. I knew who he was, though I'm not even sure why I knew that. We weren't in the same grade, and he seemed pretty much like a loner. Never saw him hanging out with any group of friends."

"Did you know if he had any enemies? Anyone who might have any reason to hurt him."

"Naw. I mean, there might have been, but I wasn't close enough to his world to even know if he did. I didn't even know he worked at that convenience store, till I heard the news that he'd gone missing."

"What did the kids at school say in the aftermath?" Hank said. "What was the buzz going around about what happened?"

"People were kinda split about it. Most of my friends figured he took the money and ran off with it. But from what I gather, only a couple hundred bucks was missing from the till. Not like you're gonna take a cruise to Tahiti with that. I was thinking it had to be foul play, but typically in a convenience store robbery, if they shoot the clerk they don't take his body with them. I mean why would you?"

"Right," said Hank. "Sounds like your detective hunches were even working back then."

"Yeah, guess they were. I was actually one of the volunteers who went out searching for him. Did it every day for a week or so, then we stopped for some reason."

"Mrs. Hopkins said a big winter storm blew in."

"Yeah, that's what it was. Not sure why, but people lost interest in the case after that. Guess that's what happens when you're a loner. No friends to keep screaming about you not being around anymore. Kind of a shame."

"Yeah, it is," Hank said. "You think maybe the fact that people lost interest back then, and that his folks moved out of town so many years ago...maybe this story won't be such a big deal now? You know, when the news breaks about it? Maybe there's just going to be a big *so what* reaction."

"Could be," Pendleton said. "But look how quickly Hazelton jumped on the story, just because of a rumor he'd heard. I'm thinking people love a good mystery, and when people find out the poor kid was probably killed the night he went missing and buried just a couple miles outside of town...they're gonna want to know what happened."

"Guess you're right." No one said anything for a few moments. Hank kinda wished he had some more probing questions to ask, just to leave a better impression, but he was coming up empty.

Pendleton stood up. "Guess that's it, then. Like I said, probably didn't shed any new light on the situation." He opened Hank's door. "Let's hope Joe was able to get Hazelton to sit tight for a few days."

"Yep. Thanks, Captain."

Pendleton walked out the door. As he did, Hank's desk phone rang. It was Janie, the gal who usually answered the non-emergency calls that came in. He picked up the receiver. "Hey Janie, what's up?"

"Sorry, to bother you Hank, but I got this lady on the phone asking some peculiar questions about the possibility of a murder that might've taken place years ago. But she's not even sure if it's real or some story some guy made up."

"Is she some kind of whack job?"

"She doesn't sound loony, more like confused. She said she wasn't even going to call but her husband convinced her she should, just to set her mind at rest."

Hank laughed. "And you think I can do a better job of that than you?"

"Well," Janie said, "it's kind of in your neck of the woods. Homicide. Took place years ago. Got that cold case ring to it."

"All right, give me her number. I'll give her a call."

"She's still on the line."

"Oh, then put her through. What's her name?"

"Let me look. I wrote it down." A short pause. "Melissa, Melissa Hendricks."

Hank waited a moment, heard a click, then Janie's voice talking to Melissa, letting her know Detective Hank Jensen was on the phone. Janie got off as soon Hank started talking. "Hello Mrs. Hendricks, this is Hank Jensen. How can I help you? I understand you have some questions about a possible murder case from a long time ago?"

"I'm sorry, Detective. I really shouldn't be bothering you with this."

Hank was expecting someone much older. She had a voice that sounded like someone more in her forties. "That's okay, just take your time. Something must have prompted you to call us."

"Well, it's not like I have a crime to report, or anything. It's more like a suspicion that a crime might have happened a long time ago."

"Where? Here in Culpepper?"

"I'm guessing so. I think that's probably where it happened, if it really happened at all. See, even saying that. I feel so stupid. I wouldn't even have called except my husband said I should."

"And why did he think that?" Hank said. "That you should call us?"

"I think it might just be to get me to shut up about this. Although, he'd never say something like that."

"What reason did he give? Why was he so insistent?" Hank hoped there might be something that at least sounded like a rational reason.

"Cliff says I've got very good intuition about things, and that when something bugs me this much, there's usually something to it."

Hearing this made Hank wonder...maybe Cliff really was just trying to shut her up. "Okay, so let's go from there. What makes you think this even might be a real thing?"

"It's just that, well, it's all because of this writers' group I'm a part of, called Word Weavers. We meet once a month at a church hall in town. Anyone who's interested in writing can come. You don't have to belong to the church. Well, anyway, there's this fellow that's been coming lately. I probably shouldn't say his name, for privacy reasons. And because, well really, I'm not officially accusing him of anything. Other than the fact that he creeps me out." She laughed. "But that's not a crime."

"And you think this...gentleman, might have been involved with a murder several years ago?"

"Something like that. No, well, it's exactly like that."

"And what makes you think this?" Hank said.

"It's this murder mystery he's writing."

Oh, geez, thought Hank.

"Everyone brings a submission to read to the group each

month," she continued. "And Andrew has been bringing this...oh, no. I just said his name, didn't I? Well, you don't know his last name."

"I'm sure that's fine," Hank said. "Go on."

"Anyway, we're only supposed to bring about fifteen hundred words, or less. So, that's like maybe a chapter or so. He's brought three so far, and each time he reads one, I get the strangest feeling that he's not making this up. Like, he's calling it fiction. But he's really writing about something that happened. It even sounds familiar to me. Like it's a case I've actually heard of before. A long time ago. But I can't remember exactly which case it was, or when it happened. This last time, he gave it a title...*An Inconvenient Death*. He wouldn't tell us why but said we'd understand why after he writes a few more chapters."

Hank looked at his watch. How much more time should he give this nice lady? He couldn't even think of a relevant follow-up question to ask.

She stopped talking a moment, then said, "This isn't making any sense, is it? That's all right, you can tell me."

"It's making sense, Mrs. Hendricks. In a way—"

"Please, call me Melissa."

"It's not that it's not making sense, Melissa. It's that I'm not sure there's anything I can do to help you. Not at this stage of things, anyway. There's just not enough information for me to act on. Or even to consider investigating further."

"I understand perfectly, Detective. Like I said at the beginning, I really shouldn't have called."

"It's okay. Maybe you just called a little too soon. Why don't you just wait till he reads a few more chapters? See if that doesn't provide us enough information to at least justify me talking to him? Or, maybe you'll remember some more specific details about why this story he's writing sounds so familiar, like when the murder happened and where?"

"That's fine, Detective. That's what I'll do then. I appreciate you taking the time to talk with me."

"Not at all, Melissa. You have a nice rest of the day."

16

F ifteen minutes later, Melissa's husband Cliff came in from whatever project he'd been working on in the garage. She'd felt so stupid now, bothering that detective with her silly suspicions. She sat in her half of the matching recliners, hand on the remote, half-watching a Hallmark movie. It might've provided a better distraction if she hadn't already seen it twice.

Cliff came up behind her. "You were talking to that detective fellow when I went out to the garage. How'd that go?"

"Not great," she said. "Makes me wish I didn't listen to you now."

"Listen to me?" he repeated.

"Yeah, you were the one kept saying I should call."

"I might've suggested it once or twice, but it was only because you kept bringing it up. Thought it might ease your mind if you talked to someone who handled these kinds of cases."

"Well, it didn't. It made me feel stupid. Now they probably think I'm some kind of old busybody, who's always butting into other people's business. Like that Gladys Kravitz on *Bewitched*."

Cliff laughed. "Unless they're in their fifties or older, I don't think anyone down there is comparing you to Gladys Kravitz. What did they say that's got you so upset?"

"There wasn't any *they*, it was just one man. A detective, and he was very nice. But even as I was explaining things to him, I could tell how crazy I must've sounded. As he asked one question after another, I realized I had absolutely nothing to offer that he could do anything about. I told him that part about how Tubbs' story sounded like something that really happened years ago but couldn't even remember a single thing that would connect it to real life."

"So, how did things end up?" Cliff said. "He suggest you get your head examined?"

"No, he suggested I wait till Mr. Tubbs writes a few more chapters. Maybe he'll say something that will help me remember."

"That sounds like good advice...*Gladys*."

"Cliff..."

"I'm totally joking. You've got almost a month before your next group meeting. Try to just tuck it away in a mental file until then." He headed down the hall.

She sat there with the remote, thinking, wondering. Could she just do that? Just...tuck it away. Men seemed to be able to compartmentalize things so easily. She tried to get into the Hallmark movie, but it wasn't sinking in. She tried changing the channel but couldn't find anything else that caught her interest. A pity how often that happened, given she had over a hundred channels to choose from.

Finally, a thought popped into her head. Really, more of an image. The face of her friend Lisa from her Word Weavers group. She picked up her phone, found Lisa's name from her Recent Calls list and pushed the button. It rang only a few times before Lisa picked up.

"Hi, Melissa. How are you doing?"

"Not too bad, Lisa. You?"

"Getting over a migraine that's been beating me up since yesterday. But other than that..."

"I'm sorry. Maybe I'll call you another time."

"Don't be silly. I said I was getting over a migraine. It's almost completely gone now. So, what's going on?"

Melissa hesitated. But it was too late now. Lisa would never let her back out of the conversation. "Okay, well...this is probably going to sound totally foolish. And if it does, you can just tell me. You don't have to humor me."

"What are you talking about, Melissa?"

"I'm sorry. It's just...well, I guess I should just say it, right?"

"Yes, you should just say it."

"Okay, remember the other night at the Word Weavers meeting, when Andrew Tubbs was reading his latest chapter?"

"I know, wasn't it just awful?"

"Well, yeah, I guess it was. But I'm not talking about the quality of his writing. I'm talking about the content, the story itself."

"Oh, yeah. That was a little disturbing. But I'm not sure if that's because I find him a little disturbing, or if the story itself was. Like, if Brian had written it, would I feel the same way?"

Melissa was relieved to hear that he creeped out Lisa, too. "I don't know. But I agree with you. I found it disturbing, too. But I'm not talking about that. I'm talking about how... well, you've lived in this town for a long time, right? Did the story itself sound at all familiar to you?"

"You know, in a way it kinda did. Not so much the first couple of chapters he read, but this last one did."

"I thought the same things, too," Melissa said. "But I'm having a hard time remembering the real-life thing it reminds me of. I thought if I called you, maybe you'd remember."

"I was thinking," Lisa said, "that it sort of reminded me of that boy who went missing in high school. I don't remember his name now. Do you know what I'm talking about?"

Melissa thought a moment. "I do. I do remember that. Not his name, but I remember it happening."

"That's one of the things that threw me, though, about Andy's story," Lisa said. "What he wrote takes place in the 70s. We were just in grade school then."

"I know. But maybe he just changed it to the 70s to make it seem like it wasn't a real story. To throw people off track."

"That could certainly be it," Lisa said. "But the other thing that threw me was the three high school guys driving around in that souped-up car. What was it, a red Camaro? Our high school class wasn't that big. Some of the guys had some really nice cars, especially the rich ones. But I don't remember any souped-up red Camaro. And what would the three guys be about? I don't remember anything about three high school guys being part of the story when that kid went missing."

"I don't, either," Melissa said. "But then, maybe Andrew

has some inside information. I mean, if he was involved in it at all. Maybe he was one of the three high school kids he's writing about."

Lisa didn't immediately reply, then said, "Could be."

"That would make it even more disturbing," Melissa said.

"It certainly would," said Lisa.

Neither spoke for a few moments. "Wait a minute," Melissa said. "What was the title he gave to his story? Remember, he thought it was something clever but wouldn't explain why?"

"I remember," Lisa said. "*An Inconvenient Death*." Just then, she gasped.

"What's the matter?"

"I just remembered...that boy went missing from that convenience store out on 270. Remember?"

Melissa did. "They thought it was some kind of robbery, right?"

"Yes, but I'm talking about Andy's story, his clever title. *An In-CONVENIENT Death*. Get it? The boy goes missing from a convenience store?"

Now Melissa gasped. "Oh, my. You think that's what this is?"

"Well, we'll know for sure at next month's meeting when he reads the next chapter. He told me the other night after the meeting that everyone would know why he picked that title when he reads his next submission."

Melissa sighed. Maybe there was something to what Cliff said about her intuition never being off. "I'm afraid if we find out that the location of his big mystery turns out to be a convenience store, we might have to go to the police."

17

December 6th, Evening, 1988
Culpepper, GA

I t was a little after six. Already dark out. An ornamental iron gate slid back behind some fancy brick pillars, allowing Ray to pull into the winding driveway of Glenn Burton's house. Like the rest of Glenn's life, it was slightly over the top. Old-timey gas lampposts illuminated the drive through the trees, which shortly gave way to the splendid panorama of the house itself. A classic two-story brick mansion with multiple high-pitched roofs, a four-car garage to the right, well-lit stone fountain in the center.

Ray drove around the fountain, pulled into one of the open spots in front of the garage. Chip's car was already there. He guessed Glenn's Monte Carlo had been tucked in for the night behind one of the closed garage doors. As he got out of his car and looked around, it did seem like the property was pretty much deserted, as Glenn said it would be, except for the lights glowing through the living areas and the large bedroom on the second floor, far left side.

Glenn's room. The place where they were supposed to meet.

Glenn said his dad was away on business, and his mom was across town having cocktails with her sister. "She won't be home for hours," Glenn had said. Ray was told to just walk right in, go up the grand staircase and head down the long hallway to Glenn's room. Ray knew the way. He paused halfway up the stairs to take in the ridiculous scene. The living area of just the downstairs was easily bigger than Ray's entire house. The furniture and decor looked like something out of a society magazine.

Fancy as could be, but everything looked so uncomfortable. He cleared the stairs and turned left, walking toward the light coming from Glenn's room.

As Ray got close to the partially-opened door, he heard Glenn and Chip debating over which band they liked as much, or better, than Aerosmith.

"I like Def Leppard even more than Aerosmith," Glenn said. "And maybe INXS, too."

"You like INXS more than Aerosmith?" Chip said. "You gotta be kidding me."

"All right, maybe not better than, but almost as much."

"How about Guns N' Roses?" Chip said. "How about U2?"

"They're both up there on my list, but somewhere just below Aerosmith."

"I can't believe we're gonna get to see these guys."

Ray walked in. Glenn's bedroom was like his room and his parents' master bedroom combined. Glenn was laying on his bed propped up with some pillows. Chip was sitting in an overstuffed recliner in the corner. They both looked at him.

"He finally arrives," Glenn said. "We're talking about who we like better than Aerosmith."

"I heard," Ray said.

"Let me guess," he continued. "You like...Rick Astley and Debbie Gibson."

"No..." Ray said.

Chip sat up in his chair, grabbed a hairbrush on the dresser beside him and began to sing: "*Never Gonna Give You Up, Never Gonna Let You Down*," mimicking Rick Astley. He was actually pretty good.

"If I hear that song on the radio one more time, I'm gonna scream," Glenn said.

"That's why I never listen to those Top 40 stations," Chip said. "The ones I listen to never play that crap."

"Well, you must listen to the bubblegum stations at least some of the time," Ray said. "You got that Rick Astley song down pretty good." He came in the room the rest of the way, sat on another upholstered chair, propped his feet up on an ottoman.

"I never do," Chip said. "But you can't avoid those Top Forty songs. They play them everywhere."

Truth was, Ray liked a lot of groups better than Aerosmith. Like The Beach Boys, Bruce Hornsby and the Range, and even Phil Collins. But he could never say that out loud. "Maybe U2."

"Yeah," Chip said. "But you'll never see those guys play the Savannah Civic Center."

"No way," Glenn said. "But boys, we are on our way this weekend to catch Aerosmith there."

"Yes sir," Chip said. "So, let's hear your grand master plan."

Back at Tony's Pizza, Glenn had said he'd tell them about it in the car. But as soon as he got in the car, Glenn's James-Bond-like car phone started ringing. His mom, telling him he needed to get home right away. So, they agreed to come back here to Glenn's house after dinner.

"Well, guys," Glenn said, "I won't keep you in suspense. My plan is, I know a surefire way to get the cash we need for the tickets. But to do this, we've got to be willing to take some risks. I'm not talking about anybody getting hurt. Not that kind of risk. But it's...let's just say...not exactly legal."

Ray looked at Chip. His face registered no change in expression. Ray was mortified. "What do you mean...not exactly legal?"

"It's against the law, Ray," Chip said. "Whatever it is."

"I know what the word illegal means," Ray said. "I'm asking, what are you wanting us to do that's against the law? What, are we gonna rob a bank?"

"Not a bank," Glenn said.

"What are we gonna rob?" Chip said. His face was all lit up.

"A convenience store," Glenn said. "And not just any convenience store, but one specific one that I know will be perfectly safe. No one gets hurt, and there's no way we get caught. We're in and out in ten minutes with plenty of cash for the tickets, the gas there and back, maybe even some Aerosmith souvenirs."

"I like the sound of this," Chip said.

Up to this point in his life, Ray had never stolen anything. Well, not from a store anyway. Here and there as a kid he'd taken the occasional toy from a friend, but only one he really wanted, and one he knew the friend either didn't care about or would never miss.

"Ray? You're awful quiet all of a sudden," Glenn said.

"I just have...a few questions, that's all. Like, how can you guarantee there's no way we ever get caught?"

"Yeah," Chip said, "I'd like to hear more about that, too."

"Easy. It's because of the store I have in mind. I drive by it all the time on my way out here. You guys passed it tonight, whether you realized it or not."

"I don't remember seeing a convenience store," Ray said.

"Me, neither," Chip said.

"See? It's perfect. You're making my case for me. But I'm telling you, it's there. On the right-hand side of the road just after that S-curve, after you go up that hill. You go by a group of trees, the ground levels out, and there it is. Hampton's Quick Stop. At nighttime, you can hardly see it. There's just one dim streetlight at the far corner of the parking lot. I hardly ever see any cars in the parking lot when I drive by at night. Except one, which probably belongs to whoever's working there. And we won't have to do it late. It gets completely dark by 6 o'clock now. We could plan to rob it at, say, 8 o'clock tomorrow night. We'd have everything we need for the concert and be home by 8:30."

"Okay," Ray said, "that's not a bad plan, but I'm not hearing anything that sounds close to a guarantee we don't get caught. What if someone does happen to stop in during the ten minutes we're there? And how do we get the guy to give us the money?"

Glenn got up, walked over to his massive closet. He walked in, grabbed some things from some built-in drawers and came back out. He put one on and tossed one each to Ray and Chip. "Ski masks, gentlemen. That's how we don't get caught. I've already checked, there's no cameras in the store. We put these on just before we go inside. We disguise our voices. Better yet, only one of us talks. Me. My voice is the deepest. The clerk can't identify us, and if anyone else happens to come in — which they won't — but if they do — they can't identify us, either."

"But what are we going to use?" Chip said, "to get the cashier to give us the money?"

"My father's gun," Glenn said. "He keeps it in a safe, but I know the combination."

"Wait a minute," Ray said. "We're gonna use a gun?"

"What do you think, Ray?" Chip said, "the guy's just gonna hand the money over if we ask real nice?"

"No, but you introduce a gun into the equation," Ray said, "you rule out the guarantee that nobody gets hurt. We wind up shooting somebody during a robbery, and we could get the chair."

"We won't get the chair," Glenn said, "and I can guarantee nobody's gonna get hurt."

"How can you do that?"

"Because the gun won't even be loaded. That's how. I'll even leave the clip in the safe."

18

The Present
Grandview Trailer Park
Culpepper, GA

I t was midmorning. The temperature outside was nice enough for Andrew Tubbs to open the windows, let some of the stink out of his trailer. He figured it must be pretty bad if he could smell it, too. He'd read somewhere people don't generally smell their own bad smells as well as others do. But it wasn't his fault, not entirely. At least half of it came from Percy's cage; the bottom of it badly needed changing. Really, the whole thing could use a makeover.

Percy was Tubbs' parrot, been his closest friend for over a decade.

Tubbs walked by the cage, situated in his little living area toward the front of the trailer. It had the most windows and Percy liked to look outside. "What you want today, Percy? Grapes or banana?" He held out both hands, palms up, with some of each fruit. Percy squawked and made his way over from the far side of his perch, which sat atop his cage. His beak checked out both options then he grabbed the banana with his right foot. It wasn't actually a foot, not technically, but that's what Tubbs called it. "Okay, you enjoy that and leave me be for a little bit. I got a flow going on this writing, and I can't stop. But I'll clean up your mess soon as I finish this chapter."

Percy didn't say anything, too busy downing that half a banana. Tubbs had taught him to say quite a few things over the years and Percy had picked up a dozen other phrases here and there, maybe from the radio or the TV. But Tubbs didn't need Percy to be a good conversationalist. It was enough that he was a good listener. Tubbs could tell by the look in Percy's eyes that he understood a good bit more of what Tubbs said than most people would give him credit for. And because he was so smart, it made Tubbs feel like he wasn't talking to himself all the time.

Tubbs sat in his comfy recliner, pretty much the only nice piece of furniture he owned. Reaching to his right, he grabbed his laptop off the end table, opened the lid and quickly navigated to the Word file for his mystery novel. A glance at the clock said he only had two good hours to write. That would give him about an hour to clean Percy's cage, and a half-hour to get ready for work. Then he'd have to hurry to his job in the painting department at Home Depot.

"But not for long, Percy," he said, as he scrolled to a clean page to start the next chapter. "I get this novel finished, get it published, and the dough will start rolling in. Finally get to move out of this dumpy place and live in a real house. Get you set up with a room all to yourself."

Percy looked down at him, nodded his head several times the way he did when he understood what Tubbs was saying. "You da Man, you da Man," he said.

"That's right, Percy. I'm the man. The man that's gonna make that happen. But first I gotta keep writing." Tubbs was really looking forward to this next chapter. This was the part when his trio of main characters actually pulled off their master plan, to rob a local convenience store and get the cash they needed to fund their trip to Vegas.

Of course, that's not what really happened. In the real story, as best as he could recall, they were only trying to get enough cash to get to a rock concert. But he liked Vegas better, for two reasons. First, he had to change things enough so people wouldn't be able to connect it to what really happened. And second, getting money for a rock concert wasn't a big enough goal to shoot for. A trip to Vegas sounded a lot more flashy.

Another major change he made was with the names. Obviously, he couldn't use anyone's real names, but to help him keep the characters straight in his head, he gave them the same initials. And then there was the car they drove. In his book, they rode a decked out, fully loaded, cherry red Camaro. Which was nothing like the black Monte Carlo used in the real story. Besides, Tubbs liked Camaros way better.

He started hammering away at the keys.

IT WAS JUST about a half-hour away from lunchtime. Jack and Rachel had graciously volunteered to make it. Baby Jack had gone down for a nap. Joe Jr. and Kristin had taken

Chance for a walk down their favorite trail. It was the last full day of their camping trip. Jack had suggested Joe and Kate go take a walk down by the lake. "We've got everything together here. You two go on."

As they neared the water's edge, Joe reached for Kate's hand.

"You've been doing that a lot the last few days," she said. "I like it."

"Like what?" he said.

"Holding hands, silly. Reminds me of the old Joe, the young skinny guy I married."

"See, the insult kinda diminishes the effect of the compliment. You know that, right?"

"What insult?" she said.

"The old fat guy one."

"I didn't call you old or fat," Kate said. "I don't think you're either. You are a bit older, and you can sometimes struggle with your weight — although you've been behaving rather well on this trip, I'll give you that. But I didn't say you're an old fat guy."

"Okay, I'm sorry. Guess I'm being a little oversensitive."

"Just a tad," she said, squeezing his hand. "The point I was making was, you've been holding my hand on this vacation the way you used to do when we were younger, and I like it. I'm hoping we can keep doing it after we go home tomorrow."

"Oh," Joe said. "Okay, I'll try to remember that. But if things start getting busy again, and I forget. Feel free to grab mine. You do, and I won't slap it away."

She laughed. "That's good to know."

They walked a couple minutes in silence, each just taking in the beauty of the surrounding scene.

Then Joe said, "I'm going to miss this. Not just this place, but...the quiet. The pace."

"Me, too. Is that what's got you a little edgy? Having to go back?"

"Yeah, but see, I don't want to be so edgy. Be the kind of guy who gets edgy so easily. I gotta do a better job at controlling that. Being out here, with you and the kids, even with Jack and Rachel, it's just been so nice. Feels like I've really been able to relax."

"Yeah," Kate said. "It really is almost like being with a new version of you. I don't hate the old version, better say that upfront. But I like this new version better. And I'm not the only one. You've really been great with the kids. They both said things to me, Joey especially."

"Really? Like what?"

"Well, just this morning when we were cleaning up after breakfast, I asked him what his favorite part of the trip was so far. Without hesitation, he said, 'Getting to spend so much more time with Dad.' I'm not saying you don't spend time with them. When we're home, I mean. Cause you do. I know it's just the nature of the work you do. Especially when you get a case like the one you're going home to. It can be pretty all-consuming. I get that. And I tell the kids that, and I think they get it, for the most part. But they really like you, Joe. They really like spending time with you. And that's a good thing. Because you're a great dad. So, I'm for anything that can keep that going, that keeps you connecting with our kids."

Joe wasn't sure why exactly, but he started tearing up.

"I'm sorry, Joe. I say something hurtful?"

He hugged her.

Still in the hug, said, "No, calling me fat would be hurtful. But what you said, made me feel...really good." Pulling out of the hug, he gently lifted her chin with his finger and kissed her. "Some kinda way, I'm going to do a better job at keeping this thing going. I don't want my kids to go through their teenage years with the old version of me."

19

The next morning, after a leisurely breakfast of fresh fried trout, eggs, and home fries, Joe reluctantly agreed to start breaking down their camp. There wasn't a ton of stuff to do, not like this was anything close to roughing it, but there was still a checklist of things he had to tend to. Jack's list was even shorter than his.

"Let me make a quick call to Hank first," Joe said to Kate. "Get him going on something that'll likely make sure we don't get interrupted on our last day." He pulled out his phone and started walking toward the lake.

Hank answered pretty quick. "Hey Joe, what's up? Wasn't expecting to hear from you till this afternoon."

"Not calling for an update. This'll only take two minutes. Seeing as I'll be back in there tomorrow morning, there really isn't any more reason to keep this thing out of the news. By the way, you've done a first-rate job on that score. Seriously, Hank. I really appreciate it. Kate and the kids even more than me."

"No problem. So, you got a good chance to unwind then?"

"I really did. Haven't felt this relaxed in I don't know how long. Anyway, I was thinking might be a good idea to call Dr. Hargrove and give him what we got, so he can officially ID the body. You and I both know it's the kid from the convenience store, but if we let him know, he can get more specific with things on his end. You know, like matching dental records and what-not."

"Good idea. I'll fax him the reports we've got, like what the kid was wearing and such. You want me to call that reporter for you, give him a heads up? Or do you want to handle that?"

"Maybe just call him, let him know we're getting real close to giving him that scoop. We'll let him know as soon as the ME confirms the kid's identity."

"Got it," Hank said. "How about I skip the afternoon update today, just fill you in the morning after you've had enough time to fix your coffee?"

"That'll work. And Hank, again, really appreciate you covering for me. I knew you could handle it."

"Thanks, Joe. Now let's hope Pendleton sees it like you."

HANK WAS JUST ABOUT to call Hargrove's office when an image flashed in his mind. It was a picture of an old, full-sized, manila envelope sitting in the evidence box for the Myron Simpson case. It had a handwritten note across the top that simply said: "From the Kid's Family." He'd only opened it long enough to see it didn't contain the information he was searching for, but now he decided he better give it a closer look.

He made a quick trip downstairs. In just a few seconds, he was glad he did. Among other things, the envelope included a copy of Myron Simpson's dental records with a note paper-clipped to the top and the date. Hank quickly figured that this info was added to the box just over a year after the boy went missing. The note said: "*The boy's mom dropped this off on her way out of town, in case her son's body ever turned up.*"

Hank didn't know why, but he felt a tinge of pain reading this. The poor lady. Leaving town. Only one reason a mother would do this. She had to be convinced her son was never coming back. She knew in her heart of hearts he hadn't run away, which could only mean one thing. He was gone.

She knew it even then.

There wasn't anything else in the envelope relevant to his phone call to Hargrove. Hank brought it with him as he headed up the stairs. Once inside his office, he lifted the receiver to his phone, then set it down again. He really should just drive this over there and talk to him in person. He could fax the documents, but not the dental x-rays. If Hargrove had these, he might be able wrap this ID thing up in a day.

An hour later, Hank was sitting in the small waiting room of the Medical Examiner's office. Not surprisingly, the other chairs were empty. He was just about to reach for a golf magazine, even though he didn't play golf, when the interior door opened.

The doctor's assistant stepped out and said, "Dr.

Hargrove can see you now. He's in his office, not the lab. Last door on the left at the end of the hallway."

Hank got up grabbed the manila envelope. "Thanks." He walked past her but kept his eyes straight ahead as he made his way down the hall. The labs where they cut up all the bodies were on the right side with big glass panels that, for some reason, would allow passersby to watch the horror unfold. He understood autopsies had to be done, but he certainly didn't want to see it and didn't know why anyone would, unless they worked here. That was the one part of the CSI TV shows he always fast forwarded through. Why in the world did the producers of those series feel the need to spend all that extra money to create fake but very realistic-looking body parts, such as lungs and livers and cracked-open rib cages?

He reached the end of the hallway, knocked on the door then opened it. Hargrove was typing something on a laptop. "Your assistant said I could come back."

"That's fine, Detective. Take a seat. I'll be right with you, as soon as I finish...this...sentence." He backed away from the laptop and faced Hank. "When she first told me you wanted to speak with me, I reached for my phone. Then she said you were in the front office. Must be pretty important for you to drive all the way here."

"I guess it kinda is. But it was also something I couldn't fax over." He set the manila envelope on Hargrove's desk.

"I'm assuming this has something to do with the skeletal remains brought in last week."

"It does. In fact, I think we know the victim's identity. We're almost certain."

"Really? Well, I finished most of my tests and was not far from calling you myself with my preliminary findings."

Hank held up the envelope. "Well, with the reports I'm about to give you, as well as what's in here, I think you'll be able to leap way past any preliminary findings."

"So, what do you have for me?" Hargrove said.

Hank handed him the copies of the police reports first. "This is the Missing Persons' Report filed for a young man — as you can see in the top field — named Myron Simpson. You'll notice the date is December 1988. I've highlighted in yellow what the boy was wearing when last seen." He waited a moment for Hargrove to read what he was saying. His eyebrows raised, as he did.

"Matches exactly the clothes we found on the body," Hargrove said.

Hank pulled out the dental records, handed them to Hargrove. "Here's something I found in the evidence box. If we're on track about the identity of this boy, these records should prove it. Apparently, his mother dropped them off at the police station a year after his disappearance, as they were moving out of town. Clearly, she was convinced he'd been killed."

Hargrove looked over the x-rays. "Excellent. This will make identifying the body so much easier."

"And Doc, there's something else...remember that class ring I asked you about earlier? From 1989?"

"You wanted to know," Hargrove said, "whether anyone ever buys such rings in advance of the year they graduate."

"Right, and you said kids do it all the time."

"Did you find a ring with the body?"

"Not exactly," Hank said. "About ten feet away. But you'll

notice the report doesn't mention that he was wearing a class ring. We think this ring might belong to the killer, or one of the killers. And that date coincides with the time the young man went missing, at the end of 1988."

"Hmm," Hargrove said. "If you're right about that ring, that would also mean the person or persons responsible for his death would not likely be a total stranger, but one of the lad's school classmates."

"Exactly," Hank said. Just then, something else dawned on Hank. He didn't know why he hadn't thought of it before. The killer wasn't just some random thief ripping off a convenience store, like a transient or drifter. It was somebody who'd lived in, maybe had even grown up in Culpepper.

Somebody who might still be living there today.

20

The Present
Victorious Life Church
Senior Pastor's Office, 11 AM

L ife was good these days for the Rev. Glenn Burton.
He'd just looked over the Tithes and Attendance Report from the church's senior administrator, good friend and confidant, the Rev. Chip Masters. Chip
sat across from him now in a plush leather office chair,
awaiting Glenn's reaction from the numbers.

"Well," Chip said, "whatta you think? Pretty nice jump
from last month, eh? And we didn't do any special offerings,
either."

Glenn smiled. How could he not? They were now regularly averaging just over three thousand in attendance every
Sunday and the money was just pouring in. Up a full fifteen
percent from last month. If he had started this church in a
town like Savannah or a suburb of Atlanta, he'd easily be

running ten thousand on Sunday, probably more. But the way he figured things, better to be a big fish in a small pond than the other way around.

And staying here in Culpepper all these years gave him the satisfaction every week of proving his parents wrong. They'd totally disapproved when he became a member of the clergy, especially his Dad. He was certain Glenn would wind up living the life of a pauper and doing a grave injustice to the family's name and reputation. Why couldn't he become a doctor like his older brother, or a lawyer like his younger sister?

But Dad wasn't thinking that way anymore, was he? Glenn couldn't be absolutely sure he made more than his siblings—such talk would be impolite. But he certainly drove a nicer car and lived in a far more elaborate home than either one of them.

"Well, Glenn?" Chip said. "Nothing to say?"

"What? I'm sorry. Yeah, these numbers are amazing."

"And did you see the column about the Online Giving? Way up over last month. I told you we'd see it go up if you started talking to the online folks more directly during the offering. Folks respond to you, Glenn. You know that. They always do. And did you see that section about the growth in attendance coming in from the radio show? That's way up, too."

"How are we tracking that?" Glenn said. "If they're just listening on the radio?"

"From the visitor cards on Sunday. I changed them the week after we launched it, made a box for 'Radio' in the *How'd You Hear About Us?* section."

Glenn set the report down on his thick mahogany desk,

leaned back in his comfy chair. "It's a great report, Chip. But have you ever heard the phrase *too much of a good thing*? Because we're not just growing our online audience. It's getting pretty tight in there...in both services. We keep tracking this way, we'll have to go to a third service. I'm not sure my voice'll hold out preaching three times."

"Way ahead of you, Glenn. Wasn't going to spring it on you yet, but since you brought it up...I've already got a plan underway to remedy that situation. We can add a third or even a fourth service if we want, won't tax your vocal cords or your energy reserves one bit."

"How are we gonna do that?"

"Through the magic of video. Fact is, we're a little behind the eight ball on this. Big churches have been doing this for years. We tape you preaching the first service, and then you're off for the morning. In the other services, we'll have a live worship band and one of the other pastors will get up and greet folks, but then we'll have this big screen come down, top to bottom, replaying what you preached in the first service."

"I don't know, Chip. Won't those folks in the video services feel like they're getting ripped off?"

"You'd think so, wouldn't you? But they don't. People are so used to watching you on video even when you're right there in front of them. We've got you on those big screens and, except for maybe the folks right in the front, everyone else is mostly looking at you on screen, so they can catch all your antics."

Glenn laughed. "What do you mean, my antics?"

"You know, all the faces you make when you talk. The way you move your arms all around. Folks like to see that stuff up close, so they look up at the screen even though you're standing right in front of them. I'm telling you, bigger churches have been doing this for a good long while, and they're not shrinking. They're growing." Chip leaned forward, took a sip of whatever was in his mug. "Seeing you preach on a big screen is not gonna shrink the church. What will shrink the church is stuff like folks not finding a place to park, or no place to sit in the service. Which is why I've been working on this the past month, so we can get ready to add another service fairly soon...before we do start shrinking."

"Well," Glenn said, "guess you better get on this then."

"You green lighting this, already? Don't you want to see the budget numbers first?"

"Nope. With all this extra cash coming in, I don't think we'll have to worry about making your idea work. Besides, if you're right, what you're talking about sounds more like making an investment in our future, rather than adding an additional expense."

"Well, Reverend," Chip said, "that sounds like something I can use when we start selling this thing to the rest of the staff. And I'm telling 'ya, I am right. We do this, and you keep putting on that quality show you somehow manage to pull off every week, this place is going to take off. We might just have to turn right around and add a fourth service a month after we launch service number three."

*Putting on that quality show...*the phrase repeated in Glenn's head. "Please tell me, Chip, when you're talking with the folks out there, staff included, you don't talk like that."

"Like what?"

"Putting on a show. I'm okay with it, when it's just you

and me, but that kinda talk could really rub some folks the wrong way."

"You got nothing to worry about, Buddy. I been at this thing almost as long as you have. I know how the game is played. Out there, I talk just like you...the upstanding man-a-God. I just like the freedom to be ourselves when it's just you and me."

"All right, then," Glenn said. "Just makin' sure."

21

The following morning, after spending the first two hours getting caught up on the case with Hank, Joe was pulling into the parking lot of Culpepper Gazette. He'd called Tom Hazelton yesterday afternoon to give him a heads up that they were ready to break the news about the convenience store case and wondered how he'd like to receive the information. Hazelton said he now had his own office at the Gazette where they could have a private chat and suggested they meet there in the morning.

While Joe's meeting was going on, Hank was getting with Captain Pendleton to bring him up to date on the case, and to unofficially pass the baton on to Joe to take the lead role from here on out. Joe opened the glass front door and walked inside, grateful that Hank had handled things so well up until now. That not only helped strengthened Pendleton's confidence in Hank, but in Joe too, since he had to talk Pendleton into giving Hank a chance.

Joe walked up to the receptionist, told her who he was

there to see. The Gazette offices were situated in one of the old historical buildings downtown. But inside it looked pretty modern. The receptionist got up and said, "Follow me. Tom told me you were coming, said to bring you on back."

Joe followed her down a hallway with a big open area of cubicles to the left and private offices on the right. She led him to the office just before one with a sign identifying it as the editor's desk. She knocked twice and opened it. "Lieutenant Boyd is here, sir." She left the door open for him and started heading back toward the front.

Joe stepped in. Hazelton was already on his feet walking toward him. He extended one hand to Joe and with the other closed the door.

"Thanks so much for coming in, Lieutenant. Sorry to be so secretive about this. It's just with social media being what it is these days, a hot story can make the rounds faster than a jackrabbit. And so far, best as I can tell, this one hasn't leaked out yet, so the Gazette will actually get the scoop on it like we used to all the time in the good old days. Go ahead, have a seat."

Joe sat in one of the two office chairs, put his notebook on the edge of Hazelton's desk. Hazelton sat in his own chair, took out a digital recorder. "You okay with me recording this? Want to make sure I don't miss any of the facts."

"Yeah, fine," Joe said. "I spoke with the ME on the way here. We had the dental records on the kid, so he was able to make a positive ID late yesterday. And I was able to reach the boy's mom on the phone. She was at work and couldn't talk, but she gets off at lunchtime, so I'll be calling her back after our little interview here. Although, I'm pretty sure she's already guessed the reason why I'm calling."

"Poor thing," Hazelton said. "She went through a lot when this all happened, and after. Her and her husband."

"You knew them?"

"Not personally. I was just starting out here at the Gazette. It was one of the first big stories they let me handle. Wound up interviewing the Simpsons quite a few times over the next year, including the last one they gave just before they moved away."

"Well," Joe said, "out of respect for them, I'd like to ask you not to release the story until I can talk to her today. I'll call you right after, let you know after we connect."

"I don't have a problem with that," Hazelton said. "So, you definitely found his body then?"

"We did, what was left of it. You can imagine the state of things, considering he'd been buried there for over thirty years."

"Can you confirm he was definitely murdered?"

"Yes."

"Can you say how? Was he shot? Stabbed?"

"I don't want to get into those details just yet."

"Can you tell me where his body was found?"

"I don't see why not," Joe said. "It was in the woods out by those rural campsites on the west end of the lake."

"Lake Samson?"

"That's right."

"Just double-checking, since there are two other lakes in the county."

"No, it was Lake Samson. But you can mention it was deep in the woods. Don't want to spook any of the people who like to camp out there."

"If it was so deep in the woods, how did the body get discovered?"

Joe laughed. "Can this one be off the record?"

Hazelton looked puzzled. "I guess...if it has to be. But it's kind of an important question, for the story I mean."

"Oh, I can give you something for the story. I just don't want the actual details made public."

"Okay...I'm listening."

"My dog found it."

"What, the body? Your dog found the body...deep in the woods?"

"Yeah, me and my family and some friends, we were camping out there. He's a beagle. Supposedly, they got the nose of a bloodhound. My son's walking him on a trail, he gets the whiff of a rabbit and takes off. I guess the rabbit must've ran past the shallow grave and my dog, Chance, now he picks up on that scent. He's digging and howling. By the time we get there, well Tom, imagine the scene. I'm standing there with my kids and the dog has just uncovered a skeletal hand."

Hazelton made the appropriate face.

"I'm sure my son might love the notoriety of being mentioned in the story, but I'd appreciate it if you could spare us that excitement. Can't you just say the body was found by some hikers walking their dog in the woods?"

"Sure," Hazelton said. "I can do that. But did you have any idea who the victim was at the time?"

Joe didn't want to point out what a lame question this was. How could anyone know such a thing at that point? "No, and I got to be a little bit careful here about how much I say. Like any crime scene, especially a cold case one, there are little details you find at the scene that only the killer would know, so we don't want to give those kinds of things away."

"I understand," Hazelton said. "So, what can you tell me about the scene and how you identified the body? You know, that it was Myron Simpson."

Joe thought for a moment. "I guess it's safe to say that once we fully recovered the remains, there were clear indications the deceased was a male—like the clothes he had on— and judging by the obvious length of time the body had been buried there, we began looking through our cold case files to ID the victim. We didn't have that many who were male, and with the dental records being available, the medical examiner was able to make a positive ID fairly quickly."

"Wow, Joe. Mind if I use that part verbatim? Don't think I can write it better than you just said it."

Joe smiled. "Go right ahead, on one condition."

"What's that?"

"That I can quote what you just said about how well I said that to my wife? She'll never believe it."

Hazelton laughed. "It's a deal. So, we got the positive ID on Myron Simpson. Any way to know if the place where you found the body was the murder scene, or if he was killed back at the store?"

"Doubt very seriously he was murdered there in the woods. No way to tell for sure, given all the time that's passed. But it's not likely. But we also can't say for sure if he was killed at the store. Not enough evidence there, either, judging by the police reports. Probably not smart to print this, but my guess is, that's where it happened. Can't think of any good reason a perp would abduct or kidnap a convenience store clerk. Especially a guy. Sad to say, but usually when that happens, it's a girl. But seeing this was a young high school kid, coming from a pretty poor family at that, makes more sense to me that whoever did this killed him, for some reason. And then for some other reason, hauled his body out there to the woods where we found him."

"Yeah," Hazelton said. "Makes sense to me, too. Guess I'll have to think of some vague way to cover that part."

"Appreciate it, if you would. And remember, I'm gonna read your report on this. If you respect the stuff I'm asking you to, I'll keep feeding you more info, as soon as it's kosher."

"I understand, Joe. Or should I call you Lieutenant?"

"Joe's fine," he said.

"I can tell you're wrapping up, but there's one pretty big part we can't skip over."

"What's that?" Although Joe was pretty sure he knew what it was.

"The obvious thing...who did it? Any ideas? Anything you can share...on the record?"

Joe quickly thought about the few items they had on that angle. Like the local high school class ring Hank found. Better keep that one to themselves for now. "It's way too early to make even an educated guess about that."

"C'mon, Joe. You gotta give me something. That's going to be the biggest part of the story. The *who* in *whodunnit*."

"Okay, I understand. So, you can say something like this...although it cannot be confirmed at this time, the location of the victim's remains leads investigators to believe the perpetrator or perpetrators of this crime were likely very familiar with this area."

"Oh, that's good," Hazelton said. "Again...quote you verbatim?"

Joe smiled. "Verbatim, yeah, you go ahead and do that."

"So, the murderer is someone local," Hazelton said. "That's pretty crazy."

"Now, that's not what I said."

"No, that's what *I'm* saying. I'll print what you said. But that's the interpretation, right Joe? What else could it mean? And when that gets confirmed, it's gonna make this story huge."

22

Joe looked at his watch. It was time to make the call. No matter how many times he'd done this over the years, he still considered it one of the biggest downsides to his job. He'd parked his car in a shady spot in the back corner of a shopping center parking lot. The only other cars in sight were at least a football field away, occupying the first few rows nearest the front of the store.

Even with the windows down, it was still pretty quiet. Nice and cool. He'd better get this over with. Setting his smartphone in this nifty little dashboard stand Kate bought him, he turned it on and set up the FaceTime app. Earlier, when he'd called the boy's mom he'd asked if she had ever used an app like this. She said she had, so he told her that's what he'd use when he called her back the second time. It wasn't as good as a face-to-face exchange, but for a situation like this, way better than just a faceless voice coming through your phone informing you that your son was dead.

He got his end set up, then hit the icon connecting her to

the call. She answered almost as soon as it rang. When her face appeared on screen, it startled Joe seeing how old she was. But then, the only picture he had of her was from the late eighties. She had to be close to seventy now. Her expression was somber.

"Hi, Mrs. Simpson...can you see and hear me okay?"

"I can. Am I coming through okay?" she said.

"Loud and clear. As I mentioned in my call earlier today, my name is Lieutenant Joe Boyd with the cold case squad here in Culpepper where you used to live."

"Nice to meet you," she said, "Well, sort of meet you. I'm still not used to this high-tech stuff. I've been kind of forced into it by my son. It does make it a whole lot easier to feel connected to family if they can see your face. He and his family live in a different state than me, you see."

"We're not family obviously," Joe said, "but that's the same reason I asked if we could talk to each other this high-tech way."

"Given the nature of the content of your call?" she said.

"Well, yeah. If you still lived here, I'd have driven to your home so we could talk face-to-face."

"I appreciate that, Lieutenant. But me and my husband had to get out of there, give us and our other kids a fighting chance to make a new start. Way too many sad memories in Culpepper."

"I can understand that. How many other children do you have?"

"One boy, my eldest, Scott, and two daughters. Well, Scott became the oldest after Myron died."

Joe was kind of stunned hearing her say this, though he probably shouldn't be. It should definitely make what he had to say a little easier to swallow. "Do your daughters live out of state, too?"

"Thankfully, no. They're here with me. My husband, Gene, though...he passed away three years ago. We had a good life together, except for those horrific years right after Myron died. There's really no getting over something like that. Not completely anyway. But we were able to move on, make a lot of nice memories with the rest of our kids. Now making some more with my grandkids."

"That's nice to hear," Joe said. "And I guess hearing the way you talk about Myron, means you're not really too surprised to be getting a call like this from someone like me."

"Oh, no. I mean...I definitely want to hear anything you have to say, but Gene and I both accepted the fact that he'd been killed when we didn't hear any word from him after that first week or so. Of course, we were devastated by what happened, but we knew right off that he didn't take that money and run off with it. We were deeply hurt when we figured out that's how the police in Culpepper were seeing things. Explains why they hardly did anything to find out what happened after the holidays were over. Boy just ran off. That's how they saw it. I get that lots of kids his age leave home, either to get free of a broken family situation or just to explore the world on their own. But you had to know Myron to know that's just not who he was. Our family wasn't broken. And he wasn't an unhappy kid."

"Yeah," Joe said. "Not sure it will do any good to hear me say it, but I'm real sorry how you and your family were treated back then. Speaking for myself, I would never let a case like this get dropped the way it did. It wasn't just you vouching for Myron's character. From what I've read, even the owners of the store agreed with you, that Myron would have never stolen anything, or run off like that. Sadly though, that's how it was handled."

"Well, thank you, Lieutenant. You aren't to blame for what others did thirty years ago, but it is nice to hear you say it. So, you mentioned you were part of the cold case squad, and I'm guessing you reaching out to me this way means there must be some new development in Myron's case after all these years."

Joe looked at her face, her eyes especially. She really was at peace with her son's death. As well as can be expected anyway. Still, he didn't want to say anything that might add to, or create for her some new measure of pain. "There has been a new development, as you say. Basically, some campers walking their dog last week in the woods west of Lake Sampson came across his remains. Well, the dog obviously discovered the body, not the campers. It was a beagle."

"I know a little about dog breeds and such," she said. "They've got quite a nose on them for being little dogs."

"They certainly do." Joe was somewhat surprised she had no visible reaction to what he'd just said.

"And you're sure the body you found was my son?"

"We are. It was confirmed by the dental records you gave us at the time."

"Oh, I forgot all about that. Okay, well, guess that's it then. It really is him. At least we'll finally have a body to bury. Any idea when you'll be able to release him back to us?"

"Not right now," Joe said. "But I'll find out for you and let you know."

"Thanks, Lieutenant. Can you...can you tell us how he died? Do you know that for sure yet?"

"We aren't releasing this information publicly yet, but I will tell you confidentially that he was shot. Somewhere in the chest. And it would seem he was only shot once, which would tell me the shot was likely fatal. I only share this because, it probably means he didn't suffer when it happened." Joe was speculating a bit here, but not making things up.

She visibly and audibly sighed. And for the first time, Joe saw a tear well up in her eyes. "Well, that's a small answer to prayer. We always hoped that he didn't suffer much."

"Doesn't look like he did."

"Well, do you have any leads yet on who might have done this to him?"

How much should he say here? "Again, we're not saying anything public on this, so please keep this confidential."

"Can I tell my kids? His brother and younger sisters?"

"Only if you know for sure they won't say anything about it on social media to anyone. You'll understand my caution when I tell you what I'm about to say. But it's very important to our case, that these things don't become public right now."

"I understand," she said. "And I'm a hundred percent confident I can get my kids to agree."

"Okay," Joe said. "We don't know who the killer or killers might be yet. But it appears clear the motive was robbery, not anything personal against your son. I know what they did was very personal to you. But I mean it doesn't seem they were out to get him. They might have shot whoever was in the store that night. And also, the evidence at the scene where his body was found leads us to believe it was definitely somebody from Culpepper. And very possibly even someone who went to the same high school as your son."

"Oh, my. One of his classmates? So, Myron might have known him, or them, if it was more than one person?"

"It's a definite possibility, Mrs. Simpson. But that's just a preliminary finding. We still have a long ways to go to bring whoever did this to justice. But I promise you, we will get there. We will find out who did this to your son and put them in prison for the rest of their lives."

23

The Following Morning

A ndrew Tubbs had just come in from fetching the morning paper. He was probably the only non-retired person in the trailer park who still had it delivered daily the old-fashioned way. Seemed like everyone these days preferred reading it on their tablet or smartphone. Tubbs understood why. It was pretty convenient. But for him, having it delivered gave him a steady supply of poop paper, as he called it, for the bottom of Percy's cage.

After closing the door, he re-tied his bathrobe which had almost come apart when he bent over to pick up the paper. Not the kind of thing most of his neighbors wanted to see out their window with their morning coffee.

Percy squawked then repeated twice, "Fetching the paper, fetching the paper."

"That's right, little buddy," Tubbs replied. "I'll let you read this one in a couple of days." It was crazy all the phrases Percy had picked up that Tubbs had never taught him. Tubbs picked up his mug of coffee and walked it and the newspaper over to his favorite chair. "Let's find out what's going on in that big bad world, Percy. Then I'll get back to writing my book."

He took a sip as he read over the events of the front page. He wasn't all that much into politics, so usually he made it through the first page pretty quickly. Had to set his mug down to read the rest of the articles. As small as it had gotten over the years, it still took two hands to hold it. As he read, every now and then, he let it drop into his lap so he could take another sip. When he finished the first section, he set it aside, took another big swig of his coffee, and picked up the local section.

"Oh, my God." He almost dropped his mug. Staring back at him was the headline:

Police Find Body of Local Teen Missing Since 1988

Then a subheading:

Possibly Murdered After Convenience Store Robbery

Tubbs' heart began racing. His hands started trembling. A cold sweat broke out across his forehead. He had to get control of himself before a full-fledged panic attack took over. He set the mug down, stood and slowly began walking back and forth between the living and dining areas, trying to calm down, get his breathing back under control. Percy started squawking and flapping his wings. "I'm okay, Percy," he said as calmly as he could. He walked up to the cage. "Really, I'm okay."

After a few minutes of this, he felt sufficiently composed to go back to his chair, sit down and read the rest of the story. He had to know what was being said, how much the police had uncovered and figure out how this crazy development might affect the book he was writing.

Potentially, it could ruin everything.

He read through the story slowly. As he did, he kept looking up at the two photos pasted right next to the headline. The first was a yearbook photo of Myron Simpson taken in his junior year. A little grainy, but pretty much just the way Tubbs remembered him. The second was a picture of the convenience store as it looked back then.

Tubbs kept reading.

When he finished, he read it through again. This time, it almost had a calming effect on him, because he realized... everything wasn't ruined. Not really. The way he'd been writing the book had been sufficiently vague enough to provide him a cover of deniability. Certainly, if this news story continued to get bigger and more evidence of the crime was revealed, it would become impossible for people not to draw comparisons. But that might actually help him. He would simply maintain that his version was entirely fiction, a figment of his fertile imagination. Or, maybe allow a loose tie-in by claiming his story, while definitely fiction, had been "inspired" by true events.

He'd seen crime shows on TV and cable that did that all the time.

He let the newspaper fall back against his knees, took a nice swig of coffee and looked up at his good friend. "You know what I think, Percy? As bizarre as it seems, this crazy story in the newspaper might turn out to be a blessing in disguise."

He'd already decided today's edition of the Culpepper Gazette would not be lining the bottom of Percy's cage. Not the local section, anyway.

MELISSA HENDRICKS HAD JUST COME inside after watering her plants in the courtyard. She saw her husband, Cliff, sipping his coffee while watching Fox News, so she knew the pot had finished brewing. Cliff was way more into the news than she was. She preferred to spend most mornings reading her devotional out in the courtyard, reading the local news on her tablet, sipping that magic elixir from her favorite mug.

"What's it like out there?" Cliff said over his shoulder.

"It's really nice. You should come out here with me."

"I will, after a while."

Which probably wouldn't happen. At least not until the news people started repeating the same stories over and over again, which they always did. Then Cliff would lose interest.

She sat in her wrought iron chair with a padded seat enjoying the shade provided by the massive oak, which she and Cliff planted themselves decades ago when it was a mere sapling. "Oh good," she muttered, remembering that the weekly church news page came out today in the local section of the Gazette. She clicked on the app then scrolled to the local section. She was just about to hit the button for "Church News" when something startling caught her eye.

"Oh my, Lord." The headline read:

Police Find Body of Local Teen Missing
Since 1988

Then a subheading:

Possibly Murdered After Convenience
Store Robbery

Her insides started tensing up as she read the story. She realized why before she'd finished the second paragraph.

Andrew Tubbs.

This was the real story he was basing his disturbing novel on. Had to be. She kept reading. The more she read, the more convinced she became that it was true. Of course, the article made no mention of three teenagers being involved or anything about a souped-up red Camaro. But as she and Lisa had surmised that part of Tubbs' story was either made up, or based on insider knowledge because... because he had something to do with it.

But there it was, in black and white, the whole story about the missing boy from their high school in 1988. Murdered after a robbery from that convenience store. There was the boy's picture and the store where it happened, just as she remembered.

An Inconvenient Death. The title of Tubbs' book.

Then she remembered something else he said at the group meeting when someone mentioned something about his title. "*Considering the location where my murder takes place, I thought it might be seen as a clever play on words.*"

Tubbs was writing about this news story. He had to

be. She stood, carried her tablet into the living room. "Cliff, I need to speak with you."

"Right now?"

"Yes, right now. And unlike your favorite news channel, where everything they talk about is BREAKING NEWS, even when it's the same thing they've been talking about for hours, *this* —" She held up her tablet. "*This* really is breaking news. Breaking *local* news."

24

M elissa walked over to her purse hanging on a hook by the kitchen door. She had just finished relaying to her husband, Cliff, all her suspicions and concerns after reading that article in the Gazette a short while ago. He agreed the similarities between the article and what she'd told him about Tubbs' story seemed convincing enough to take it further. But considering how much she beat herself up after the last time she called the police, Cliff had suggested she call her friend Lisa and run the whole thing by her.

So, that's what she would do. She pulled her phone from the front pocket of her purse, turned it on and found Lisa's number from her Recent Calls list. Lisa picked up after a few rings.

"Good morning, Melissa. Nice to hear from you again. How's your day going so far?"

So chipper and upbeat. "I'm guessing you haven't read the article," Melissa said.

"I guess not. What article?"

"In the local section of the Gazette this morning. It's on the front page."

"We don't get the Gazette delivered anymore," Lisa said.

"Me, either. I read it online. Have you ever gone on their website?"

"A few times, but not recently."

"Well, you just have to read it," Melissa said.

"Why don't you just tell me what the article said?"

"No, Lisa. Really, you should read it. Tell you what...I'll hang up and reheat my coffee in the microwave. You go online and read the story and call me back when you're through."

"Okay, I can do that." She seemed a little reluctant.

"Believe me," Melissa said. "You'll be glad I called as soon as you read it." She hung up and brought her coffee mug to the microwave.

Ten minutes later, Lisa called her back.

"Oh, my goodness," was the first thing she said. "Can you believe it? They're writing about the very thing we've been talking about."

"So, you think so too?" Melissa said.

"How could I not? It's so obvious. They found the boy's body, Myron Simpson. After all these years."

"You know what I'm talking about, right?" Melissa said. "Not just that they found his body after all this time. I'm talking about the story Andrew Tubbs has been reading at our Word Weavers meetings. You know, *An Inconvenient Death*."

"I'm talking about that, too," Lisa said. "I just can't believe the timing. Here Andy Tubbs decides to write a novel for the first time in his life, and he picks this murder from thirty years ago — a murder that really happened — to base it on. A few months later, the police find the body of the boy whose murder he's writing about. Don't you think that's crazy?"

"I do."

"It's like a God thing," Lisa said. "What's that Scripture...*Be sure your sin will find you out*? It's somewhere in the book of Numbers, I think."

"So, you think Andrew killed Myron Simpson?"

"I don't know," Lisa said. "If not, seems like he at least has to be involved in some way. Why else would he write about it?"

"Maybe...maybe he just picked it as a premise for his story, but he's not involved at all. Remember that workshop we went to last year, where that bestselling author talked about drawing from your own life experiences when writing fiction. You know, *write what you know*. It helps your writing seem more credible and realistic. Maybe that's all Andrew is doing."

"I agree," Lisa said. "He's writing from his own life experiences. *Because he was involved*. He's just changing things up enough, so that it seems like he's writing about something else."

A part of Melissa wanted to believe what Lisa was saying. In fact, a part of her did. But what if they were wrong? "So, what are you thinking we should do?"

"I don't know," Lisa said. "Seems like one of us should go to the police. Tell them what we know?"

"But what if we're wrong? We could ruin a man's life. We don't really have any evidence, just our suspicions."

"It's not up to us to find evidence," Lisa said. "That's the police's job. We're just supposed to be citizens doing their civic duty. Right? You know, see something, say something?"

"Maybe," Melissa said. "I just don't know if I'm ready to take that step just yet. I already called them a few days ago, but then felt so stupid afterwards. Like some old busybody. Remember Gladys Kravitz?"

"From *Bewitched*?" Lisa said, then laughed. "You're being silly now, Melissa. You're nothing like Gladys Kravitz. Besides, when you called them a few days ago, it was before this story came out this morning. To me, that kinda changes everything. We're not talking about accusing Andy of murder. Just letting them know about this very strange coincidence, see if they want to pursue it or not. After that, it's not up to us."

"I guess," Melissa said. "I'm just not sure."

Then she got an idea of somebody else to call instead of the police.

AFTER LISA HUNG up the phone with Melissa, she went back and reread the article about the police finding Myron Simpson's body. Slowly. By the time she finished, she was more convinced than ever that one of them should call the police. Isn't that likely why the police released the story to the media? To ask for the public's help? The police were quoted several times as being the source of the information.

If Melissa wouldn't do it, Lisa would. She had to. There was a reason both she and Melissa were equally disturbed by Andy Tubbs' story when they read it at the meeting. It was called discernment. She googled the Culpepper police non-emergency number, then dialed it. After a woman answered the phone politely, Lisa said, "Hi, my name is Lisa. I'm calling about an article that appeared in the Gazette this morning. You know, the one about the police finding the body of that boy that went missing in 1988."

"You mean, the Myron Simpson case?" the woman said.

"Yes, that's the one."

"You have some information relevant to the case?"

"Very possibly," Lisa said. "Could I please speak to the detective in charge, or really anyone who's working on that case?"

"Hold on a minute. Let me see if I get one of the detectives on the phone."

A few moments later, Lisa heard the voice of a pleasant-sounding man with a slight southern accent. "Hello, this is Detective Hank Jensen. Who am I speaking with?"

"Hello, Detective. My name is Lisa. If it's okay, I'd rather not give my last name just yet."

"Okay. I understand you might have some information regarding the Myron Simpson case, something about the article that came out in the paper today?"

"Yes, that's right. I'm not sure if it was you, but a friend of mine called a few days ago and spoke with one of the detectives about a murder mystery someone in our writing group was writing that she found disturbing."

"She was wondering," Hank said, "if whether or not the writer was talking about an actual case versus one he was making up? That was me. I took that call."

"Oh, good. Well, I was at that same writer's group and heard this man in our group read the same story. And I was just as concerned about it as my friend. So, you can imagine our shock when we read that story in the newspaper this morning."

"Wait," Hank said, "are you saying that your friend was calling about the Myron Simpson case? That this man from your writing group was actually writing about that murder, as though it was a fiction story he was writing?"

"Yes," Lisa said. "That's exactly what we're saying. We can't be sure it's the same story, but some of the coincidences are, let's say, remarkable. At least from the things I remember about what happened back then. What was reported on the news, I mean. And with the chapter he read at our last meeting, well...he introduced three new characters into the story. Three high school boys. One of them drives a shiny red Camaro. It's pretty clear from what he wrote, he's hinting that these three boys had something to do with the robbery and murder. You might want to ask him about that. We're not saying this man from our writing group had anything to do with that young boy's murder. It just seems like...well, maybe you should have a talk with him. Let him explain where he got the inspiration for his story. Maybe it's nothing. But maybe it's...I don't know. I'll leave that for you to decide."

"Well, thank you, Lisa. We won't jump to any conclusions, but information like this may prove helpful. Can you give me the man's name, maybe a description of what he looks like? Oh, and what is the story he read to you all? Did it have a title?"

"Yes," Lisa said. "His name is Andrew Tubbs. He's around my age, so late forties. I don't know his address, but he lives in a trailer park. The title of his story is, *An Inconvenient Death*."

Hank wrote all this down.

"And one more thing, Detective. Is there any way you can leave my name out of this when you speak with Mr. Tubbs?"

"Sure, we can do that. And thanks again for the call." He hung up and instantly called Joe. As he waited for Joe to pick up, he thought about what Lisa said, about three high school boys possibly being involved. A picture of that Culpepper High School Class ring flashed into his mind.

Joe picked up. "Hey Hank, what's up?"

"You're not gonna believe the phone call I just had," Hank said. "The article's only been out a couple of hours, and already we've got our first lead. Maybe a good one."

25

A s soon as Melissa hung up the phone with Lisa, she looked up the number then called the office of Victorious Life Church. She was sure her pastor, Glenn Burton would know what to do. It was clear from his sermons that he really had the wisdom of God. She'd never tried calling him before, but this was a pretty big thing. She waited through a handful of rings then a pleasant young girl answered the phone.

"Good morning to you, this is Jasmine at Victorious Life Church. How can I serve you today?"

"Hi, Jasmine. I'm not sure if we've ever met. My husband and I have been attending for almost three years and became members just over a year ago. My name's Melissa Hendricks. I'm sure he's a busy man, but is there any way I could speak with the pastor?"

"Well, thanks for calling, Melissa. May I ask which pastor you wish to speak to? We have seven on staff."

"Oh, I'm sorry. I'm talking about Pastor Glenn, the one who preaches every Sunday."

A pause. "I see," Jasmine said. "You know, Melissa, Pastor Glenn wishes he could speak directly with everyone who calls. He really does. But as you said, he's a very busy man, and it's just not possible for me to put you through with him, unless he has personally asked you to call him. Is that what you're saying?"

"Oh, no," Melissa said. "I'm not sure we've ever even had a conversation before. Although I've greeted him several times and shook his hand. I was just hoping I could talk with him. There's this really pressing issue I'm dealing with, and I wanted to ask his advice."

"Well, you know Melissa, Pastor Glenn has handpicked all the other pastors on staff. Many of them are excellent counselors. I'm sure we could find one who might be able to take your call, hear what you're going through. At the very least, they could pray with you. But they may even have some great advice for you, too. Would you like me to try?"

"I suppose so," Melissa said. "Especially if Pastor Glenn picked the other pastors himself."

"Can I ask what this is in reference to? You don't have to give me any details, just enough for me to know which pastor to contact."

"Well, it's kind of hard to explain. I actually went to the police about this a few days ago, but then I read that article in the Culpepper Gazette this morning, and it really bothered me."

"Did you say the Gazette?"

"Yes, the newspaper. You know, the local one. But I read the story online. We don't get the paper delivered any—"

"Then I'll put you through to Pastor Chip. He handles all the calls that have to do with the media and things online. Could you hold please?"

"Yes, but —" Then Melissa realized, Jasmine had already put her on hold. She was going to say, she didn't need advice about media or online things. Oh, well...hopefully this Pastor Chip would know what she should do.

CHIP MASTERS LOVED HIS JOB. Sure, there were downsides. All jobs had them. But this was hands down the best job he'd ever had. Always something new every day. Never a dull moment. Great pay. The best benefits of any company in town. And they were big enough now where Chip could delegate all the crap assignments to one of the newer pastors. Let them pay their dues, like he had in the early years.

Basically, his main priority was...do whatever it took to make his boss and buddy, Glenn Burton, a success. Glenn wins, everybody wins. And they had been winning a lot these past few years. Now they were getting the kind of resources to really do things right.

Sure, there were still problems. Life was full of problems. Even the Bible said that. But when you've got plenty of money and the right kind of people to throw at those problems, even the bigger ones were starting to feel more like wrinkles. Or speed bumps, as he liked to call them. That's all they were.

And look at this view he had from his desk. Rolling hills, bordered by deep forests and the big blue sky. Who needs an office painting when you got a scene like this out your window?

His desk phone rang. Line two. That would be that cute blonde, Jasmine, manning one of the front desks. He pressed the button. "Hey Jasmine, how's life treating you?"

"Just fine, Pastor Chip," Jasmine said in that sweet southern accent of hers. "I've got a Melissa Hendricks on the line here. One of our church members, she and her husband. She called wanting some advice from Pastor Glenn about some pressing issue she's facing."

"And you remembered how we trained you to respond to such requests, right?" Chip said.

"I did. Like most folks, she was a little disappointed at first, but now she seems happy to talk to one of the other pastors."

"Okay..." Chip said. "So, why are you putting her through to me?"

"Well, I was going to put her with one of the other staff pastors, but then she mentioned her problem had to do with something she read in the paper this morning."

"In the paper?" Chip repeated. "There's something in the paper about us?"

"Uh, I'm not sure about that. If it's about our church, I mean. I didn't think to ask her that. But I know you're the pastor that handles all the media and online issues. That's why I'm coming to you first. Did I handle that wrong, Pastor Chip?"

Chip decided to go easy on her, seeing as she was so easy on the eyes. "Let's just say, this is one of those gray areas. Just a little speed bump, that's all. But in the future, feel free to ask another question or two on something like this. Could be what she read has nothing to do with us. She might just be bothered by some story that has no connection to the church. But don't worry about it, Darlin'. You go ahead and put her through. I'll see if I can help her out some way."

"Why, thank you, Pastor Chip. I'll remember that. I'll go ahead and hang up now. She should be on the line when I do. That's Melissa Hendricks."

"Got it, Melissa," Chip repeated. He heard a few clicks then a more mature woman's voice came on the line.

"Hello? Pastor Chip, are you there?"

"I am, Melissa. I just spoke with one of our receptionists, Jasmine. She mentioned there was something you needed some advice on, something to do with an article you read in the newspaper this morning?"

"That's right, Pastor. Did you happen to read the Gazette this morning? The local section, I mean?"

"No, I have not. My mornings are usually filled up doing the Lord's work these days. Not much time for getting caught up on the Gazette. Why, is there a story in there about our church?"

"Oh, no," she said. "Nothing about our church. But it's about that young boy who went missing thirty years ago. I'm pretty sure you don't remember me. I was such a wallflower back then. Still am in a lot of ways. But I went to Culpepper High around the same time as you and Pastor Glenn. Of course, you guys weren't pastors then. I'm not even sure we even knew each other. I just remember Pastor Glenn talking about your high school days in a couple of his sermons. I could tell by what he said we were going there around the same time."

"Excuse me, Melissa, don't mean to interrupt you but..."

did you say you read a story about a boy who went missing thirty years ago?"

"Yes, in 1988. Something to do with a robbery at a convenience store out on 270."

Chip's heart skipped a beat. Felt like he'd just been gut-punched. "What... what else did the article say?"

"Well, apparently, sometime last week some campers found his body in the woods. The Medical Examiner made a positive ID. It was that missing boy, Myron Simpson. I don't know if you remember him. I barely do. But I remember when he went missing."

Oh, no. Oh, God no. This was horrible.

"Well," she continued, "they're saying he was definitely murdered. And as upsetting as this news is, that's not really what I'm calling about, or what I need your advice for."

"Advice? That's right, you're calling about some advice." Chip had to get himself together. But his head was spinning with this news. His insides were all churning up. "What kind of advice do you need, and how is it connected with this... terrible story?"

"Well, see Pastor, I may have some information about someone who may have had something to do with this... with this murdered boy, I mean."

"You do? How?"

"Well, it's kind of a long story. The short version is, I go to a monthly writers meeting, called Word Weavers. And there's this fellow who's been coming the last few months, someone we went to high school with, so he's the right age for when this happened, and he was definitely living here at the time."

"And why do you think he had something to do with this?" Chip said.

"Because he's been writing a murder mystery that we've been reading chapter by chapter the last few months, and it sounds like a fiction version about the real story of what happened to that boy, Myron Simpson. And I've been thinking, now that this story has come out, that maybe I should go to the police, tell them what I know. But what if I'm wrong? What if he had nothing to do with it, and I'm just being a busybody. I could be creating all kinds of problems for this guy."

"I see, Melissa. And I can understand why this is troubling you. Could you tell me a little bit about the story this man is writing? And why you think it connects to this story in the paper?"

So, she did. And the more she said, the more concerned Chip became. Especially, hearing the part where—in his story—he has 3 young men from the victim's high school involved. Which, she was quick to point out, *"might just be made up, because that part wasn't in the papers."*

When she finished, Chip asked, "Do you mind telling me who this fellow is, the one writing the story?"

"I guess I don't mind telling someone like you, in confidence. His name is Andrew Tubbs. He says he's a Christian, but he doesn't go to our church."

Tubbs, Tubbs, Andrew Tubbs...the name definitely rang a bell. But Chip couldn't come up with a face. "Well, Melissa, I'm glad you called. I've been taking notes and writing down everything you said. Let me have some time to pray and think about this, but I don't think you should go to the police about it. They usually require hard evidence on things before they take any action."

"I think I know what you mean," she said.

"But that name does sound familiar to me. He may be somebody I knew in high school, too. Let me look into this for you. Maybe I could pay him a visit, see if there's anything to this. And if there is, and he's a believer, perhaps I can convince him to go to the police himself. How does that sound?"

"That would be wonderful, Pastor. It would take such a load off my mind."

"Then that's what we'll do. You don't worry about contacting the police. You let me handle this. But first, I think I should read this story myself. You said it was in the Gazette?"

"Yes, the local section."

They said their goodbyes. Chip instantly opened his laptop.

This situation was way more than a speed bump. Had the potential to very quickly become a raging fire.

26

J oe glanced down at the GPS screen in his car. He had to turn at the next light. He and Hank were on their way to the trailer park where Andrew Tubbs lived. Back at the office, after Hank had briefed Joe on his phone call with Lisa, they decided to check this guy out. Especially after reading everything they could about him online.

Andrew Tubbs was not what you'd call a private person. Although he was in his late forties, the volume of things he posted about his life on Facebook and Instagram was more like something you'd expect from a millennial. Tons of pics, especially with him and his parrot. Quite a few selfies of him typing away at his laptop, even talking freely about the fact he was writing a book. A few people commented on these posts, asking for details about the book but Tubbs always replied the same way: "*I can't spill the beans. It's a murder mystery. You just have to wait and buy the book when it comes out.*"

Hopefully, Hank and Joe could get him to spill at least some of those beans very shortly. Joe made the turn and saw that the trailer park was just up ahead on the right.

"We might be well on our way after talking with this guy," Hank said.

"You got a hunch?" Joe said.

"Yeah, I got a hunch. But more than a hunch, I think. Did you see he went to Culpepper High? He was there the same timeframe as Myron Simpson. And now, here he is writing a fictionalized version of the story, after all these years. Could be he's trying to alleviate his guilty conscience?"

"Could be," Joe said. "Or he's just some sad sack of a guy who lives in a rundown trailer park all by himself, trying to spice up his life a little. Best I could tell from Facebook, he doesn't seem to have any close friends."

"Well, he's got that bird."

Joe turned into the trailer park. The GPS gal mentioned he should turn at the next left and then his destination would be on the right. It wasn't a bad little trailer park. He'd seen much worse. A bit on the older side. Lots of what they used to call single-wide's, little awnings, the occasional screen room. But nothing like some of those fancy manufactured home parks he'd seen in the nicer parts of town. He wouldn't mind living in some of those. Perfectly manicured lawns, nice big clubhouse and pool, and the homes themselves looked like regular houses.

When they got to the trailer whose mailbox matched the address they had for Tubbs, Joe noticed it had to be the oldest and most poorly-maintained trailer in the park.

"Geez," Hank said, "what a dump. So, what's our strategy going in? You want to be the good cop or the bad one?"

"Let's both start off going easy on him. See how far that gets us?"

They got out of the car and walked over a handful of cement squares that led into an aluminum carport. A metal set of steps sat under a fairly banged up front door. They were both startled by a loud squawking bird.

"CALM DOWN, PERCY," Tubbs said. "Nothing's going on." He'd been banging away at his laptop something fierce, had a real flow going. That newspaper story this morning really got him stirred up.

But Percy wouldn't calm down. He was like a watchdog that way, so Tubbs looked out the front windows, noticed a car had pulled up out front. A dark sedan, but he didn't see anyone. Then a knock at his front door. He walked around to the window to the right of the door, see who it was. Two men, dressed pretty nice. Looked too old to be Mormons. Maybe JW's. Should he ignore them? Sometimes if he did, they'd just go away. He needed to keep writing, keep the flow going. He was finishing up a real exciting chapter, too. The one where the three boys actually robbed the store.

Tubbs stood very still. Percy was staring at him, wondering what he was up to.

Another bang at the door.

"Andrew Tubbs? This is Hank Jensen, a detective with the Culpepper PD. We'd like to ask you a few questions."

The police? What in the world were the police doing here?

"Mr. Tubbs?" Another knock.

Percy started squawking again. He'd better answer the door. "I'm coming," he yelled. "Give me just a minute."

Walked over to Percy. "It's all right," he said calmly. "Everything's okay." Was he saying that to Percy or to himself? He
walked back to the front door and opened it. "Could I please
see some ID? Can't be too careful these days."

"Not a problem," the younger man said. Both of them
took out their wallets, held up their ID badges.

"Okay, come on in then." He backed away from the door,
noticed his laptop. Quickly walked over and closed the lid.
He turned to see both men step into the living area. The
older of the two closed the door behind them.

"As I said, I'm Detective Hank Jensen, and this is my partner, Lieutenant Joe Boyd."

"A Lieutenant?" Tubbs repeated. "Bringing out the big
guns, eh? Well, come on in. Have a seat. You can just set
those newspapers on the coffee table. Sorry for the mess, I've
been kinda busy. Working on a book actually." He sat in one
of his dinette chairs, closest to Percy's cage. "So, what brings
you here? Don't think I've ever had the police knock on my
door before. Least not detectives in street clothes."

Both of the detectives sat on the couch, but on the edge
like they weren't planning on staying very long. Which was a
good thing far as Tubbs was concerned.

"As Detective Jensen said, we're with the Culpepper PD.
With a cold case squad, to be more specific. We're investigating a homicide."

"A homicide?" Tubbs repeated. "In this trailer park? Only
thing that kills folks around here is old age."

The younger of the two laughed.

The older one smiled. "No, the homicide didn't happen
here. I don't know if you read the local newspaper yet this
morning." The Lieutenant looked down at the coffee table,

noticed the newspaper. "Here it is, right here." He moved the sections around. "I don't see the local section."

Tubbs instantly tensed up, hoped the look on his face hadn't changed too much to show it. "Uh, I usually do read the paper in the morning, but I didn't today." He stood, backed up toward his laptop. Could they possibly be here because of *that* story? "I think the local section's over here. I was gonna put it on the bottom of Percy's cage, since I didn't have time to clean it."

"Well," the younger one, Hank, said, "if you hold it up, we're here to talk to you about this big story on the front page."

Tubbs felt his heart start to beat faster. "Really?" he said. He picked the newspaper up, pretended to read it for the first time. "Oh, my." He pretended to read the first few paragraphs. "You know, I remember this case. I used to go to school with that boy, the one here in the article." He set the paper down, looked over at the detectives. "But what in the world does this story have to do with me? And why would you even think to come here to talk to me about it?"

The older of the two stood, walked toward Tubbs. He wasn't smiling anymore.

"Let's cut the crap, Mr. Tubbs," he said. "I think you know exactly why we're here, talking to you about this case."

27

Tubbs looked stunned...by both the words Joe had just spoken as well as the tone.

"I...I don't know what you mean," he said. "I don't know anything about this story in the paper, or why you think I would."

Joe deliberately came closer, stared him right in the eyes. "Is that right, Mr. Tubbs? That your story, and you're sticking with it?"

Tubbs smiled weakly, like he recognized the line Joe used from that comedian on Saturday Night Live. But Joe didn't smile back.

"Why would you think I would know anything about this?"

Hank stood up. "We don't think, Tubbs. We know you do."

Tubbs didn't reply, like he was scrambling for something to say.

"You know that writers' group you been going to once a

month?" Joe said. He turned to Hank. "What's the name of it?"

"Word Weavers."

"That's right," Joe said. "Word Weavers. That ring a bell?" Joe could see in his eyes it did. He knew he'd been caught lying to the police.

Tubbs set the newspaper down on the table. His head stayed looking down.

"Not a good thing to lie to the police, Tubbs," Hank said. "See, we know people only lie when they've got something to hide."

"Or something they're ashamed of," Joe added.

"Maybe something they feel guilty about," Hank said.

Tubbs looked up. "Well, that's not what's happening here. I don't feel ashamed or guilty about nothing."

"That because you're a sociopath, Mr. Tubbs?" Joe said. "You know what a sociopath is?"

"I know what a sociopath is. People that don't feel any guilt when they do wrong. But I haven't done anything wrong. I'm just writing a book. Nothing wrong with writing a book."

"No," Joe said, "nothing wrong with writing a book. But you're not just writing *any* book. You're writing a book about a murder that just so happens to be the murder we're investigating. One that took place over thirty years ago. And from what we hear, the things in your story bear an uncanny resemblance to the things that actually happened back then. Now, how do you suppose something like that happens? Just by chance? You made some lucky guesses?"

"No, I don't know. But it's not because I had anything to do with it...if that's what you're suggesting. I happened to

live here back then. I went to school with the kid who got
killed. I read all about it in the papers. And as most fiction
writers do, I have an active imagination. I decided to loosely
base my mystery on something that really happened.
Mystery writers do that all the time. It's not a crime. Doesn't
mean they were involved."

"Loosely based?" Hank said.

"Yes."

"Then how do you know the victim was killed?" Joe said.
"We only knew that last week when we found his body, and
it's only been reported to the public since this morning. For
all these years, he was only listed as missing."

"Well, everyone knew Myron had been killed. Nothing
else made any sense."

"Some people believed that," Hank said. "Not everyone.
Quite a few people were sure he stole the money and took
off with it. Did you know Myron personally, Mr. Tubbs?"

"No. I didn't. I don't know if we ever even talked to each
other."

"But you know for a fact he was killed," Joe said. "But
there's way more than that going on here. Isn't there, Tubbs?
You write in your story that three high school friends are
involved. Not friends of the victim, but friends with each
other. How would you know that? That information was
never discussed in the news. That kind of information is
something only the killer would know. The killer and the
police."

Tubbs' eyes bugged out. A genuine expression of fear
came over his face. Joe's wild leap seemed to have just paid
off. He and Hank had no proof that three high school friends
were involved, but Tubbs didn't know that. His reaction to

that info confirmed, though, this part of Tubbs's story was *not* fiction.

Tubbs looked away then down at his laptop. "I didn't kill that boy. And I wasn't involved in any way. It's just a story."

"It's way more than just a story," Hank said. "And you know that, too. You're writing about it as if it was a made-up story, but you know for a fact it really happened. Because you were involved. You figured it would be safe to draw from it after all this time, because you figured no one but you and your other two friends would ever know the truth. And for some reason, they've stayed quiet all this time, so you figured —"

"Would you just stop?" Tubbs all but yelled. "That's not what happened. And that's not how I knew the stuff I'm writing about. The stuff you say only the police and the killer would know."

"If we're wrong, Tubbs," Joe said, "then you better start telling us how."

"I don't know, Joe," Hank said, "maybe we should move this conversation downtown."

Tubbs dropped into the dinette chair. "No, wait." He sighed deeply. "I'm not lying when I say I wasn't involved. Because I wasn't. But I think I might know the guys who were."

"You think?" Hank said.

"Yes, but I'm not sure. I didn't even know the part about the three guys being involved was definitely true until you guys just said it now."

Now, Joe was confused. He looked at Hank. He was, too. Because Joe had only inserted that into the story, because of what Lisa had told Hank. She said Tubbs had written about it, but that she'd never read anything about three boys in the newspapers before. If Tubbs was involved, why wouldn't he know this point for certain? "Okay Mr. Tubbs, let's back up a second. Let's just say for the moment that you weren't personally involved in the robbery and murder."

"I wasn't. I swear it."

"Okay, assuming that's true, then someone who was involved — personally involved — must've told you what happened. I'm talking about the parts that were never discussed in the news."

"The parts that only the killers and the police would know," Tubbs said.

"Right," Joe said. "Those parts. If you weren't involved, then someone who was involved gave you that information."

"We need to know who that person is, Mr. Tubbs," Hank said.

"I...I can't say."

"Can't say, or won't say," Joe said.

"In a way, both," Tubbs said.

"Tubbs..." Joe said sternly.

"What I mean is, yes, someone who may have been involved—and I stress...*may*—confided in me about this case a long time ago. Way back when we were still in high school. His name is Ray Dodson. We were next-door neighbors. I guess we were friends, too. Sort of. But he told me what he told me a few days before his family moved out of town. We were kind of hanging out for the last time before they left. I don't know how the subject came up, but we were talking about Myron Simpson being missing all that time. By then, it had been over six months. I said something trying to guess at what might've happened, then Ray got real quiet. He got this look on his face, a real serious one. And then he said, *maybe that's not how it happened at all. Maybe it happened more like this...*then he tells me this whole story of what happened, but the whole time he's talking in hypothetical terms. So, it wasn't actually a confession. But the way he said it, the look in his eyes...I was sure he was telling me what really happened."

"And you didn't think maybe you should tell somebody what he said?" Hank said.

"No. Like I said, it wasn't a confession. He wasn't admitting to anything. And even if he had, I was pretty freaked out. I mean, the guys that killed this kid knew who I was. And *they* weren't moving out of town. In fact, if it's the two guys I think really did it, they still live in this town. I don't want them coming after me."

"Then why are you writing this stupid book?" Hank said. "If you're afraid they'll come after you."

"Because, up until this morning it was a totally forgotten story. Nobody's talked about it for years. Nobody was investigating it, and I had no reason to believe that would ever change. I doubt the guys who did this will ever even read my book, and if they did, they'd see how I changed many of the details that would implicate them. But *now*...now that you guys found the body, and it's in the news...it's a whole new ballgame. So, I'm not gonna do a thing that might give these guys reason to want to shut me up."

"So," Joe said, "you're not going to help us get these two guys who you say actually did the crime?"

"I want to," Tubbs said. "It's not that. But I'm not hearing you offer to set me up in that Witness Protection Program, so no, I'm not volunteering any more information."

"Would you be willing to send us the file?" Joe said, pointing to his laptop. "The fiction story you're writing. Just as far as you've gotten up to this point. And maybe any research files you got."

"No, I wouldn't."

"We could get a warrant," Hank said. "Force you to give it to us."

"Then I guess that's what you'll have to do. At least then, it'll be obvious that I didn't do it willingly."

No one said anything for a few moments. Joe looked at Hank. "I guess that's what we'll do next, Mr. Tubbs." He started walking toward the front door.

"Don't even think about deleting that file, Tubbs," Hank said. "Our computer guys will still be able to find it, no matter what you do."

Joe opened the front door, then turned and faced Tubbs. "You said the guy that told you this tale back in high school was named Ray Dodson, right?"

Tubbs nodded.

"And you have no idea where he lives now?"

Tubbs shook his head no.

ONCE THEY WERE BACK in the car, Hank said, "Whoa, we're coming out with a lot more than I expected."

"Yeah," Joe said. "Me, too." He started the car.

Then Hank said, "But I gotta ask you something...about what you said before we went in."

"What's that?"

"What happened to the, *Let's both go easy on him then, see how far that gets us* bit? Think I missed the *going easy on him* part completely.

Joe smiled. "What can I say? I had a hunch."

"A hunch, eh?"

"Yeah, something like that."

28

Chip Masters had read enough. It was time for action.

He closed his laptop and headed out the front door of his office, toward the last office suite at the end of the hall. It belonged to the senior pastor and his good friend, Glenn Burton. The door was closed, which was not unusual. He paused briefly to touch base with Glenn's personal assistant, Maria. "Is Glenn in?"

"He is, Pastor Chip, but he's kind of busy. He's meeting with that writer the two of you talked about, the one who's going to start converting some of his best messages into books."

"Is the meeting just getting started, or have they been at it a while?"

"They've been in there for over an hour. According to the schedule, Pastor Glenn should be taking a break in about ten minutes to take the writer out to lunch. If you'd like, I could tell him to come see you before —"

"No, something very urgent has come up. I'm going to need to interrupt him right now."

"Are you sure? He'll only be —"

"I'm sure." Chip opened his door. "I'll take any heat for this, if there is any." He stepped inside and closed the door behind him.

Glenn was startled by Chip's sudden appearance but quickly recovered. They'd been at this long enough for Glenn to recognize by the look in Chip's eyes that something big was up. The writer turned in his chair to face Chip.

"So sorry to interrupt you gentlemen," Chip said.

"Gary," Glenn said, "let me introduce you to a good friend of mine and our church administrator, Pastor Chip Masters. It's good for you guys to connect anyways. Chip will be the one you'll be working with on the contract and business end of things."

The writer, Gary, stood and offered his hand. Chip shook it. "Like I said, I'm very sorry to have to butt in like this, but something pretty serious has come up and I need to speak with Pastor Glenn about it...in private."

Gary looked at Glenn, who nodded and said, "That's all right. We can pick up the rest of our conversation at lunch. Will this take long, Pastor Chip?"

"Shouldn't be more than ten minutes."

"Then Gary, why don't you wait out in my outer office area with Maria while I chat with Glenn, and I'll be right with you."

"Great," Gary said. "No problem. Nice to meet you, Pastor Chip."

Chip smiled and nodded as the man walked past him

and out Glenn's office door. He hurried over and sat in one of Glenn's upholstered office chairs.

Glenn's whole demeanor instantly changed. "What's going on, Chip? Must be something serious for you to bust in here like this."

"Sorry, Glenn, but it doesn't get any more serious than this."

Glenn sat back in his chair. "Wow, okay. Let's hear it."

"Maybe you should read it first, then we'll talk."

"Read what?"

"I sent you a link. Check your email. Should be right at the top."

Glenn opened his laptop lid, clicked on his email tab, saw the email from Chip and clicked on that.

"That link is to the lead article in the local section of the Gazette this morning." Chip stopped talking to watch Glenn's eyes as he read. First, his eyebrows arched high on his forehead, then a scowl. Then he got real serious, and his head shook back and forth slowly. He leaned back and sighed. "Man, you weren't kidding." He sighed again, shook his head again. "Can't believe they found his body, after all these years." He looked up at Chip. "But I guess, in a way, this is a good thing. At least, it will give the boy's family some closure. Something we were never able to do."

"Glenn, there's more going on here than just that story showing up in the papers."

"What? What do you mean?"

"Aren't you gonna ask me how I found out about this story being in the Gazette today? It's not like that's a news-paper I read, unless we've got some ad in there, or else there's some story about the church."

"Okay, how did you find out about it?"

Chip took the next five minutes filling him in on the details of his conversation with Melissa Hendricks. When he got to the part about Andrew Tubbs writing a murder mystery using this case as his premise, Glenn's expression completely changed. Then he mentioned the part of Melissa's story that wasn't in the Gazette piece, the part about him introducing three boys from the victim's high school as being the ones who did it.

Chip didn't need to waste another word persuading him after that.

Glenn got it.

After a long silence, Glenn said. "Why is that name familiar, Andrew Tubbs?"

"He was in our class at Culpepper High, same year. Looked him up in the yearbook. Kind of a nerd. Not somebody we would've hung around with. I don't know what he looks like now."

"Then how in the world," Glenn said, "does this guy Tubbs know what happened back in '88? Because I never said a word to anyone."

"Me either, Glenn."

"You think it was Dodson?"

"I don't know," Chip said. "Guess it had to be. He's the only other one who knew. But why he would blab about it to someone like this guy Tubbs is beyond me."

"Well, you know how he was," Glenn said. "He wanted no part of it after... after it happened. He just walked away into the night, left the two of us to deal with the mess. Then after that, he started pulling away from us."

"I know," Chip said. "But I still don't get why he'd talk

about it to anyone. Remember that little meeting we had a few days later, when we cornered him behind the gym?"

Glenn nodded. "You got a little too rough with him, as I recall. We were supposed to just meet there to talk."

"I had to get through to him, Glenn. You know that. Make him see...just because he walked away afterwards and wouldn't help us bury the body, didn't make him any less guilty than us. He was there. He helped us plan it. As I recall, while I had him pinned to the wall, you got in his face pretty good. *Better get your act together, Ray. You tell anyone about this, and you're going down for it, too. Same as us.* Remember?"

"I remember. And I remember he said he got it and swore he'd never tell a soul."

"Well," Chip said. "He must've told this guy, Tubbs, at some point before he moved away. How else would Tubbs know enough to write what he did? It's obvious from what this gal Melissa said, he didn't use our real names in the book he's writing. Or else we'd be hearing from the police already. But if he was just making stuff up from the information available back when it happened, he'd have never come up with three local high school guys being the culprits. He had to have talked to Ray. Only thing that makes sense."

"I agree," Glenn said. "Even though he didn't use our real names, think this guy Tubbs knows them?"

"I don't know, Glenn. Depends on how much Ray told him, I guess. But I don't think we can take that chance."

"No, we can't. We've got to know the answer to that question. And we need to know it now." He leaned back, looked up at the ceiling and sighed. "Man, this could really get bad."

"Yes, it could," Chip said. "Very bad."

"We could lose everything, Chip. All of this. Everything

we've built here all these years. Our reputations would be shot. Our pension funds...they're tied up in this church."

"Our pension fund?" Chip said. "Forget about that, we'd spend the rest of our lives in prison. There's no statute of limitations on murder. You were seventeen, and I was eighteen. We'd be tried as adults. We can't let that happen, Glenn."

"No, we can't." He leaned forward, rested his elbows on the desk. "I guess if there's one consolation to this mess, it would appear that Ray hasn't talked to anyone else about it since. Otherwise, we'd have heard about it before this."

"Probably true," Chip said. "Turns out, talking about it once was enough. So, what do you want me to do...with this guy Tubbs?"

"Only thing you can do. Put the fear of God in him. Make sure he knows, he talks to anyone about this — especially the police — it'll be his last conversation on earth."

Chip knew exactly what Glenn was saying. "Will do." He turned, headed for the door.

"Oh, and Chip...whatever else you do with Tubbs, you get hold of that laptop and any backup files he made of his little...book."

29

"Oh, shoot."

Andrew Tubbs was getting ready to go to work when he heard a car pull up in his little driveway. He never got visitors. Must be the cops coming back. But they couldn't have gotten a warrant that quick, could they? He was in the bathroom, so he walked down the hall, ducked into the middle bedroom where he could see out the window to the driveway. "What the heck?" Couldn't see who it was, but that was definitely not a cop car. Judging by the fancy grill, looked more like a Jaguar. Now, there's a car he'd never seen in the trailer park before.

Whoever it was, they were gonna make him late if they didn't make it quick. Percy started squawking as soon as they started knocking on the door. "Be right there," he yelled, then finished wiping off the shaving cream from his neck. He put his shirt back on, started buttoning it up as he headed back into the living room. "It's okay, Percy. Everything's just fine."

As soon as he opened the door, he knew...everything was not fine.

It was big Chip Masters standing right there in an expensive suit. One of the many bullies who'd tormented Tubbs' during his middle and high school years. But worse, Tubbs was near positive he was one of the two other guys involved in Myron Simpson's murder, besides Ray Dodson. He was supposed to be in ministry now, though he didn't dress like it. He looked more like a scary mobster.

"You don't recognize me, Andy. Do you?"

"Uh, yeah actually. I think I do. Chip Masters. We went to high school around the same time."

"Yeah, that's right," Chip said. "You gonna invite me in?"

"What? Yeah, sure. But I can't talk long. I'm just getting ready for work. Have to leave in about ten minutes, or I'll be late."

"This won't take long."

Tubbs looked down, saw he was holding a newspaper in his left hand. Feelings of panic began to simmer. The story about the murder. Had to be why he was here. Tubbs backed away from the door, held it open as Chip walked in. Percy started pacing back and forth in his cage.

"Nice bird. Some kind of parrot, right?"

"Yeah, I've had him for years. Sometimes he gets nervous when I get company." Tubbs walked over to his cage, stuck his finger between the bars. Percy walked right to him and lowered his head to let Tubbs scratch it. "It's okay, Percy. Everything's fine." He tried to sound convincing.

Chip looked around at Tubbs' place. It didn't show on his face, but how could he approve? Weren't the nerds supposed to rule the world, and the bullies wind up living like this?

He glanced over at Tubbs' laptop. "Hear you're writing a book. Guess you're going to some kind of monthly writers' group."

"You heard about that?"

"Yes, I did. Just this morning, in fact. Wouldn't be right to divulge who told me, seeing as it was in confidence. You know, things said to a clergyman are a private matter"

"Okay, I don't mind someone telling you that. Not exactly a secret." Tubbs decided his best bet was to play it stupid, as if he had no idea why Chip had come to see him.

"Well, apparently what you've been writing about is causing a little bit of commotion and concern with some people."

"Really? I can't imagine why. It's just a murder mystery. I've only read a handful of chapters to the group so far. Haven't even gotten to the really tense parts yet."

"My source seems to think you're basing your novel on a true story," Chip said. "And not just any true story, but the story that's taken up a good part of the first page in the local section of today's paper." He held up his copy of the Gazette. "You read this story yet?"

Tubbs was just about to deny it when he noticed his copy of the paper was still sitting next to his laptop. "Uh, yeah actually. I did. And I'll be honest, I was basing my story — just in part, mind you — on the story that came out today. I'm sure you've read it, seeing as it's right there in your hand. I was quite shocked to read it actually. I was thinking that me drawing from it the way I've been doing was no big deal, since I haven't heard anybody talk about that situation for, I don't know, twenty years or more. I wasn't even sure anyone still remembered it."

Chip set the newspaper on the edge of the table. "Yeah, I was pretty shocked to read it myself. Since we're being honest. But even more shocked to hear this church member of ours sharing how disturbed she was between the similarities in your story and this newspaper article."

"Well, I don't know why that would be," Tubbs said. "There are similarities. There would be, since I'm drawing from that true story, like I said. But I'm changing a lot of it, so that it isn't exactly the same. I mean, it's not even close to the same. And I've been thinking, ever since I read that story this morning, of changing even more things than I was going to. Now that the story's come out in the public eye. I'm sure you've seen movies that have said, *Inspired by True Events*. I was thinking of something like that."

Chip didn't say anything, but the look on his face got real serious. "I've got another idea, Andy. Why don't you come up with another idea for your murder mystery altogether? What I mean is, pick a different crime. I don't care if it's true, or one you made up in your head. Just pick a different one... and stop making it about this one." He pointed to the newspaper.

It didn't sound like a suggestion.

"Can I ask you why? Like, why would you care if I did or didn't change it?" Tubbs was almost positive he knew why, but wanted to see what Chip would say. "The reason I ask is, I've been working on this for quite a while, and I got the whole outline almost finished."

"Well, Andy, it's like this. The church member who shared what you've written so far said you've included some parts that weren't in the newspaper."

"Well, there would be, right? That's because some of it's fiction. There'd have to be because —"

"Let me finish. The parts she mentioned included something about three high school friends being involved in the crime. You know what I'm talking about?"

"Well, yes. There is that..."

"Yeah, see, that's unacceptable to us."

"Us?" Tubbs said.

"Yes, Andy. Us. Pastor Glenn Burton and myself. And the reason is, someone back in the day, back when this whole thing happened, was circulating a vicious rumor that Pastor Glenn and me had something to do with the robbery and murder of that boy. And we can't have your story coming out now, giving this news story all kinds of fresh publicity, which then resurrects this old rumor about Pastor Glenn and me. Next thing you know, the police will want to take a look into that rumor, since they'll be looking to hang this on somebody. And wouldn't they just love to stir up a big scandal and try to bring Pastor Glenn down and smear his name all over the media. We can't have that, Andy. We just can't."

The more he spoke, the louder he got, and the closer he stood to Tubbs. The alarm bells started going off inside. He felt like he had to tell him. "The police already know about this, Chip."

"What? What do you mean? How?"

"They were here this morning. Talking about this story I'm writing. I guess either that member who talked to you or another one went to them, thinking that maybe I had something to do with the murder, and that's why I was basing my story on it. So, they came here asking me all kinds of questions, trying to see if there was anything to it."

The look on Chip's face made Tubbs feel suddenly afraid.

"Did you give them a copy of what you've written?"

"No, but they said they were going to get a warrant to seize and search my laptop."

"Well, we can't have that, Andy. That won't do at all." He walked over and picked up Tubbs' laptop. "You got the files for this book or any research for it backed up anywhere?"

Tubbs shook his head no. "I've been meaning to, but never got around to it."

"Well, here's what you're gonna do. I'm taking this with me. And because we're not bad guys, I'm going to take this back to my office and make a backup of all your files, except any files that had anything to do with this story or your book. Those I'm going to destroy. And you can never write about this again, do you hear me?" His finger was right in Tubbs' face.

Tubbs nodded.

"Then sometime later today, you're going to call the police and report a burglary. Tell them anything else you want, but make sure you say this laptop was stolen. They can't search something that doesn't exist. And like I said, because we're not bad guys, you can come by the office in a couple of days, and I'll have a brand-new Apple laptop waiting for you, loaded up with software and all your old files from the backup I made. You figure out some other crime to base your novel on, and you and me will have no problems after that. Are we good?"

What else could Tubbs say? Considering how bad this could have gone, felt like he was coming up pretty good. "Yeah, we're good. I don't have a problem doing any of that."

"Good. I'm gonna need any password or login info you use to sign on to your computer."

"I don't use any. I know I probably should but..."

Chip started walking with the laptop toward the door. He turned and said, "You might be wondering how any of what I've said to you squares off with the idea that I'm a man of God now. I can understand that. But there's a verse in 1st Chronicles, chapter 16, that says: *Touch not the Lord's anointed and do my prophets no harm.* To me, and to our entire church, Pastor Glenn is the Lord's anointed. And the Lord has appointed me to protect him from anyone and anything that would ever try to do him harm. I will do anything I have to, to make sure he stays protected. Do you follow me? Do you understand what I'm saying? Anything I have to do."

Tubbs understood.

Chip Masters walked out the door, drove off in his deep-blue Jaguar.

30

T he following day, about midmorning, Joe left his desk to get a cup of coffee. He didn't know why, but the coffee made by the folks who sat near his old office was just better than the stuff he could get in the lounge. He walked past his old office, now Hank's spot. Didn't bother to look in on Hank. He knew he was on his way to the courthouse to pick up that warrant to search Andrew Tubbs' laptop.

After fixing his coffee, one of the newer patrolmen came up. Joe had forgotten his name.

"Hey, Detective Boyd," he said. "Did I hear your partner say something about getting a warrant for the cold case you guys are working on?"

"That's where he's at now," Joe said.

"Wasn't the guy's name Tubbs? I remembered it because it's kind of an odd last name."

"Yeah, that's it. Andrew Tubbs. Why?"

"Guess you should call Hank, tell him to forget about it.

This guy, Tubbs, called 911 about an hour ago to report a burglary at his place. I wasn't the one who checked it out, but I took a second call from him about ten minutes ago. He called on the non-emergency line, asked us to get a message to you or Hank, let you know that his laptop was one of the main things stolen. So, there probably wasn't any reason to waste time on the search warrant. That's what he said anyway."

"How convenient," Joe said. "Thanks for the message. I'll call Hank."

"Think he's bluffing?" the patrolman asked. "I could look into it, check with the guys that visited his trailer."

"I doubt he'd be stupid enough to make something like that up. But thanks for the offer. I'll see what Hank wants to do about it." Joe took a satisfying sip of his coffee and took out his cell phone, called Hank.

"Hey, Joe, what's up?"

"How far did you get with that warrant?"

"I'm at the clerk of the court's office. It's supposed to be ready, but I'm waiting for them to bring it out. Why?"

Joe explained to Hank what just happened.

"Yeah, that's just a little too convenient," Hank said. "Are you buying it?"

"I don't know. Way too coincidental for me. But I can't imagine he's stupid enough to make something like that up."

"Well, I could see about changing the warrant to search his place instead, see if he's just hiding it. You know, since I'm here at the courthouse anyway. He seemed highly motivated to keep us from seeing what he'd written about the story."

"I don't know," Joe said. He thought a moment. "Yeah, go ahead and do that. But instead of heading right over there, maybe we'll drive by his place in a couple days, pay him a little visit then. Something he wouldn't expect. You could tell from what we saw on his Facebook page, he's very into writing this book. If he is bluffing about it being stolen, I can't imagine him not getting it out in a few days to start writing again. So, if we find it there, then we can arrest him for filing a false report. Might give us some leverage to get him to spill a few more beans."

"All right, will do."

"Meanwhile, I'm going to contact that lady from the writing group, Lisa. See if she won't mind answering a few more background questions about this guy, see if she remembers anything more specific about what Tubbs shared with the group about his book."

THIRTY MINUTES LATER, Joe had just driven through the entrance of a shady little subdivision of villa-style homes. The main road curved back-and-forth and around a series of tree-clusters, which Joe found rather charming. It was nice to see a builder who'd gone out of his way to keep as many trees intact as possible when he laid out the roads.

He was following the GPS instructions from the address Lisa had given him when they'd talked on the phone. She sounded happy to meet with him and would be willing to answer any questions he had.

When he finally pulled into her driveway, he saw two women standing on the sidewalk that led to the front door. They were hugging and greeting each other. Apparently, one of them had just arrived moments before Joe pulled in. He got out of the car. Both women appeared to be in their late forties, which would make sense if they'd been in high school in 1988, when the murder had been committed.

"Hello, Detective Boyd. I'm guessing that's who you are." The shorter woman with darker hair waved to him. "I'm Lisa, the one you spoke to on the phone."

"Hi, Lisa. Yep, that's me. Detective Boyd. But you ladies can just call me Joe, if you'd like. Or just Detective. Either one works for me."

"Okay...Joe," Lisa said. "This is my friend, Melissa Hendricks. I hope you don't mind. I invited her over to join us. She only lives a few minutes away. We both go to the same writers' group, the one Andy Tubbs goes to. In fact, we were both in the small group he was in both meetings. And we were both in high school around the same time as when the murder took place."

Joe walked up and shook each of their hands. "No, don't mind at all. The more information I can get, the quicker we can figure this thing out."

As they walked toward the front door, Melissa said, "I was a little nervous about coming when Lisa called. Not because of you, or anything. It's just, I'm the one who called and spoke with Detective Hank a few days ago, before the story came out in the paper. After that, I felt so stupid because I almost felt like I was being some kind of tattletale, and I didn't really have any evidence."

Lisa opened the door, and they walked in. "Well, Hank, my partner," Joe said, "he told me about your call. You have no reason to be embarrassed, Mrs. Hendricks. Especially now, since this story's come out. It would appear you were actually on to something."

"Well, thank you. And please, call me Melissa."

Lisa led them into a warmly decorated living space, a dining area on the left that opened to some comfy-looking leather furniture situated around a large screen TV. On a coffee table, he saw a fresh pot of coffee, cream and sugar and a plate of cookies. Hardly seemed like the setting to be discussing a murder.

"Sit anywhere you like," Lisa said. "I'll sit in my favorite spot, here on this loveseat. Feel free to have some coffee and cookies. I have some iced tea or juice in the kitchen, if you'd like."

"No, this is great," Joe said. "Just don't tell my wife about the cookies."

They both laughed.

"So, how can we help you?" Melissa said as she fixed her coffee. "Lisa said you were wanting to ask some questions about the story Andrew Tubbs had shared at our group."

Joe sat on the edge of the couch near the center. "Yeah, we ran into a snag after meeting with Mr. Tubbs yesterday. He was cooperative to a point and admitted that the book he'd been writing was loosely based, to use his words, on the crime we're investigating. And he had read the article in the paper yesterday morning."

"It's crazy, the timing of all this," Lisa said. "Don't you think?"

"Yeah," Joe said, "but crazy in a good way for us. We would never have expected to be this far along already. But like I said, we also already ran into our first snag. Mr. Tubbs was very apprehensive about giving us a copy of the chapters he wrote in his book that connect to this case and said we'd need to get a warrant if we wanted to see them."

"Really?" Melissa said. "I wonder why, because at our

meetings he shares them without hesitation. Like he's proud as can be to have us read them."

"But Melissa," Lisa said, "that's before this story came out in the Gazette."

"Yeah," Joe said. "And, of course, he denied being involved in any way, and he hinted that the real killers were likely from this area and still live here."

"Do you think he just said that," Melissa said, "you know, to deflect attention away from him? We were wondering if maybe he might have been involved."

"Could be," Joe said. "At this point, we can't rule out anything. But the snag I mentioned gets even worse. He phoned in to us this morning reporting a burglary at his place, saying the laptop — with the full contents of the story — was stolen. So, now we have no way of knowing what he may have shared or written about it."

"Which is why you need our help?" Lisa said.

Joe nodded. "Is there anything you can remember about this story, from the things he shared with the group that might be relevant to our case?"

Both ladies each took a few minutes giving their best summaries of what the first few chapters of Tubbs' book seemed to be about. But other than the part about Tubbs introducing three high school friends as being involved in the crime, there really weren't any pertinent facts shared beyond what the newspapers had already reported. Melissa said, "He hadn't really even gotten to the part where the robbery and murder at the convenience store happens."

"Yeah," Lisa added, "he gave us the impression, though, that the actual crime would take place in the next chapter, the one he'd read at next month's meeting. And in that chapter, his so-called clever title would make sense. You know, *An Inconvenient Death*."

"I wonder now if he'll ever finish it," Melissa said. "Doesn't sound like he is."

Joe took some notes, although it was mostly for show. Sadly, he wasn't learning anything new. Then a thought popped into his head. Something Tubbs had said yesterday. "Now, both of you went to school at the same time as this murder, and Tubbs was there, too. Right?"

They both nodded.

"When we asked Tubbs where he got the idea for the story," Joe said, "he mentioned a high school friend of his had told him. I think it was his next-door neighbor. But then he said this kid moved away a few months later, and he hasn't heard from him since. Do either one of you remember a young man by the name of Ray Dodson?"

Neither one immediately replied. Then Lisa said, "I'm sorry. Doesn't ring any bell with me."

But Melissa started shaking her head up and down. "I do remember Ray. We weren't close friends, but I did have a couple of classes with him. I'd forgotten completely about him because, like you said, he moved away so long ago. But hearing his name, it's definitely coming back to me. I don't remember where he moved to, or anything, but —" She gasped. Then a startled look came over her face. "I just remembered...he used to always hang around two other boys. I used to always see the three of them together." She thought a moment, then shook her head no. "But...I can't remember their names."

Joe did write this down. "Can you try? It could really be important."

She was racking her brain trying to remember. But it was no use.

Then Lisa said, "Melissa, didn't you tell me you still had our high school yearbooks? Maybe if you looked through them, you'd remember who they were."

"I do," Melissa said. "Would you like me to do that, Detective?"

"Definitely, Melissa. The sooner, the better."

31

Chip Masters had driven back to the church, parked in his reserved spot, his soft leather brief bag hanging from his shoulder as he walked to his office. Inside, was Tubbs' laptop. He'd made sure he appeared as nonchalant and outgoing with everyone, as always. Not a care in the world. As he walked down the hallway where most of the staff pastors' offices were located, an idea popped into his head.

An important one.

He remembered the youth pastor had taken a few days off to visit his mother out of state. She was getting surgery, or something. The thing was, that meant his computer was unattended. And Chip had set the computers up, so that none of the junior staff had private passwords. For account-ability reasons, he'd told them, so they wouldn't be tempted to store inappropriate things on their computer. He looked around, saw no one was looking, and quickly ducked into the empty office.

After waiting for the computer to come alive, he searched on Google: *How to completely destroy a laptop hard drive, so the information on it can never be retrieved.* He remembered seeing on the news when some popular criminal trial was being covered, that police often checked the things people searched Google about during their investigations. It wouldn't do to have a Google search like that on his computer.

Chip scanned through the various articles listed and scribbled down a bunch of handwritten notes. Then he shut the computer down, checked the hallway, and eased himself out and straight to his own office a few doors down. One of the more humorous articles he saw was titled, *Get Rid of Your Data the Hillary Way.* The good news was, there was a variety of ways to do it safely, giving him the assurance that after today no one would ever see the story Andrew Tubbs had written, or ever make any connection between it, him and Glenn.

Chip wasn't exactly a high-tech gadget guy, but he knew his way around the computer and fairly quickly located all the files Tubbs had created for his story. Obviously, Tubbs had no reason to think anyone would ever come after these files, so they were all located in one folder, called: *An Inconvenient Death – First Novel.* Chip noticed the latest entry was that morning. He looked at the time. Tubbs had actually been writing the latest chapter less than thirty minutes before Chip stopped in at his trailer.

Too bad for Tubbs. This thing had to be done. He was just about to delete it, when he had a thought. Maybe he should read what Tubbs had written first. See how close his story actually resembled what happened.

Chip was a fast reader, so it only took him about fifteen minutes before he'd gotten to the end. But what he read was way too close for comfort. It was obvious that Dodson had confided in Tubbs. Then he looked back at the last page, the chapter that actually described the robbery and murder, when something very disturbing suddenly dawned on him.

The three boys in Tubbs' story had the exact same initials as him, Glenn and Ray Dodson. Could Dodson have really been that stupid and told Tubbs their real identities? He sighed, tried to calm down. It really didn't matter anymore.

Not after today.

He selected the folder and hit the delete button then found the trash can icon, right-clicked on it, and deleted the entire contents in the trashcan. After double-checking to make sure the files were gone, he closed the lid. Just as he did, his office door opened.

It was Glenn. He slipped in, closed and locked the door behind him. This was totally unlike him, to chase after an update. It told Chip how much this mattered to him.

"So, how'd it go?" Glenn said. "You get with that guy, Tubbs?"

Chip held up his laptop.

"What's that?"

"Tubbs' laptop. Picked it up from his trailer this morning. Made sure there were no backup files. Everything he'd written that had anything to do with that convenience store situation was on here, and now it's deleted."

"He just gave it to you? You didn't have to —"

"He required a little persuasion, but not too much. I could tell he was majorly intimidated the moment I walked through that door. So, I just played on that, and he cried uncle pretty quick." Chip told him about the goodwill gesture he'd offered Tubbs, giving him back a new laptop with all of his files restored, minus the ones about the book.

"How confident are you that this is the end of it?" Glenn said. "That he's going to keep a lid on this thing going forward?"

Chip decided not to tell Glenn about the issue with Tubbs' characters having the same initials as the three of them. "Totally confident."

Chip also decided not to tell Glenn about the fact that the police had already been there and spoken with Tubbs. "I made sure he understood why he could never write about that story again, because of that nasty rumor someone spread about us back in the day, about us having something to do with that convenience store case." He was speaking facetiously about that last part, and Glenn got it. "Seriously, Glenn, this is a done deal. The fire has been put out. That's why I offered him the new laptop, offset him giving up all that work he'd already done on his book."

"I think that's wise," Glenn said, a relieved smile now appearing on his face. "What are you going to do with that thing?" He pointed to the laptop.

"Utterly destroy it. As soon as I back up the rest of his files, so we can put them on his brand-new laptop."

"Great, Chip. Knew you'd handle it. Well, I better get." He unlocked the door, slipped back into the hallway.

WHEN JOE GOT BACK to the police department after meeting with Lisa and Melissa, he stopped in to see Hank, give him an update. "How did you make out with the warrant?"

"It's coming, but I don't have it yet. They need to amend it to include searching his residence. But I explained all the reasons why, and they don't seem to have a problem with it. Should be able to pick it up tomorrow."

"That'll be fine," Joe said. "Maybe we'll wait till the day after that to stop by. By then, I figure Tubbs will imagine this has all blown over and feel like the coast is clear to start writing his book again on that laptop."

"We'll see," Hank said. "How'd you make out with the gal from the writing group?"

"Turned out to be two gals," Joe said and explained why. Then said, "But all I got out of it was a nice cup of java and some homemade cookies."

"Really, they couldn't remember anything about Tubbs' story?"

"They remembered plenty. Just nothing new. But then before I left, I remembered what Tubbs said about that kid in high school who supposedly told him the story."

"The next-door neighbor?" Hank said.

"Yeah, with the hypothetical tale. Ray Dodson. One of the ladies, Melissa — the one who called you first — did remember him from high school. Then she gets this look on her face, says she remembered he used to hang around two other guys a lot."

"Really?"

Joe nodded. "But there's a problem...she couldn't remember who they were. So the other gal, Lisa, suggests she look through her old yearbooks. See if that doesn't stir some fresh memories."

"That might help."

"Yeah, it could," Joe said. "But I think this Ray Dodson angle is a better thread to pull. What are you doing now?"

"Just waiting on your orders, sir." Hank smiled.

"Good, you still know your place." Joe smiled back. "How about while I go meet with Pendleton, give him an update on everything, you put on your private eye hat, and see if you can locate this guy Dodson? His family moved away in the early summer of 1989. I know you're pretty good turning up things on the internet. See if you can turn up where this guy landed. I don't care where he is. We need to meet with him... face-to-face. I got a hunch he's gonna be our meal ticket on this case."

32

fter Melissa got home from her meeting with Lisa and Lieutenant Boyd, she made lunch for herself and Cliff. As they ate, she filled him in on all that was said, including the urgent task at hand...searching her high school yearbooks to see if she could figure out who those two friends of Ray Dodson's were.

"Well, look at you," Cliff said. "This is just like one of your mystery movies on Hallmark, where all those ladies get involved in solving the crime."

She hadn't thought about it till then, but he was right. She and Lisa really were making a difference in this case, however small.

Cliff couldn't be of any help, since they'd met in college and he'd gone to high school in South Carolina. But it was fun to see how interested he'd become in what she was doing, especially considering how this situation began with that first call to Detective Hank. "Well, I've got to find those yearbooks, then I'm gonna retreat into the living room flipping through the pages till I either strike out or figure out the identity of these two boys."

"So, you're saying to leave you alone for a while."

"Guess I am," she said. "You should've seen the look on the Lieutenant's face. He really wants this info ASAP."

"I get it," Cliff said. "Won't hear a peep out of me."

She got up, kissed him on the forehead and set her dishes by the sink.

"I'll clean up this little mess," he said, "you go on and solve this mystery."

Melissa washed up and headed for their third bedroom to begin her search. For all practical purposes, they were already empty-nesters. Their son and only child was away at college. The second bedroom was for him, for those occasional trips back home. Their house had no cellar, so the third bedroom served that function.

She opened the door and surveyed the scene. Neither of them were hoarders, thankfully, so this task wouldn't be a nightmare. But it could take some time. She probably hadn't looked at those yearbooks, since the last reunion she'd attended over ten years ago.

"Better get at it," she muttered aloud and set to work.

THIRTY MINUTES LATER, she'd finally located the box. She had all three yearbooks but only pulled out the one for her senior year, 1988. The year Myron Simpson was killed. She carried it to the living room, stopping briefly to fetch a bottle of water out of the fridge. In their house, the living room was for company, for entertaining guests and such, so there was no TV. And really, since they rarely had company the room was barely used.

She sat on the big comfy leather chair closest to the big window, opened the yearbook and slowly started turning the pages. Instantly, old memories began to fill her mind. It was funny how pictures from so long ago had a way of awakening specific moments in time that you'd completely forgotten about.

Most of them were pleasant. With those, she allowed herself to drift along enjoying what they had to offer. Of course, she would see certain people's faces and situations that triggered more challenging emotions. For those, she quickly turned the page and moved on. She had a job to do and kept resetting her focus on that task.

She decided to look up Ray Dodson's senior class photo to refresh her memory about his face. Then started back through the book searching for that face in the variety of pics taken of student groups or during high school events like football games, dances, plays, field trips and the like.

Two-thirds of the way through the book, she still hadn't found anything. Found the two pics of her and two more of Lisa, but none of Ray. Then she came across a picture that caught her eye for another reason. It was six of the hottest cars owned by male students spread across the bottom half of one page and standing in front of each car were the six "hot" male students they belonged to.

Melissa didn't have a car given to her in high school, or even have access to one, so she remembered being slightly jealous whenever these wealthier kids would strut around in theirs. But she had to admit...they really were nice looking cars...and some really nice-looking guys. Then suddenly, her eyes locked onto one nice looking guy and one of the hot cars...a shiny black Monte Carlo. Standing in front, leaning up against the hood was a very familiar face. She read the list of names at the bottom, left to right, to make sure.

It was definitely him. It was her beloved pastor, Glenn Burton.

She knew they had gone to high school at the same time but had totally forgotten what he looked like, or who he really was back then. It didn't really matter. Remembering what Pastor Glenn had said when he shared his story about how he came to the Lord, it happened during his college years. Because clearly, this wasn't a pic of the Christian Club.

Another image flashed through her mind, but not from a yearbook picture. It was Glenn, this younger version of him sitting in that Monte Carlo at the curb near their high school gym. Ray Dodson was walking toward him. They waved at each other. Next to Ray was a bigger guy, short blondish hair. It was a younger version of Chip Masters. They got to Glenn's car, pretend-wrestled about who would sit in the front seat. Ray lost and sat in the back. They were all laughing and chatting like good friends.

Oh, no. That's who Ray Dodson's two good friends were. Her pastors, Glenn Burton and Chip Masters.

MELISSA FELT EQUAL PARTS DEPRESSED, confused, and afraid.

Depressed to think it was even possible that Pastor Glenn and Pastor Chip could have had anything to do with that horrible crime in 1988. It had to be wrong. It couldn't be true. She was confused about what to do with this information. It seemed like she had to share it, but if she was wrong, this would be ten times worse than her original phone call about Tubbs to Detective Hank. Talk about ruining someone's life unnecessarily. And she was afraid because of all the uncertainty this revelation had stirred.

This was way too big a deal. She no longer had any desire to be a part of this makeshift investigative team. What should she do?

Just then, Cliff looked in on her. "I'm gonna make some coffee, want some?"

She sighed. "Sure, that would be nice."

"What's wrong?"

She held up the yearbook. "This. This is what's wrong."

"So, you found out who the bad guys were?" He was smiling, the way you do when you're trying to be upbeat.

"Maybe I did. Or maybe I didn't. I don't know. I'm so confused."

He came in and sat on the matching chair beside her. "All right, tell me about it. I probably won't have the answer, but I know it helps to talk things out."

She told him everything she'd found, what she'd remembered, what she thought it all could mean.

"Wow." That's all he said at first. After maybe a minute, "You're really sure it was them? No doubt in your mind?"

She shook her head no. "I'm not saying I'm sure they were involved or had anything to do with the crime. Just sure they were the two friends who hung around with Ray Dodson."

"Did you find any pictures of them together in there?" He pointed at the yearbook.

"No, and other than his senior year photo, I didn't find

any other pics of Ray Dodson at all. A couple each of Pastor Glenn and Pastor Chip, before they were pastors obviously. But even as I looked at these pictures, then looked at their senior class photos, I kept having flashbacks of the three of them walking around school together, or driving off in Glenn's black Monte Carlo. It was definitely them. They were the two friends I remember being with Ray Dodson."

"The Three Amigos, eh?" Again, that comforting smile.

"What should I do? Part of me wants to just forget about it. But even if I did, I know Detective Boyd will call me at some point asking me if I found anything in the yearbooks."

"Yeah, he certainly will. And when he does, you're gonna have to tell him the truth. Doesn't seem like you have any choice. But you don't have to take my word for it. Call Lisa, if you want. Run it by her. See if she agrees."

Melissa thought a moment. She knew Cliff wasn't saying this with any mixed motives. He wasn't a big fan of Pastor Glenn or Pastor Chip, or even the church in general. He was only going because she really wanted to. He wished they'd stayed at their old church.

"I may call Lisa," she said, "just as a friend to fill her in. But I know you're right. I need to call Lieutenant Boyd and tell him what I found. Or I should say, what I remembered. It's up to him what he does with it after that."

33

J oe had been walking the distance between his office and Captain Pendleton's to update him on the case when his cell phone rang. He pulled it out of his pocket and saw it was Melissa Hendricks. He was going to let it go to voicemail, call her back later, but figured she may have something that he'd like to include in his update with Pendleton "Hello, Melissa, this is Joe Boyd. How can I help you?"

"Hi, Lieutenant. I don't know if you're the person I should talk to, but I have some information that might help the case you're working on."

"Really?" She didn't sound very enthusiastic. "Does it have something to do with your yearbook research?" He started walking back toward his office.

"I'm afraid so."

"You're afraid so? I don't understand."

"You might after I tell you what I found."

"Okay, I'm listening."

"So, I was trying to remember the two friends who used to hang around with Ray Dodson."

"Right."

"Well, I think I know who they are, the two friends. In fact, I'm sure I do."

He had reached his office, so he stepped inside and closed the door. "I'm tempted to say that's great news, but you don't sound too happy about it."

"That's because I'm not. It's because of who they are."

"I'm guessing you know these two people. Now, I mean, not just their identity."

"Yes," she said. "Well, I know who they are and actually see them every week. But I'm not really close friends with them."

"Okay, so...who are they? Somebody I know?"

"I'm not sure. Have you ever heard of Victorious Life Church?"

"I think so," Joe said. "It's not the church we go to but, I've heard of it. A pretty big church, right? The pastor's on the radio and in the news sometimes. I forget his name."

"Glenn Burton," she said. "That's his name, Pastor Glenn Burton."

"Yeah, that's it."

"Well, that's him."

"What's him?"

She sighed. "The friend of Ray Dodson. It's him. He's one of the two friends. And the other one is named Chip Masters. He's on staff with Pastor Glenn."

Oh, boy. "I see." Now, Joe sighed. "How sure are you of this?"

"Sure as I can be, I'm afraid. How I wish I wasn't."

"So, I'm guessing this is where you go to church?"

"Yes. We're members there, me and my husband. And up until now, I've loved it there."

Joe felt bad for her. He didn't want to mention that he and Kate had visited that church a few years ago when they were looking for a new church home, but neither one of them liked it at all. It was way too showy, and Joe was totally turned off by the pastor's flamboyant style.

"Now, I'm not saying I think they had anything to do with Myron Simpson's murder," Melissa added. "I can't imagine that being true. All I'm saying is, when I remembered talking about Ray Dodson always hanging around two other guys... turns out, it was them."

Then she gasped.

"What's the matter?"

"I just realized something." A long pause. "This is terrible."

"What's terrible, Melissa?"

"A few days ago, when the story came out in the papers about y'all finding the body, I was struggling about whether to call you about Andrew Tubbs. You know, the fellow from our writers' group who's writing a story about the murder."

"I remember," Joe said.

"Well, I decided to get some advice first, so I called the church. Our church. And wound up talking all about it with Pastor Chip. You know, Chip Masters. One of Ray Dodson's two friends."

Well, this just got very interesting. "I see," Joe said. "And what advice did Pastor Chip give you, if you don't mind me asking?"

A pause. Joe heard her sigh again.

"He said he remembered Andrew Tubbs from high school, and that maybe he would pay him a visit. See if he could get him to voluntarily go to you all himself. And he suggested I not go to the police, that he would handle it. So, that's what I decided to do, but I didn't know Lisa had decided to call you anyway. That's how I got back involved again."

"I understand," Joe said. "And I can see why that would be a little troubling for you, Melissa. But this all could be very innocent."

"You think Pastor Chip visited Andrew Tubbs to talk about this?"

"I don't know." But instantly Joe wondered if he had, and if that had anything to do with Tubbs' laptop mysteriously being stolen yesterday.

"I want to think that Pastor Glenn and Pastor Chip had nothing to do with any of this," she said. "It's making me sick inside thinking...you know, what if they did?"

It wasn't making Joe sick inside, but if they were involved, this investigation would be ten times more complicated than before. "Well, listen Melissa. You did the right thing calling. Really. And you should know, we don't jump to conclusions around here. We proceed very slowly and carefully, and only go where the facts lead. We will look into this as carefully as we can. I know it's a delicate situation. In fact, when you called, I was on my way to meet with Captain Pendleton, our police chief and my boss. I'll get his advice on this also. So, don't worry."

"Thank you, Lieutenant."

Then Joe thought of something. "Can I ask you one more question?"

"Sure, anything."

"When you were looking through those yearbooks, did you find any pictures with the three of those boys together? You know, Ray, Chip and Glenn?"

"No, I didn't."

Rats.

"I saw a picture of Glenn standing in front of his shiny black Monte Carlo. It was a really nice car, then I instantly had flashbacks of seeing the three of them together in that car and standing around it. They used to drive in it all the time."

"And you're absolutely sure? These memories are solid, not even a little bit iffy."

"I'm afraid not."

"Okay," he said. "That's helpful." Of course, he knew, it would've been way more helpful — especially for Pendleton — if she had found a photo.

A thirty-year-old photo is way more reliable than a thirty-year-old memory.

34

Joe headed back to Pendleton's office to update him on the case. Man, this thing just got a little crazy.

He hadn't made an appointment, but unless Pendleton had something big going on, he'd usually see Joe on the spot. Joe asked Pendleton's secretary what the chances were to meet with him now.

"For you, Joe, they're pretty good." She buzzed Pendleton, and he agreed to let Joe in.

Joe walked through the door, found Pendleton typing away at his laptop. Before Joe took a seat, he stopped what he was doing and closed the lid.

"I'm glad you stopped by with an update. I was just about to call you to get one. Especially now that the story broke about the dead kid. Everybody I talked to is asking about it."

"Really?" Joe said. "Like who?"

"Like the mayor. Like two different City councilmen. Like even the guy who cuts my hair."

"Guess I don't get out enough," Joe said. "No one's said Boo to me about it."

"So, tell me you and Hank have made some progress."

"Actually, way more progress than I would've expected by now."

"That's what I like to hear. Anything we can tell the press yet?"

Pendleton, Joe thought. Always looking for the publicity. "Not yet, I'm afraid. Everything's still too soupy, but it's coming together."

"Okay then, let me hear it. Anything even close to resembling a suspect?"

"Do you want to know my hunches, or only what I can prove?"

"Let's start with your hunches," Pendleton said. "They're usually pretty good."

"Okay, if we're talking hunches, I think we may already know who killed this boy."

"You're kidding me."

"I'm not," Joe said. "We're a mile away from making an arrest, but some very serious leads have emerged. The biggest one, not ten minutes ago."

"Ten minutes ago? How's that?"

Joe filled Pendleton in on the various progress points he and Hank had made, as well as some of the snags. Mostly the developments surrounding the two ladies from that writer's group and Andrew Tubbs, and the things that sprung from the book he'd been writing. Joe held back the latest news about the pastors.

"That all sounds pretty good," Pendleton said. "And I guess the idea of it being high school kids jives with the class ring Hank found. But I'm not hearing anything that sounds like you figured out who the killer is."

"I'm getting to that part," Joe said. "But here's where things get real sticky."

"You think it's this guy Tubbs, the one writing the story?"

"No, I don't. And neither does Hank."

"Then who?"

"Okay, I'll start with where this lead came from. Before Tubbs stopped cooperating, he told us where he got the idea for doing this book. Specifically, who told him what really happened the night of the murder. It came from this kid, his next-door neighbor at the time, named Ray Dodson. Now, Dodson wasn't exactly making a confession. Tubbs said he told the whole thing using hypothetical terms, but Tubbs really did believe him. His whole demeanor and the way he said everything...nothing else makes any sense. Why would a kid fabricate such a detailed story about something so serious? And he tells Tubbs all this just before his family moves out-of-state."

Pendleton made a face, like he was thinking it through. "I can see that. That adds up. What else?"

"In Dodson's story, there are three high school friends who pull off this robbery and murder, which is how Tubbs wrote it in his book. Then when I'm talking with these two ladies from the writers' group, I ask them if they remember a kid named Ray Dodson. They all went to high school at the same time. Anyway, one of them does. Then she gets this look on her face and suddenly remembers...this Dodson kid always hung around with two other guys."

"So, now you got your three guys," Pendleton said.

"Right. It keeps lining up. But then it turns out, she

doesn't remember who the other two guys are. Her friend says, why not check out the yearbooks, which she does. And just before I come in here to see you, I get interrupted by a phone call from her."

"She remembers who the other two guys were," Pendleton added.

"Right, she does. Only..."

"Only what?"

"Only you're not gonna like who these other two guys turn out to be."

"What do you mean, I'm not gonna like who the other guys are? Why should I care?"

"Because of how you reacted in that Dresden case, when it turned out that the Senator was involved."

"You saying these two guys are big names in local politics?"

"No, not politics. Church."

"Church? What are they...priests?"

"No," Joe said, "ever heard of Victorious Life Church?"

Pendleton repeated the church name aloud. "Yeah, I've heard of it. A pretty big church for a town this size. That pastor of theirs, what's his name... Burton? He's on the radio all the time. You saying one or both of these killers works at that church? That would be a shame if you are. Like that BTK killer. Turned out he was a church deacon the whole time."

"It's worse than that," Joe said. "I don't mean worse than the BTK killer, I mean worse than being just a deacon. The two friends of this kid Ray Dodson are Burton, the senior pastor, and another guy on his staff, named Chip Masters."

The look on Pendleton's face told Joe he had not over-hyped this thing. He leaned back on his chair, sighed audibly. "Yeah, that's not good."

"No, it's not," Joe said. "But the gal I talked to, the one who went to school with them all...she's positive on this ID. Said she remembers seeing the three of them together quite a bit in high school."

"She find any pictures in that yearbook to back her up?"

Joe knew that question was coming. "No, she didn't. But she's totally sure it's them. And you could tell, she really didn't want it to be them."

"Does she think they could've done this?"

Joe wasn't sure how to answer that. "I think she's pretty conflicted about it. She doesn't want to believe it's possible. But she also wasn't ruling it out. She was, more or less, saying all she can do is tell the truth. Which is, they were Dodson's friends. And if we think Dodson was telling this guy Tubbs how it went down that night, it only makes sense that he was involved, along with these two pastors."

Neither one said anything for a moment as the reality of this settled in.

"I don't know, Cap...seems like I gotta talk to these two guys, these pastors. I don't see any other way around it."

Pendleton still didn't reply. He was looking off to the side, like he does when he's working something out.

"You know we would," Joe said, "if this was some small no-name church with some no-name pastor. We wouldn't hesitate."

"I know," he said. "Problem is, this is one of the biggest churches in town and one of the best-known clergyman. I wouldn't be surprised if the mayor and half the city councilmen go there."

Joe paused. "Like I said, I told you it was going to be sticky."

Pendleton sat up, looked at Joe. "I know you might have to talk with these guys —"

"*Might* have to talk with them?"

"Hear me out, Joe. Maybe you do. Maybe they did it. And if they did, they need to go to jail. But look at what we've got right now...a thirty-year-old memory from one woman, and a fiction story about the crime based on a hypothetical story told to someone who you don't even believe was involved. If she even had a photograph or two of them together, that would be something at least. But we don't even have that."

"Well, I wasn't suggesting we go in there accusing these pastors of anything. Just ask them some questions, gauge their reaction, see if anything turns up that might lead to something else."

"I know, Joe. But you do that, and the cat's out of the bag. The press will get hold of it, or it will turn up in social media, and the scandal begins. I don't want to go there unless we have something much more solid than what we've got now."

"I hear you, Sir. I really do. This isn't something I want to do, either. And if you recall, at the beginning, you said you wanted to hear my hunches, not just what I could prove."

"I did. You're right. And your hunches may be right. But we can't move out on those hunches. Not yet anyway."

"Then I have another idea," Joe said. "Something that may make all the uncertainty go away. But it's gonna cost you some money."

"What is it?"

"Authorize a trip for Hank and me, to go interview this guy Ray Dodson, in person. We do it right, and we might have someone who might be able to clear this whole thing up, and give us the kind of rock-solid evidence we're looking for."

"Where's he live?"

"I don't know. Hank's digging it up."

"Then do it," Pendleton said. "I don't care if he lives in Tahiti."

35

J oe headed back to his office but decided to stop in and see Hank, see how he was making out in his search for Ray Dodson. He got to Hank's door, knocked twice, and opened it. Hank was reading something on his laptop, turned and greeted Joe.

"How's the search coming?" Joe said. "Any sign of our mystery man?"

He spun his laptop around to face Joe. "Here he is right here. Meet Ray Dodson, according to his Facebook page, born in Culpepper, Georgia. Graduated from Culpepper high school in 1989. Don't imagine there were too many other Ray Dodsons in the world sharing that exact same background."

"So, you found him on Facebook, eh? I could've done that."

"Sorry my investigative techniques aren't more sophisticated or complex. I always start with Facebook. That or Google. It doesn't always work, but it often does when you're looking for people who have no reason to hide their identity."

"Which Dodson didn't have," Joe said. "Why would he?"

"Right," Hank said. "Seems like he's done pretty well for himself. Has a wife and two kids and a pretty successful business restoring historic homes in Charleston."

"Really, Charleston. I was hoping he might've moved to someplace more exotic and further away."

"Why's that?" Hank said.

"Because, I just got the okay from Pendleton for us to interview Dodson face-to-face, all-expenses-paid. Would've included airfare, meals, staying at nice hotels."

"Sorry to disappoint. It's only about a four-hour drive from here to Charleston. Wouldn't make sense to fly. But we can still do the other things.

They've got some really nice restaurants and hotels in Charleston, especially in the historic district."

"You been there?" Joe said.

"Yeah, couple of times. Great little romantic getaway. And I love Civil War history. Plenty of it in Charleston, and the surrounding areas. But I guess we're not gonna get too much time for sightseeing."

"Probably not," Joe said. "But now I'm tempted to bring my metal detector. I've become quite a fan of Civil War stuff myself. But we need to get there soon, get some face-to-face time with this guy, Dodson. The Captain's not going to green light the idea of going after these pastors unless we have something more solid than Melissa Hendricks' memory."

"Not too gung-ho about that kind of publicity," Hank added.

"Nope, he's not. So, you up for a nice drive tomorrow morning?"

"Sure. Should I tell my wife we'll be staying overnight, driving back the next day?"

"Yeah," Joe said. "Give me a little time to scope out this place, see if I want to bring Kate back there sometime."

"I know you guys would love it. We're planning to go back again sometime. Want me to book us a place?"

Joe's cell phone rang. "Sure. Let's plan on leaving at 8 AM. I better get this." Joe stepped into the hallway. The call was from Dr. Hargrove, the Medical Examiner.

"Dr. Hargrove, nice to hear from you. Got something for me on this Myron Simpson case?" Joe kept walking down the hall toward his office.

"As a matter of fact, I do," Hargrove said. "Something pretty significant I think. Although it doesn't have to do with the victim's medical analysis. All the tests on that are simply confirming what we've already discussed. But I'm calling about the murder weapon. I'm assuming your partner, Hank, briefed you on our conversation on that matter."

"He did, when I came off vacation. And I read his notes. He said you were something of a weapons connoisseur, if I remember."

"That's correct. Think I said it just like that."

"He also said you were pretty impressed with the bullet you removed from the boy's remains, said it was something out of the ordinary. If I remember, the phrase was, an unusual bullet often comes from an unusual gun. Hank really liked that."

"Right," Hargrove said. "Well, that's what I'm calling about. I was able to spend some time researching the situation, and I almost say with certainty that this bullet came from a very unusual gun. In fact, while I'm sure you'll still have to do your usual ballistics tests if you do finally find the weapon, it will undoubtedly be a pretty rare and now pretty valuable pistol, called the Bren Ten. Have you heard of it?"

"The Bren Ten," Joe repeated. "Can't say as I have. I do know my way around firearms, but I'm no connoisseur."

Hargrove laughed. "Well, I had heard of this gun though I've never seen one in person. Perhaps you're old enough to remember the Miami Vice TV series from the 80s."

"Yeah, I loved that show when I was a kid. Why?"

"Well, the Bren Ten — a hard chromed version — was the main pistol used by Sonny Crockett throughout the first and second seasons of the show. Sonny was the main star, played by Don Johnson."

"I wouldn't have known enough about guns then," Joe said, "to notice the difference between that and any other pistol, I guess."

"They somewhat resemble the popular 1911 semiauto-matic pistol, although firearms aficionados would likely take offense at hearing that. The Bren Ten had some very unique characteristics. Sadly though, for a variety of reasons, it's manufacture ceased in 1986, after only fifteen-hundred guns were produced."

"So, Sonny got one of the first and last Bren Tens?"

"He did, and they are very hard to find nowadays," Hargrove said. "But the most salient point of all this is...if you find that one of your suspects in this case happens to be in possession of a Bren Ten, I would stop looking at anyone else and put my entire focus on him. Because the bullet we removed from the body of Myron Simpson could only have come from one of these fairly rare pistols."

"Wow, Doc. That really is some very useful information. I am sure it will come in very handy in the days ahead."

"So, you're making progress then?"

"Yes, we definitely are."

Now, if Joe could only figure out some way to find out if this Pastor Glenn Burton owned a Bren Ten.

36

7 PM Victorious Life Church
Education Building

Melissa Hendricks sat in her car in the church parking lot staring at the front doors, as a steady stream of fellow church members entered the building. It was Wednesday night, time for the church's Life Action Groups. Really, just a creative name for their small group ministry. Melissa belonged to one. She should be joining the throng heading inside. But all this talk about murders and yearbooks and the suggestion that Pastor Glenn and Pastor Chip could possibly be involved had been eating away at her peace all afternoon.

Prior to this terrible situation, she had loved coming here on Wednesday nights, almost as much as Sunday mornings. But her joy had been tarnished somehow. Sitting there alone, she wondered if the same thing was happening to Cliff. She had shared everything with him and, when it came time to leave, suddenly he wasn't up to going. It was obvious by what he said, he was having the same kind of struggle as her, believing it could be true.

But it had to be a mistake. These were men of God, not killers. Even thinking it through now helped her see what a foolish notion it was. She opened the car door, grabbed her purse and Bible, and forced herself to head toward the doors. If she bumped into either man, she'd just act like everything was the way it had always been.

By the time she made it through the doors, most of the crowd had already funneled into their various classrooms. She veered left from the lobby down the hall toward the classroom where her small group met and was startled to find Pastor Chip talking to someone right by the door she needed to enter. Halfway there, his conversation with that man ended, and he turned around and headed right toward her. She felt her insides tense up then forced herself to calm down.

He saw her and for just a moment looked away. She thought he might walk right past her, but he looked at her again and smiled.

"Melissa, nice to see you," he said. "How are you doing this evening?"

See, she thought, he's acting perfectly normal. So should she. "I'm just fine, Pastor Chip? By the way, did you ever meet with that fellow from our writers' group, Andrew Tubbs?" Now, why did she say that?

He seemed momentarily stunned by the question. "Uh...no, not yet. I've been very busy since we met. But it's on my calendar."

She decided not to press it, since it really didn't matter

anymore. She and Lisa had already met with Lieutenant Boyd to discuss it. "Well, don't worry about it. I was just curious." She was going to end the conversation and keep walking but instead found herself talking some more. "I guess that news story about them finding that boy's body in the woods, you know the one we went to school with..."

"Uh...Myron Simpson," Chip said.

"That's the one. I guess reading about it after so many years got me thinking, so I took out our old yearbook. You are in the class of '89, right? Like me?"

"I was," he said. "But I don't have a yearbook. Don't know if I lost it, or what."

"I saw some pictures of you in there...and Pastor Glenn. Remember that fancy car he drove?"

"The black Monte Carlo?"

So, he remembered it, too. "That's the one. There's a picture of him standing in front of it in the yearbook, with a bunch of other very nice cars and their owners."

Chip nodded. "I remember that picture. As a matter fact, I was there when it was taken, standing off to the side."

"That's right," Melissa said. "You and Pastor Glenn were good friends even back then."

"We were. Through thick and thin ever since."

For some reason, she wasn't nervous anymore and decided to press one more matter. "You got to ride in that car quite a bit, as I recall. There weren't any pictures of that in the yearbook, but I have memories seeing the two of you in there."

"You have a good memory, Melissa. Yeah, I had access to a crummy car my parents owned, so we rode in Glenn's car every chance we got."

"By any chance, when you say we, do you mean Ray Dodson? Remember him?"

"Dodson, Dodson," Chip repeated.

"Because," she continued, "when I saw you and Pastor Glenn in that Monte Carlo, I also remember seeing Ray Dodson in there with you."

"Ray Dodson?" he said. "I do remember Ray. Gosh, it was so long ago, I completely forgot about that. But he hung around with us sometimes, at least for part of the year. Then he moved away somewhere, I think, after we graduated."

"I think you're right. That's probably why you don't remember him. That and it was thirty years ago."

Chip looked up, over her shoulder, got a look on his face then said, "Well, there's someone I'm supposed to meet. And I think you're going to be late for your group."

She looked at her watch. "You're right. Guess I better go too."

"Nice talking with you," he said, and hurried around her back toward the lobby.

As soon as he left, Melissa's heart sank. She felt like she'd fallen into a hole. He'd just confirmed it. He and Pastor Glenn were friends with Ray Dodson. Her memory was accurate.

But, wait a minute. That didn't mean anything. It only meant they knew each other. It didn't mean they collaborated on a robbery and murder. She hurried into the room where her small group met, quietly snuck in the back and took a seat.

Chip Masters walked through the halls as fast as he dared, did his best to smile at church members passing by, while giving off the impression that he really had no time to stop and chat with anyone. He came to the church office building, which was mostly empty at this hour. But he knew Glenn was in his office, so he headed there. A couple of quick knocks, and he walked in, locked the door behind him.

Glenn was reading something and looked up. "Hey, Chip... what's up?"

Chip steadied himself, so he wouldn't sound as disturbed as he felt inside. "Just had an interesting chat with Melissa Hendricks over in the education building. You remember her, right?"

"The gal we went to school with, the one who called you to talk about Andrew Tubbs. Speaking of Andrew Tubbs, where are things at with him?"

"Holding steady," Chip said. "He came by this afternoon just before dinner to pick up his new laptop."

"How was his demeanor?"

"Like he was real excited to get that laptop. It was easily twice as expensive as the one I took from him."

"So, you think we can lay that one to rest?"

"I think so."

"You think?"

"No, I know. Tubbs will be fine. But that chat with Melissa just now has me a little rattled, if I'm being honest."

"Why's that? Have a seat."

Chip sat down. "I don't know, she's clearly the extremely curious type. After reading that story in the Gazette about that boy, it got her thinking about the days of auld lang syne. So, she gets out her yearbook from our senior year, starts browsing through it. Next thing you know, it's stirring up memories of all kinds of things."

"What kinds of things?" Glenn said.

"How about you and me and Ray Dodson riding around in your shiny black Monte Carlo?"

"No, really?"

Chip nodded.

"Did that conversation go anywhere...unhealthy?"

"Fortunately, no. But it's making me wonder...there are so many people in this town from our old high school days. How many more of them are going to have their memories freshly stirred by this newspaper story?"

"Is that going to be a problem?"

"I don't know. I hope not. But it's got me thinking about Ray Dodson. I'm thinking maybe one of us should contact him. Make sure he understands how very important it is, to his welfare too, that he keeps his trap shut. That is, should anyone bring this up with him."

"I think that's a great idea, Chip. Considering the stakes, better to play it safe."

"You know where he moved to?"

"Somewhere out west, not sure which state. But then I heard after he got married, they settled down somewhere in Charleston."

"South Carolina?"

Glenn nodded. "Can't be too many Ray Dodson's in Charleston."

"That's only a four-hour drive from here," Chip said. "Think I should get over there, pay him a little visit. Make sure the lid stays on tight."

Glenn nodded. "You remind him...he gets the urge to come clean, his neck is in the noose right there with ours."

37

Historic District
Charleston, SC

It was just after 1PM on Thursday. About an hour ago, while Hank drove down I-26, Joe had received a call from Melissa Hendricks, saying last night she had a chat with "Pastor Chip" who'd confirmed that he and "Pastor Glenn" had hung around with Ray Dodson that last year in high school. It wasn't as good as a photograph, but Joe felt it definitely gave them a stronger hand to play in their upcoming interview with Ray Dodson.

Joe walked up to the register, left a nice tip on the card for their server at a tasty eatery on Market Street with a great chicken wing buffet. Their first of several charges to the Culpepper PD's expense account over the next two days. Joe was really liking Charleston. They had been here just over an hour, and already he could tell...Kate would love this place. They had come in from I–26 onto Meeting Street, then headed south. Almost immediately, you could see a presence of historic houses, but when they got past Calhoun Street, it was almost like driving back in time.

Except for the cars, traffic lights and paved roads, Joe could just imagine how this place must've looked during the Civil War. All the surrounding buildings seemed to be from that era. They stepped into the sunlight on Market Street in search of their car. Right there, across the street and running from one end to the other, was the historic City Market. "I think Kate could spend half a day just walking up and down in that place," Joe said.

"When we were here, we did," Hank said. "But it wasn't just Elaine liking it, there's plenty of fun stuff in there for guys, too." They turned left on the sidewalk toward the river. Their car was parallel parked on the same road one block up.

Since Hank had been here a few times before, Joe decided to let him drive. "How far is this house where we expect Dodson to be?"

"Not far. Maybe a few blocks," Hank said. "I'm pretty sure he's gonna be there. That's one of the upsides to social media sites like Facebook. People like Dodson use it to promote their business and even to interact with customers. His construction company is restoring one of these historic homes over on Logan Street. So, he's got all kinds of pictures of it on his Facebook site. Judging by the comments he made, the owners must be out of town, so he's showing them how things are going. The last pic he posted was just before lunch."

They got the car, carefully dodging all the tourists walking about, got back on Meeting Street and turned left.

"See up ahead, that big steeple?" Hank said. That's St. Michael's church. It's on the corner of Broad. We're going to be turning right, but if you look left toward the end of the road you can see the Old Exchange and Provost Dungeon. George Washington visited there. In fact, think he went to this church up ahead, too. Remember the movie The Patriot with Mel Gibson?"

"Love that movie," Joe said.

"They filmed part of it here, right on Broad Street. Just covered the roads with dirt."

They reached the intersection of Market and Broad. Joe was just taking it all in. They were waiting behind a horse-drawn carriage. It went straight to the light, and they turned right.

"Logan Street is just a few blocks up," Hank said. "Ever hear of the term South of Broad?"

"I have, but not sure why."

"It's what this whole area is called that runs south of this road. And it was the title of a bestselling novel by that big-time author Pat Conroy."

"Now him I heard of," Joe said. "Seems to me, Hank, you ever get tired of doing this, you could get a job giving tours on one of those carriages."

Hank laughed. "Elaine said the same thing. Only I'm not so sure she was kidding."

As they moved down Broad, it became less commercial and more residential. "Man," Joe said, "look at these places."

"They're nice," Hank said, "but they even get nicer, and some a lot bigger." He reached Logan, but it was a one-way road going the wrong direction for them. "The house Dodson's working on is right down there. I'll have to go down another block, so I can come in from the right direction."

Joe didn't mind the detour one bit. Hank was right. The further in he drove, the more he liked the houses. It was like some storybook place. Finally, they reached Logan Street again and turned left. They didn't have to wonder which house Dodson's company was working on. You could see the work trucks and a temporary dumpster parked right in front. Hank pulled in just as a dusty pickup truck pulled out. "That worked out," Joe said. "I was afraid we were going to have to park a block away" They got out of the car and walked up the sidewalk till they were standing right in front of it.

There was a sign: *Dodson's Restorations*. He could hear sawing, drilling and what sounded like a nail gun going off. A young black guy with a nice smile came out the front door and walked down the steps toward them. Looked like a tradesman of some kind.

"Can I help you gentlemen with something?"

"Looking for the owner," Joe said. "Ray Dodson?" He decided not to show their ID badges. Didn't want to give the staff some unnecessary things to talk about. At least not yet anyway.

"He's right inside, but probably better if I go in and get him. Be right back."

"Appreciate it," Joe said.

The man disappeared but was back in less than a minute. "He'll be out soon. I gotta make a quick trip to the store. You men have a nice day."

Joe looked around at the houses up and down the street. "So, what do these places go for, Hank? You know?"

"Get it out of your head, Joe. We couldn't afford the

smallest house on this street if we went in on it together, and one of us won the lottery."

"You're kidding?"

"I'm not. We checked. They start at about 1.2 million and go up to about 15 million. Ones at that price aren't on this street, but just a few blocks from here."

Just then the front door opened and a much older version of a boy's face from a yearbook photo came walking toward them.

"Hello, gentlemen. I understand you'd like to see me. My name's Ray Dodson. My company's restoring this lovely house." He stuck out his hand.

Hank and Joe shook it. Joe decided it was time to shift gears a little...from nice and friendly to homicide cops on a mission. "We're not prospective customers, Mr. Dodson. My name's Lieutenant Joe Boyd, this is my partner, Detective Hank Jensen." They both took out their badge IDs. "We're here from the Culpepper Police Department, part of the cold case squad...on a homicide investigation."

Joe could've sold tickets to folks for a chance to see the look on Dodson's face.

"One might almost think you were expecting us," Hank said.

Dodson quickly tried to recover his composure. "No, why would that be?"

"You do seem a little startled," Joe said.

"Could we not talk here?"

"You have a better place in mind?" Hank said.

"Not really," Dodson said. "It's just that we're standing here right in the path where the workers come and go."

"Is that all it is?" Joe said. "Let's walk down a few houses, closer to where our car's parked.

"That would be better, thanks."

Hank led the way. As Dodson walked he looked around nervously.

"You keep up with the news from back home?" Hank said.

"Back home?"

"Culpepper," Joe said. "Where you were born."

"Where you went to high school," Hank added.

"Uh, no. Not really. We moved away right after I graduated."

"We know," Joe said. "Some of the folks who knew you back then told us. So, let me get right to the point of why we've driven all this way to chat with you, Mr. Dodson. You remember that boy who worked at a convenience store out on 270? The one who got robbed and murdered just a few weeks before Christmas in your senior year?"

He sighed. "Yeah, hard to forget something like that."

"So, you say you haven't heard any recent local news?" Hank said.

"No, don't really have any connections in Culpepper anymore."

"That's funny," Joe said. "You say you remember this kid who got robbed and murdered back then, but see, when you left Culpepper, no one knew the kid had been murdered. None of the newspapers reported that. He was only reported as missing. Supposedly, no one knew what happened to him."

"So," Hank said, "why don't you tell us, Mr. Dodson, how come you remember him being murdered?"

He didn't reply. Joe noticed...there was that same look again.

ABOUT A HALF-BLOCK AWAY, sitting in his blue Jaguar under a shady tree, sat Chip Masters watching Ray Dodson talking with two men wearing relatively cheap suits. His stomach was churning in knots. He didn't recognize one of the men but certainly knew who the other one was. The older one. The one doing most of the talking. From the numerous interviews he'd given on the local news, both in print and TV, he knew it was Lieutenant Joe Boyd.

Ray Dodson was talking to the cops.

This was about as bad a scene as Chip could imagine. For everyone's sake — especially Ray's — Chip hoped he was keeping his mouth shut. Involuntarily, he reached over and touched his semi-automatic pistol in its concealed holster, hidden under his sportscoat.

38

Ray Dodson looked back toward the house he and his crew had been working on, as if to make sure no one was watching.

"So, Mr. Dodson," Joe said, "I'd like to hear your answer to my partner's question, too. How did you come by this inside information that Myron Simpson had, in fact, been murdered?"

Dodson looked down at the ground, sighed. "Okay, I'm guessing you guys haven't driven all this way from Culpepper just to see how I'm doing after all these years. And I don't really know what any of this is about. I'm guessing it has something to do with the Myron Simpson case, but I have no idea why you're asking me about it."

"That's how you gonna play this?" Joe said. "I could tell you what was recently reported in the Culpepper Gazette, but I have a good feeling that you know more than anything written in that article."

"What?" Dodson said, "Someone found Myron's body?"

"Right where you guys left it," Hank said.

"I have no idea where Myron's body was buried," Dodson said. "And that's the God's-honest truth."

"Yeah, we found it," Joe said. "In the woods a few miles from the convenience store he went missing from. As you can imagine, it's created quite a stir back in Culpepper. All these folks who remember the case from back in the day. Some of them, folks you went to high school with. Remember Andrew Tubbs?"

The look in Dodson's eyes said a definite yes. Like he made the connection about how Joe and Hank knew to come looking for him. Then his look softened. "If I recall, that was my next-door neighbor. But we weren't all that close."

"But close enough to confide in about your deepest troubles?" Hank said.

Dodson feigned confusion.

"Let's cut the nonsense, Ray?" Joe said. "I call you Ray? That okay? You call me Joe. I know you know we talked to Tubbs. He's not the only one in your class we talked to, but he said you were definitely the one who told him how the robbery and murder went down."

"What?" Dodson said loudly. "That's crazy. I never told Andy that. We were talking about what might've happened to Myron, and I said something about... maybe it happened like this. That's all it was. I wasn't confiding in him. We were just two kids talking."

"Just two kids talking, eh?" Joe said. "Funny how the story you told him turned out to be right on the money, lining up perfectly with the evidence we're uncovering."

"We found evidence on the scene confirming the culprits

were school classmates of his," Hank said. "Tubbs said you told him there were three of you involved."

"We've got testimony from other classmates," Joe said, "who said you used to hang around with two guys in your same class all the time. Glenn Burton and Chip Masters. Used to always drive around in Glenn's shiny black Monte Carlo."

Dodson's eyes bugged out hearing those two names, even more when Joe mentioned the car.

"That was the car you guys drove in that night, wasn't it, Ray?" Hank said. "And we just got confirmation on the murder weapon. A very unique and expensive pistol. Not the kind of gun your run-of-the-mill punk carries around in his waistband."

Joe played a hunch. "More like the kind of gun some high school kids get from their rich Daddy's gun safe."

"Look," Dodson said, "it wasn't my gun. I had nothing to do with shooting that boy." There was a different kind of emotion showing in his eyes now. Looked like he was blinking back tears.

"But you were involved, Ray," Joe said in a softer tone. "That's the point. You know that's why we're here. Don't you think it's finally time to give Myron's poor mom some closure? I'm looking around here at the kind of man you've become. Looks like you turned out pretty good. Had a nice life. A wife, some kids, a nice business. A beautiful town to work in. But see, things didn't go so well for Mrs. Simpson, Ray's mom. She lost her boy one night thirty years ago and had no idea what happened to him. She's had to live all this time not knowing. She never bought into the idea that he was missing. Told me so herself. He was too faithful a son, too hard-working and honest, to ever do that to them. Maybe you didn't shoot that boy."

"I didn't," Dodson said.

"But you were with the two kids who did," Hank said. "In the eyes of the law, with multiple suspects involved in an armed robbery with a homicide —"

"I know what happens," Dodson said, looking down again. He sighed. Looked around.

Joe could see it. He didn't want to give all this up. Who would? "Listen Ray, I did some checking. Went by the house you used to live in, just before you moved. I doubt your dad could've afforded the kind of gun used in the shooting. I also drove by the house — really, the mansion — where Glenn Burton lived. I'm guessing it was his Daddy's gun. And maybe it was either him or Chip Masters did the actual shooting, but like Hank just said..."

"I know, I know."

"Then you know," Hank said, "your best outcome in this comes from fully cooperating with us, and giving up the other two guys. I checked. You guys aren't even friends on Facebook. I'm guessing you don't even stay in touch anymore. So, what is it to you if they're held accountable for what they did?"

Dodson looked right at Hank, then at Joe. A different look in his eyes. Stern, serious. "My best outcome, did you say? No, that's not good enough. I'm not willing to give up everything I have, everything I've done with my life these past thirty years, just to give you guys an easy case to solve. It's clear to me, you have figured some of this out and gathered some of the evidence you need to build a decent case. But you're nowhere near ready to go to the DA or press charges. I've watched some shows about cold case homicides. Some new clue surfaces, and they think they're close. Then nothing happens. And years go by until, maybe, another new lead surfaces. That could happen here. Or, I could get involved and cooperate fully. But if I do that, it won't be for *my best outcome*. It'll only be if you can guarantee me, in writing, full immunity from prosecution for anything that had anything to do with this case. You get me that? My attorney reads it, and agrees that's what you're offering? Then I will definitely tell you everything I know."

Joe thought a moment. This guy was no dummy. "That's a very real possibility, what you're asking, Ray. But if we're going to talk to the DA and get him to give you a sweetheart deal like that, we've got a be able to tell him the kind of difference your testimony will make. You follow?"

"I do," Dodson said. "You tell him, I will be able to tell you exactly what happened. A reliable eyewitness to the whole thing. You will be able to put the real culprits behind bars, the ones who actually robbed, killed and buried Myron Simpson in that convenience store in December, 1988."

"And you're saying," Hank said, "that wasn't you? You bear none of the blame?"

Dodson looked at Hank. Tears welled up in his eyes. "I do bear some, for sure. And my part has haunted me ever since. But my mistake was getting talked into a stupid teen scheme by some misguided friends, doing something I never wanted to do in the first place. But I had nothing to do with the killing of that boy or what followed after, and I will not allow my life to be destroyed for something I did not do. So, you get me that deal, and I'll tell you everything I know."

"Okay, Ray," Joe said, "we'll let you get back to your work.

And we'll be in touch very soon. But just so we're clear on something...the two guys you're talking about, the misguided friends. We're talking about Glenn Burton and Chip Masters, right?"

Dodson nodded, turned and walked away.

39

R ay Dodson headed back toward the house they were restoring on Logan Street. He wasn't doing well at all. Over the years, he'd been able to successfully tuck all this ugliness away, like old photo albums you stick in a box and hide in some corner of the attic. These two detectives had just grabbed that box and threw it down in the middle of the dining room table.

No avoiding it anymore.

His insides were a mess. His mind a carousel of conflicting, dark memories. He had to get out of there, get some time alone. He walked up the stairs and found his project supervisor, Bill, made some excuse about something that just came up. Ray had to take care of it now, would be back in an hour or so. He headed back outside, down the sidewalk till he reached his Dodge pickup. He carefully pulled out of his spot along the curb and headed north toward Broad Street.

Turning right on Broad, he headed for the River, the Old

Provost Dungeon just up ahead. He was headed for the Waterfront Park, a seriously attractive use of taxpayer money a few blocks long, built just north of the Battery. Lots of shady trees and decorative shrubs, fancy brickwork walkways, plenty of Charleston benches to sit on. This time of day it should be pretty easy to find a spot to call his own.

As luck would have it, someone was pulling out along the curb just as he turned down the road toward a nearby parking garage. He slipped in the space, got out and headed for the park. Once there, he walked south a bit, away from the big Pineapple Fountain, until he found the section where he could be alone. He sat on the bench, slouched a little and stared out the water. Man, how he loved this place.

Everything was going so good. His business, his relationship with his wife, Jennifer.

Jennifer. How was he going to explain all this to her? Would she ever look at him the same way again...once she knew...the truth. Involuntarily, the scenes from that dreadful night replayed in his mind.

It was December 6th, 8 PM at Hampton's Quik Stop in Culpepper. The three of them, all dressed in dark clothes, wearing dark gloves provided by Glenn, were driving through the dark winding roads along 270 toward their destination.

Hamptons Quik Stop.

This time, Ray didn't argue with Chip about who got to ride shotgun in the Monte Carlo. Ray was happy to take the back seat. Honestly, he wished he hadn't gotten into the car at all. He liked *Aerosmith* and certainly wouldn't mind an opportunity to see them in concert. But not like this. This was crazy. He'd always felt like Glenn was a little off, but Ray just chalked it up to him being raised as a spoiled rich kid with no discipline. But this — what they were doing here — was no crazy school-age prank.

They could go to prison for doing this.

Glenn stopped at the last intersection before they reached the convenience store. It took all of Ray's strength not to open the door and flee. It would be a long walk back to fetch his crap car at Glenn's place, but maybe he should —

"Glenn," Chip yelled, "slow down. Don't want to give any reason for the cops to pull us over."

"Chip, look around. There's not another car on the road. We've only seen two since we left my house. This is the boondocks. Only people live out here are the rich folks like my parents and a bunch of local yokels who, apparently, go to sleep very early. I never see anyone on this road this time of night."

A few more twists and curves and *Hampton's Quik Stop* suddenly appeared up ahead on the left

"Okay, boys," Glenn said, "time to put these on." He slipped on his black ski mask, handed one each to Chip and Ray.

Ray did as he was told. Guess there was no turning back now.

"Yo, Glenn," Chip said, "it's just like you said, the place is deserted. Only that one car at the far end."

"That's the car the kid who works there drives," Glenn said. "He goes to our school. Kind of a nerdy fellow. Myron, something, I think."

"Myron Simpson?" Ray said.

"Maybe," Glenn said. "We've never talked. I only know his first name, because it's on a badge he wears at the register. You know him?"

"Not really," Ray said. "If it's the same guy, we had a couple of classes together over the years. None this year, though."

"Well, just in case," Chip said. "You don't do any talking."

Glenn pulled in but parked at the opposite end in the shadows. He pulled out the gun. "Okay, boys. This is it. We do this right, we're in there and out in five minutes with plenty of cash for the concert."

"You bring any rope?" Chip said.

"What we need rope for?" Glenn said.

"To tie this Myron kid up with. After we're done. We can't have him following after us as we drive off. He'll ID the car, call the cops."

"You're right. Should've thought of that. I'm sure they got rope in there. They've got a whole aisle of hardware stuff. Well, let's get it on." They got out of the car. "Remember, let me do all the talking."

Everyone looked all around, confirming there was no one else in sight. Glenn led the way.

Ray followed behind Chip. He looked through the windows and didn't see anyone else in the store. But there was Myron behind the cash register. His back was facing them. Probably reading a book or something.

Glenn took one more look around the parking lot and street and burst through the front doors with his gun drawn. Chip and Ray came right in behind him. "Don't get excited,

Boy," Glenn said in a deeper and more southern accent then he owned. "But this is a stick up."

Myron spun around, and his eyes bugged out at the sight of the three masked men. Then a look of fear when he focused on the gun pointed at his chest. "What do you guys want?"

"The money, idiot!" Chip blurted out. "What do you think we want?"

His voice, sounding every bit like Chip. No attempt to disguise it. Ray could tell Myron recognized it, but he didn't reply.

Myron stepped behind the cash register and was just about to open it.

"And we want all of it," Chip demanded.

"Chip," Glenn muttered sternly, an attempt to get him to shut up.

But it was too late. Myron heard him.

He looked up at Chip, a slight smile coming over his face. "I thought that voice sounded familiar. Chip Masters, right? Am I right? Is this some kind of prank you guys are pulling?"

"This ain't no prank, kid," Glenn said in that same fake voice. "Now, open that door and give us the money."

"So, if that's Chip Masters," Myron said, "then you must be Glenn Burton. I always see you guys together at school. And I'm guessing you might be Ray Dodson." He looked up past them toward the front window. "You guys come here in that hot Monte Carlo?"

Glenn thrust the gun closer toward Myron's chest. "We ain't fooling with you, Boy."

"What are you going to do, shoot me?" Myron said. He reached for the end of the pistol and Glenn jerked it back.

BAM !!

It suddenly went off.

Myron flew backward against the back counter. His eyes got huge then all the life went out of them, as he slid to the floor.

For just a second, time froze. No one else moved.

Ray could not believe what he had just heard and seen.

"Glenn," Chip said in a panicked voice. "I thought you said it wouldn't be loaded."

Glenn turned, his face stunned. "It wasn't. It isn't. Look, there's no clip. I left it home like I said."

"One in the chamber," Ray said.

"What?" the other two said in unison.

"One in the chamber. Must've been one in the chamber." Ray hurried around the counter to check on Myron, but he knew instantly from the look in his eyes that he was already gone. A widening stain of red spread across his abdomen, from the chest down. He checked his pulse anyway.

"Is he..." Glenn said.

"Yeah," Ray said. "He's dead. You killed him, Glenn. I knew I should never have gone along with this."

"I didn't mean to. The gun just went off. He grabbed for it, and it went off."

"Doesn't matter, Glenn, what we meant to do," Chip said. "He's still dead. And we better do something about it...quick. Anybody comes in here in the next few minutes, and we're all dead."

"Okay," Glenn said, taking charge. He put the gun back in

his waistband. I'll get the money out of the drawer. You pick up Myron. We're taking him with us."

"Why we going to do that?" Chip said.

"Because of the evidence. Look at the wall. The bullet didn't go through him. We leave his body here, they'll be able to trace the bullet to this gun. So, we're taking him with us."

"Then we better put this on him," Chip said. He held up a padded red vest. "I've seen him wearing this at school."

Glenn was grabbing the cash. "Okay, put it on then, and hurry."

Ray was just standing there, in shock. He couldn't think straight. Didn't know what to do. His only thought was to flee.

"Give me a hand with him, Ray," Chip said. "Help me get this vest on him."

Ray did, then stood, backed away a few steps.

Chip lifted Myron up on his shoulder. A set of keys fell out of the vest pocket. "Ray, get those for me."

Ray handed them to Chip.

Glenn was done emptying the drawer. "Let's get a move on it, start heading outside."

Once on the sidewalk, everyone was relieved to see there were still no cars in sight.

"I got an idea," Chip said. "There's a place a few miles from here, deep in the woods, not far from the lake. We used to go up there sometimes to get stoned. There's a little trail. If I had a flashlight, I could find it. We could bury him back there, and no one would ever find him."

"Good," Glenn said. "We can swing by my house, grab a shovel and a flashlight. Ray, why don't you get the keys from

Chip, you follow us in Myron's car. We shouldn't leave that here, either. After we bury him, we'll find a nice winding road further up in the hills and push it off. The woods will swallow it up."

Ray didn't answer. He heard the words Glenn said but didn't process them.

"Ray, did you hear Glenn?" Chip said, holding out the keys in his hand.

"No, I'm not doing that," Ray said. "I'm not going along with any of this anymore." He started walking out to the parking area. "I'm all done."

"Ray," Glenn shouted. "What, are you just gonna leave us? Just like that? You can't do that."

Ray kept walking into the darkness. Wasn't sure where, just in the general direction of Glenn's house. One thought. Get his car. And get home.

"Ray," Chip yelled. "Where you going, Man?"

Ray didn't answer.

40

Riverfront Park, Charleston, SC
The Present - Thursday

C hip Masters had followed Ray through the streets
of Charleston and watched him parallel park his
pickup on a side street near the water. He'd stayed
in his car at the end of the block until he was sure he knew
where Ray was headed, then parked in a nearby garage
where you paid by the hour. There, he changed into a
jogging outfit, complete with hoodie.

It took him a few minutes to find Ray and, for a while,
Chip thought he'd lost him. But then he saw him sitting on a
park bench that faced the water, underneath some shady
trees. Chip waited a while to see if he was meeting someone
there, but after ten minutes or so, it was clear he'd gone there
just to be alone. Wasn't even on his smartphone. Just staring
out at the water in a daze.

Guess that visit from the two Culpepper detectives had

really shaken him up. Good. The more unnerved he was, the better. A handful of people were walking throughout the park area, but none hung around the section where Ray was sitting. Which was perfect. Chip walked around the area, checking for security cameras but didn't see any in the immediate park area. Probably due to the myriad of oak trees lining the walkways.

He started walking toward Ray, his eyes roving in every direction to make sure there was no one coming. When he got within ten feet, from behind he said, "Afternoon, Ray."

Ray jolted in his seat and turned toward the voice.

"Were you deep in thought or just startled by a blast from the past?"

It took Ray a few moments before he recognized his visitor. "Chip, is that you?"

"It's me, little buddy." Chip walked toward him.

Ray looked around nervously.

"Just me. No one else." Chip came over, sat beside him on the bench. "Really nice place. And what a view. I can see why you come here."

Ray looked at him, no expression on his face.

"I came by that house you're working on over on Logan Street, but you had company. Two guys wearing suits."

"Yeah, just some business people I'm doing a quote for."

"Really? Business people? You know, lying's still a sin, Ray. I may not look the part now, but Glenn and me are clergy now. Did you know that?"

"Heard something about that," Ray said. "Quite a while ago, right? Didn't figure either one of you to go in that direction."

"Well, you know how it is. Traumatic things have a way of

shaking things up, get you looking at life in ways you never planned. Know what I mean by traumatic things?"

Ray nodded.

"I guess you moving away when you did gave you a chance for a fresh start, too. Didn't it?"

"Guess it did."

"But it would appear, you handled the trauma a little different than Glenn and me. We wound up turning to God, and I guess you decided to unburden your soul at the confessional."

A look of confusion on Ray's face. "We're not Catholic.

"Didn't say you went to a priest. You unburdened your soul to your next-door neighbor before you left, didn't you, Ray?" Chip saw fear in Ray's eyes for the first time. Good. "You remember his name? Andrew Tubbs. Remember Andy? Guess what you said made a real impact on him. Even after all these years. So, you know what he does? He takes everything you told him and starts writing a novel about it. Joins this writer's group. Introduces it like it's a story he made up. But lo and behold, some of the ladies remember the story as being eerily similar to the same traumatic event the three of us went through back in the day. Then you know what happens? I'll tell you what happens. Some campers find Myron's body buried in the woods. Can you believe that? Couldn't have come at a worse time. For us, that is. Because now, it's got everybody talking. It's even got the police talking. They're snooping all over the place, trying to pull on all these loose threads, see where they lead."

Chip took a breather, checked on Ray's disposition. He was listening intently, though now looking down at the ground. He continued. "Yep, those detectives are like two hound dogs. And because of your blabbing to old Andy Tubbs, that led them to drive all this way from Culpepper to find you. We both know that's who those two gentlemen were you were talking to back at your house project. You going to have the decency to at least admit that to your old friend, Ray?"

"Yeah," he said, deflated. "That's who they were."

"Yeah, if I'm being honest, I was pretty shocked to see them talking with you like that. Thought I had plenty of time to get with you first myself. So, I could prepare you for the likelihood of their visit. But, I was a tad too slow. No matter. I'm here now. The only question is, since they got here first to talk with you, did you make a very unwise decision to talk back to them? What I mean is, what are they leaving with? What kinds of things did you give them about our...traumatic event?"

Ray looked up at him. "Nothing, Chip. I didn't tell them anything. But you should know, they've just about got it all figured out already. Even without me telling them a thing."

"I know they're good. Especially the older one, that Lieutenant Boyd fella. He's been in the papers a number of times solving all kinds of cases. They put him in charge of a cold case squad. That's what they call a situation like ours. Now, he may be good, but like every cop, he's only as good as the evidence he gathers and the witnesses he gets to testify. Without evidence and without witnesses, even the very fine Detective Boyd can't put a case together. See Ray, right now, he's got nothing. Just a made up story by some wannabe novelist who had nothing to do with what happened. But you're the kind of nut he can crack. My guess is, if you really haven't given him what he wants, he's gonna go back to the DA and get you some kind of deal."

Ray's eyes changed. A look that told Chip...paydirt. "I'm right, aren't I? You didn't tell him anything, because you're waiting to see what kind of a deal he's willing to make with you."

Ray didn't answer. He looked down again.

"That's okay, Ray. You don't need to say it. I can tell by the look on your face that's what happened. The thing is, I'm here to make you a counteroffer." Chip stood, in such a way that he was towering over Ray. "See, if you don't testify, he's got nothing. He can't come after you, or Glenn and me. So, let me offer you an incentive to call him back and tell him he can forget about any deal. That you're all done talking." Chip pulled out his gun from the pocket of his hoodie. He didn't point it, just showed it to Ray

Ray's eyes popped out at the sight.

"Recognize this?" Chip said. "I see you do. It's that Bren Ten, the gun we used that fateful night." Chip showed him the handle. "But unlike that night, I got a fully loaded clip in it. See, Glenn inherited it twelve years ago when his dad died. He had no use for it, so I bought it from him. But then I bought a nice little addition for it." Chip slid out the silencer from the other pocket. "Had it custom-made. I've gotten to be quite an expert with it."

He looked around. The furthest person was easily fifty yards away. "I could double-tap you right here. Just take a few seconds. No one would know. I'd set you up like some guy taking a nap on a bench, then casually walk away. By the time anyone knew you were dead, I'd be an hour outside of town."

Ray looked up at him. "You'd really shoot me, Chip?"

Chip leaned down way too close to his face. "Oh yeah, buddy. I would. In a heartbeat." He straightened back up. "See, I would do anything to keep the life I've built intact. Not just for me, but for Glenn, too. And for our families. And for our church. Because if you talked, you would ruin it all."

"But how can you say that?" Ray said. "If you're supposed to be some man of God now? You just said it...part of the reason you'd kill me is for the good of your church? What sense does that make?"

"I'm not saying it would make any sense, Ray. In fact, I'll admit it would even be a sin. Not an unforgivable one, mind you, but still a sin I don't want to commit. So, don't you make me. Keep your mouth shut, Ray, and you won't tempt me to commit this serious sin. And even better for you, and your family, you won't be dead."

41

Joe and Hank were about an hour down the road heading west on I-26. After their visit with Ray Dodson, they both agreed they needed to head home right away, postpone their little overnight stay at a fancy Charleston hotel. But Joe had already seen enough to know...Kate would love this place. He was definitely bringing her back for their next romantic getaway.

He and Hank had spent the last hour going over the details of the case, adding all the new info generated by their conversation with Dodson. Not just the things he said, but discussing the things he probably meant by what he said, and the kinds of things he probably would say if he could talk freely. "He's not just a good witness," Hank had said, "because of all the things he saw and knows, but he really comes across well. Very articulate and credible."

Joe had agreed. "Yeah, he'll do great on the stand. We gotta get him on our side. I'm going to call Pendleton now." Joe set the call up on the car screen, so he could be hands-free. After a few rings, Pendleton's secretary answered. When Joe stressed how urgent it was that they talk, she was able to put them through.

"What's up, Joe?" Pendleton said. "You guys still in Charleston?"

"On our way back."

"Does that mean things went good or bad with Dodson? He's the reason you went there, right?"

"Yeah, he is. We think things went very good with him."

"He agreed to testify?"

"Yes and no."

"He wants a deal then?"

"He does. And not just a basic deal. He wants total immunity from any and all charges this case might bring about. He wants it in writing and wants his attorney to read it before he'll say a word."

"You think what he has to say is worth that kind of deal?"

"Yeah, I do. We both do. The case is shaping up nicely, especially for how much time we've put into it so far. But without him, we're miles away from going to the DA. We get him to fully cooperate? I think we're there. I think we'll have enough to arrest the other two guys involved."

"The two pastors," Pendleton said.

"Yeah, them."

"So, this guy Dodson — who's been out of town for thirty years — gets off scot-free, and the two local guys go to prison for life. How you think that's going to sell, from a PR standpoint?"

Joe glanced at Hank, knew what he was thinking. Thank God somebody's worrying about the PR side of things. Joe shook his head, glad this wasn't a video call. "Well, sir, when you put it that way, we might get some blowback back in town, but —"

"Some blowback?" Pendleton said. "Joe, you're forgetting who these guys are. Especially, Burton. His whole church will be in an uproar. Not to mention all the people from other churches in town who listen to his radio program. Or all the other pastors he's connected with, locally and elsewhere. We really gotta have our case against him locked up tight."

"I know that, sir. Which is why we need this immunity deal for Dodson ASAP. See, Hank, and I don't think we're making some kind of deal with the devil here. Him getting off scot-free, as you call it, might actually just be something pretty close to justice, the way we're seeing things. We haven't heard his testimony yet, but from all of the facts we do have, coupled with what our instincts and intuition is telling us, Dodson really had nothing to do with the killing of that boy. He was friends with Burton and Chip Masters, and may have driven to that convenience store with them, but we think everything else that happened that night was on them. There's a reason why they're best buds, and he hasn't spoken to either one of them in thirty years. And then there's the murder weapon, that Bren Ten that Dr. Hargrove told us about. That's no ordinary gun.

Kids like Dodson and Chip Masters wouldn't have access to something like that. That's a rich kid's toy."

"So, you think Burton brought the gun to the store?" Pendleton said.

"Without a doubt," Joe said.

"Any ideas on how to locate that gun, or prove the gun was his?"

"Not yet, but I'm working on an idea I hope will pan out once I get back in town."

"All right then," Pendleton said. "I'll call the DA as soon as we get off the phone, get that immunity deal set up."

"Thank you, sir. Any chance you can make that happen very soon?"

"I think he'll get right on it. The story is getting bigger by the day."

Just then, Joe's phone call was interrupted by another. He looked at the screen. "I've got Ray Dodson calling, sir. Probably should get it."

"You go on then. I'll see you both back in town."

Joe hung up, pressed the button to take Ray Dodson's call. "Hey, Ray. We were just talking about you. What's up?"

After too long a pause, Dodson said, ""Yeah, I've been doing some thinking since you left."

Joe could already tell, this wasn't going to be good. "Well, like I was saying, we were talking about you just before you called. We report directly to the Chief of Police, and we've explained everything to him. He's already working on getting that immunity deal we talked about."

"Yeah, about that... here's the thing. I've changed my mind."

"From what to what?" Joe said. "What are you saying?"

"About testifying against Chip and Glenn. I'm not gonna do it."

"You're not? Why not? What's changed in the last hour or so?"

"Nothing, just... had more time to think. I'm down here at Riverfront Park, came right after you guys left. And I... I just realized, I'm not ready to do this, even with the immunity deal. I like my life here in Charleston. I'm not ready for everything to be turned upside down."

"Well, Mr. Dodson," Joe said, "everything doesn't have to be turned upside down if you testify. Other than the people you tell in Charleston, I don't think anyone else will even know. Might be a big deal back in Culpepper, but this isn't the kind of story that's gonna make national headlines. You might have to be here for a week or so, but the kind of deal we're talking about, once you're done doing your part, it's over. You're in and out. You can go back to the life you've made for yourself there, and it'll be like nothing ever happened."

Hank leaned forward. "Mr. Dodson, this is Detective Jensen, Hank, Joe's partner. "Even if somehow people do find out there in Charleston — not saying they will — but if they do, shouldn't be any kind of scandal for you. I mean, the only way this goes down is that you came back as a witness to a crime that happened back when you were in high school. Nobody can fault you for that."

"I'm not worried about a scandal," Ray said. "But thanks for explaining that."

"Then what?" Hank said. "What changed your mind? Because you know, if you don't cooperate now, and later on we get evidence to pursue this case without your help, there won't be any deal on the table then. You'll be right in there facing the same consequences as Burton and Masters."

"Guess I'll just have to take my chances," he said.

Then it hit Joe... what was really going on here. "Did someone get to you, Ray? Someone call you or meet with you after we left, threaten you in any way?"

A long pause. Too long.

"That's it," Joe said. "Who was it? Someone from the church? What did they say? Whatever it is, don't let them intimidate you from doing the right thing." Ray didn't respond. "We can protect you, if that's what you're worried about. So, who was it?"

"One of the killers," Ray said. "I'm sorry, but I can't do this."

He hung up the phone.

42

A few hours later, Hank and Joe arrived back in Culpepper. After that disappointing phone call from Ray Dodson, Hank asked if they should call Pendleton back and put a hold on the DA working up that immunity deal. But Joe wasn't ready to give up on Dodson yet, so he decided to let it go through. "We'll give him a night to sleep on it," Joe had said. "Maybe call him back tomorrow when the deal's all set. See if he's at a better place."

Joe was heading back to the station, so Hank could get his car, when he thought of something. "Maybe we should head over to Andrew Tubbs' place before we call it a night. Instead of going there tomorrow. See if he's back to writing that book on his supposedly-stolen laptop."

"Sure, why not?" Hank said. "Enough time has passed. He probably thinks he's in the clear."

Joe knew what was prompting his change of plans. Dodson was his best hope for a quick resolve to this case. Without him, Tubbs was the only card he had left to play.

That and the murder weapon, if he could locate that some-how. "You got the search warrant with you?"

"I do," Hank said. "In my briefcase."

"When we get there, you get it out while I knock on the door."

"Will do. Maybe we'll get lucky, and he'll still have the files for his book on there."

"That's my hope," Joe said.

They were there in ten minutes. Joe parked at the same spot then walked to the front door. He waited till Hank had the warrant in his hands before knocking. Joe saw the front window was partially open. "Mr. Tubbs? It's Lieutenant Joe Boyd and my partner, Hank. We need to speak with you again."

Tubbs' parrot started squawking up a storm. They could hear Tubbs coming down the hallway, trying to calm him down. "Be right there." Moments later, the front door opened. "How can I help you, gentlemen?"

Hank held up the search warrant. "Last time we were here, you said we'd need to get a warrant to search your laptop. So, we did."

"I know," Tubbs said, "but then my laptop got stolen." He suddenly seemed a little edgy. "I called down at the station, told them to tell you fellas, so you wouldn't be wasting your time."

"We got the message," Joe said. "But we decided to get the warrant anyway. Just to be thorough."

"You mean, you don't trust me. You think I'm lying about the laptop being gone. Well, I'm not. See for yourselves." He stood back, let Joe and Hank inside.

As soon as they got in, Joe's eyes scanned the area and

quickly focused on a laptop sitting on the dinette table. Right where it was before.

"What do you call that?" Hank said pointing to the same thing.

Tubbs walked over to it, picked it up. "I call it a laptop. But as you can plainly see, it's not the same laptop as the one that was here before. See? It's a MacBook Pro, made by Apple. The other one was bigger, and a PC. Totally different animal."

"I can see that," Joe said. "And I'm no tech expert, but I'm pretty sure that laptop cost at least twice as much as the one you claim was stolen."

"I didn't claim anything. It was stolen."

"That must be some kind of amazing insurance policy you have, Mr. Tubbs," Joe said. "Process your claim that fast and give you enough money to buy a computer twice as nice as the one you lost?"

Tubbs didn't answer. His face grew more agitated. Or maybe just more nervous.

"Yeah," Hank said. "Mind if I ask what company that is? I might like to switch mine."

"Uh...I, I didn't go through my insurance company. My deductible would've been too high anyway."

"So, you got that kind of money just laying around?" Hank said. "You seem like the kinda guy who, like most people, live paycheck to paycheck."

"Well, I do. I guess. I wouldn't live here if I was rolling in it. And I certainly wouldn't be working at Home Depot."

"So, how'd you afford such a swank laptop as this?" Joe said.

"I, uh...didn't buy it. It was, uh...a gift. Someone who heard about my laptop getting stolen gave it to me."

"Really?" Hank said. "You got some nice friends. Mind if I ask who? Who likes you that much to spend fifteen-hundred bucks buying you a new laptop?"

"Well, yes, actually. I do mind. I don't believe I have to answer that question. Do I? That's not what that warrant's about. I'm not under arrest, and you came here for a laptop that no longer exists. So, I think I'm all done talking with you gentlemen for today."

Hank looked at the warrant. "Funny thing, Tubbs. This warrant doesn't spell out a specific laptop. It just says a laptop belonging to Andrew Tubbs at this address." Hank walked toward the laptop. "So, I guess we'll just have to seize this one. Take it back to the station, see what's on it."

Tubbs quickly stood in front of the laptop, blocking Hank's access. "You can't take that one. I need it to write. Besides, there's nothing on this laptop that you want. Aren't you looking for the files for the book I was writing about, the convenience store murder?"

"I suppose we are," Joe said.

"Well, they're gone. They're not on this computer. Here, I'll show you." He quickly turned around and sat down, opened the lid and typed in his password. He flipped on the Finder icon, which opened a big box on screen showing all files and folders on Tubbs' computer.

"That's quite a lot files for laptop you've just had for a day or two," Hank said.

"They're not new files. They're from a backup drive. All the files from the other computer are now in this one, except for the ones for that book. I deleted those."

"What?" Joe said. "You deleted all the files for the book? Why would you do that? What possible reason could you have?"

"I... I, uh... I decided... not to write it anymore. It didn't seem like the right thing to do, now that they found Myron's body."

"Really?" Joe said. "I find that pretty odd, Mr. Tubbs, if I'm being honest. Seems like — if your goal is to be a successful writer — you'd want to take advantage of all the publicity created by the situation. Maybe write it as a true crime novel now, or based on true events. I mean, you've already said you barely knew the guy, and it's not like he has family in town who'd be offended. So, I'm finding it a little hard to believe that you would backup every other file from the old laptop onto this brand-new one — the one a mysterious person gave you as a gift — except the main passion of your life these past several months, writing the story that you've been reading to that writers' group."

"Yeah, Tubbs," Hank said. "Hearing it the way Joe just put it, I'm not buying it, either."

"Well, you don't have to buy it. It doesn't matter if you believe me."

"That's your story, and you're sticking to it. Is that it, Tubbs?" Joe said. "Let me tell you what I think is really going on here. You're lying about your laptop being stolen. Someone from the church, that Victorious Life Church, maybe that pastor Chip Masters, heard about your story. And he paid you a little visit."

A look of fear came over Tubbs' face.

"And he intimidated you," Joe continued, "maybe even threatened you, about what would happen if you didn't get rid of that story. And maybe — just maybe — he agreed to swap out laptops with you, so he wouldn't come off seeming like such a bad guy. How am I doing?"

Tubbs stood up, forced a new expression on his face. "I'm all done talking to you. To both of you. If you have any more questions, you can talk to my lawyer."

"You even have a lawyer, Tubbs?" Hank said.

"Now please leave my home." He walked to the front door and opened it.

"Should we take his laptop with us?"

"Nah, leave it," Joe said. "May be the only truthful thing Mr. Tubbs said to us here today. I really think that file is gone, probably for good." He and Hank headed down the steps, through Tubbs' carport toward their car. "Oddly enough," Joe said. "I think we've made some progress here."

"I don't know, Joe. Maybe. But it makes me wonder...what the heck kind of a church is that anyway? How did it get to be this big, fast-growing church with pastors like these guys?"

Joe was wondering the same thing.

43

After dropping Hank off to get his car, he called Kate to let her know he was on his way home. She could tell he was kind of down. He told her he'd fill her in when he got home. Turned out, since she expected Hank and Joe to stay overnight in Charleston, she'd already eaten and fed the kids but wouldn't mind hearing him out over some heated up leftovers. They sent the kids upstairs, so they could have privacy.

Took Joe about an hour to update her and talk through what was eating at him. Her advice? "I could tell you what I think, but I think you'd feel a whole lot better running all this past Ed."

Ed was their pastor. Unlike most pastors Joe had known, Ed preferred church members to just use his name without any title in front. So, Joe called Ed, who said he had some time right now if Joe wanted to head over.

Joe made the short ride, pulled into the driveway of Ed's home. That's where Ed wanted to meet. Joe had been there several times before. He rang the doorbell, heard Rufus barking, then Ed's voice telling him to quiet down. The door opened and both Ed and Rufus greeted him warmly. Rufus was part lab, part something else. As soon as he saw Joe, he lightened right up.

"Come on in, Joe. Mary's visiting one of her friends, so it's just you, me and Rufus. So, we can get comfortable in the family room instead of meeting in my home office." Ed and Mary were in their mid-50s and empty-nesters.

"Thanks for seeing me on such short notice," Joe said, as he walked through the foyer, following Ed.

"Happy to. I know you don't usually call unless it's something that counts."

"Well, I guess that's one way to describe what's bothering me." They entered into a nice-sized living area with a fireplace and vaulted ceiling. Decorated more for comfort than to impress.

Ed headed for his favorite chair. "Sit anywhere you like, Joe."

Joe picked out the stuffed chair closest to him. "What I want to chat about, guess I should mention, needs to be kept between us. You can talk with Mary, but... I don't know, I guess you'll understand my hesitation once you hear what I have to say."

"Okay, I have no problem with that. What's on your mind?"

"It's this case I'm working on, Ed. You been following the news on the Myron Simpson murder?"

"Pretty much, though not as close as Mary. But hearing her, seems like everyone in town is pretty curious about this.

We weren't here back when all this happened, but I guess everybody loves a good mystery."

"Yes, they do," Joe said, thinking about why Pendleton was so concerned about how this played out in the press. "Well, I'm about to share something that will probably shock you. And I normally wouldn't share this level of detail with anyone on a case we're still working on, but if I don't, you won't be able to help me."

"Okay, I'll brace for the impact."

"Well, here it is. My partner Hank and I feel almost certain we know who did this. Who committed the robbery and who killed Myron Simpson back in 1988. Problem is, they are both well-known clergymen in this town. Well, one is way more popular than the other. We don't have all the evidence in yet, not enough to press charges, but certainly enough to say what I just said."

"I see," Ed said. "And why is this a problem for you, Joe?"

"Because these guys are pastors, Ed. They've been pastors for quite a while. The main guy — very possibly the one who did the shooting — is preaching every Sunday to a sizable congregation and he's on the radio several times a week. Preaching from the Bible, talking about Jesus, praying out loud, regularly asking folks to donate their money, as though they're giving to God."

"Now Joe, you know that pastors aren't perfect people. I know lots of guys, me included, who've done quite a few things they aren't proud of when they were young. That's part of the reason they needed Christ. I mean, the gospel's all about redemption and forgiveness."

"I know, Ed. But do any of the pastors' salvation stories that you know of include armed robbery, murder, then burying the victim in the woods? And then not telling a soul about it, leaving the kid's family in torment for thirty years? I get that Jesus came to save sinners, not the righteous, but aren't the sinners supposed to come clean and repent for what they've done?"

Ed smiled. "No, I don't know any pastors who were killers, and you're right, that's not the kind of thing you can just say a little prayer and sidestep around."

"Right, and then you just become a pastor and start a church, like nothing ever happened? How can they do that? I thought pastors were supposed to be guys who have integrity and have high moral character."

"They are, Joe. But you've seen your share, I'm sure, of even well-known guys who got way off-track and fall into serious sin. They wind up stepping down and bringing reproach on the whole church."

"I have, Ed. But my guys, if everything we're seeing is true, they never were on track. The whole foundation of their ministry is a sham, isn't it? I've read in the Bible terms like wolves in sheep's clothing. Could that be what we're dealing with here?"

"We very well could be, Joe."

"Is it the size of the church?" Joe said. "Because it seems like a lot of these corrupt guys pastor huge churches?"

"It's not the size, Joe. I mean, think about the early church. After Peter preached on the Day of Pentecost, the church grew by over three-thousand people. God wants us to reach thousands and thousands, millions of folks. So, size is not the corrupting thing. I know some seriously good pastors of some mega-churches who are really straight shooters. Guys I respect and admire. If I lived in their cities, I'd probably retire and go to their church."

"Then what's the deal, Ed? How do guys like this get into ministry, and how do so many people get duped into following them? And I haven't even told you some of the most disturbing things about these guys. Because, they're still doing it. So far, not killing people. But one of them, probably both of them, knowing that we're on to them, have threatened the lives of those who are cooperating with us in the investigation."

"You're kidding?" Ed said.

"I wish I was. So, you see what I mean? What bugs me about this?"

"I do. You're actually touching on something of a sore spot for me. One of the reasons I envy what it must've been like in the days of guys like Peter and Paul. See, in this country because of the freedom of religion — which we still have for now — anybody who wants to can start a church. And unlike lawyers or doctors, there's no significant oversight for these people. No one to take them down if they're corrupt. Even if they have no business being in ministry in the first place. There's no one to call them out. Although some denominations provide some small measure of accountability, but even that doesn't seem to cut it so much of the time. So, these charlatans can get away with an amazing amount of nonsense before they're found out."

"How was it different in the days of Peter and Paul?" Joe asked.

"Well, for one thing they talked plainly and openly about this danger. Jesus talked about false prophets who'd come in sheep's clothing, but inwardly were ravenous wolves. Paul warned Christians in Ephesus in a similar way about false teachers who'd come in like vicious wolves, not sparing the flock. And he wasn't talking about outsiders, either. Because he said, *Even from among your own group.* He talked to the Corinthians about people who preached to them a different Jesus, or a different gospel than the one he'd preached to them. And he didn't use soft words when describing them. He called them deceitful workers who disguise themselves as God's servants, then said we shouldn't be shocked by this because even the devil disguises himself as an angel of light."

"Wow, Ed. Yeah, you're right. Don't hear too many Christian leaders these days calling anyone out like that."

"And these are just a few examples, Joe. I could go on and on. There are so many more warnings like this."

"Then how are ordinary Christians supposed to avoid being taken in by these people?"

"It's tricky," Ed said. "But the Bible does talk about that, too. You ever heard of something passing or not passing the smell test?" Joe nodded. "Well, it's kind of like that. Jesus said, we'd know them by their fruit. Meaning, the conduct and character of their lives. Paul urged Christians to observe those who lived the same way he lived and imitate their faith. So, it's about how leaders *live* behind the scenes, in the day-to-day situations. And, to a certain extent, the things they teach. Do they pass the smell test? The way I handle it is this...if I hear or see some Christian leader teaching or doing something you'd never see Jesus, or guys like Peter and Paul teaching or doing, then it's probably not legit. Because we're called to be like them, and to teach the things they taught, emphasize the things they emphasized."

Ed looked like he was done, then got another thought. "Something else I should say, Joe. Even with everything else I've said, there's really no foolproof way of discerning everyone who's not legit. Sometimes it takes God doing something on His own to expose the really clever ones. But He'll do it. May take some time, but eventually, He'll bring down the phonies."

Joe didn't say anything for a second.

"Man, Ed, seriously...that's really helpful stuff. So, you'd be okay with me going after these guys, when you hear about it in the news? Because these guys? They definitely don't pass the smell test."

"Totally, Joe. You go wherever the evidence and the truth takes you."

44

Joe pulled into the police station the following morning feeling pretty good. His talk last night with his pastor settled several nagging concerns. His mood improved even further after filling Kate in on everything that was said. She completely agreed with Ed. Neither one of these guys were "men of God" in her book. She only felt bad about what all this would do to the members of their church, once the news broke.

As Joe walked through the main entrance area, the receptionist flagged him. "Hey, Lieutenant. Captain Pendleton called me a short while ago, said for you to head back and see him as soon as you got in. He said it was good news."

"Thanks." That's what he liked to hear first thing in the morning. He headed straight back to Pendleton's office. His secretary wasn't at her desk, so Joe knocked a couple times on the Captain's door and poked his head inside.

"Come on in, Joe. Close the door. You can have a seat if you want, but this won't take long."

Joe came up, stood in front of his desk. "What's the good news?"

"Heard back from the DA already on that immunity deal. You know, for your buddy in Charleston...Dodson. Full, transactional immunity. Just like he wanted. Of course, he's gotta come totally clean on everything and give the DA enough to sink these two guys."

"That's great, Captain." Joe decided not to tell him yet that Dodson had changed his mind and backed out of the deal. He could always do that later. Besides, Joe hadn't given up on the idea flipping Dodson back to their side. "How does he want to work this, with Dodson being in a different state?"

"I asked him about that. You run this by Dodson, get the contact information for his attorney. Get that to the DA, and he'll fax a copy to Dodson's attorney to review. Then he'll probably want to interview him on video, make sure he's gonna deliver the goods. Once he's satisfied, we'll want to see him here in town for a formal deposition and sign off on everything. After that, we'll get the warrants out and you and Hank can make the arrests. How's that sound?"

"Sounds great," Joe said. "I'll get right on it."

"And Joe, not a word of this to anyone except Hank. There'll be time enough to fill Hazelton in at the Gazette when this deal is locked up tight."

Joe headed out the door toward Hank's office to fill him in, which was the easy part. Then back to his office for the hard part...convincing Ray Dodson to get back in the game.

After briefing Hank, Joe tried calling Ray Dodson several

times but kept getting voicemail. He didn't leave a message, figuring Dodson wouldn't return the call and would probably not answer it anymore once he recognized Joe's number.

The third time was the charm.

"Dodson's Quality Restorations, Ray Dodson speaking. How can I help you this morning?"

"Probably the best way you can help me is not hang up when you find out who's calling?"

A pause. "Okay...who is calling?"

"It's me, Ray. Lieutenant Joe Boyd from the Culpepper PD."

"Oh. I see. Lieutenant, I've said everything I have to say."

"Then don't say anything. Just hear me out. Won't take two minutes." Joe waited. Dodson didn't reply, so he continued. "I know you wanted out of this thing, but the immunity deal you asked for was already underway when you called back saying you wanted out. Well, I heard back this morning from the DA. He wants to hear what you have to say on this case, and is willing to give you exactly what you asked for, in writing. And you can have your attorney preview the deal before you agree to say a word. That's full, transactional immunity, Ray. A total, get-out-of-jail-free card."

"That's good to know, I guess," Ray said. "But that doesn't really help me out of the situation I'm in. I told you before I hung up what's happening."

"You really didn't, Ray. Maybe you think you did. But all you said was one of the killers had talked to you after we left. Obviously, he threatened you. My guess, it was Chip Masters. Can't see the main guy getting his hands dirty. But that's all I know."

"Then, the way I see it," Ray said, "you know enough. What else is there? I'm looking at two threats here, Lieutenant. One is the quick and violent end to my life now if I cooperate with you, the other is the possibility that you might arrest me several years down the road, if I don't. What would you choose if you were me?"

"Is that what you're facing, Ray? A quick and violent end? What did Masters say to you, exactly?"

Ray sighed. "Well, for starters he showed me the gun he would use to kill me, as I was sitting out on a park bench by the river. Then he showed me the silencer he had custom made for it. Said if I cooperated with you he could double-tap me right then and there in two seconds. No one would hear a thing. He'd set me up, so that I looked like I was napping and be an hour down the road before anyone knew I was dead."

Man, Joe thought. Some pastor. "And you're sure he wasn't bluffing?"

"This was no bluff, Lieutenant. I have no doubt Chip would shoot me if I helped you. He's got way too much to lose, and he's got some kind of sick way of justifying everything he does, so that somehow God doesn't mind too awful much. And I know that gun he'd use packs a lethal punch."

"How do you know that?"

"Because it was the same gun used that night to shoot Myron Simpson at the convenience store."

"What?" Joe said. "The Bren Ten? Masters showed you the Bren Ten?"

"I don't know what that means. But it was definitely the gun Glenn used to shoot Myron that night. Chip showed it to

me, because he knew I'd recognize it. One shot and BOOM...
Myron was gone."

"So, Burton was the one who did the shooting?

"Yeah, and the whole scheme was Glenn's idea in the first
place."

"Ray, that's huge. Game-changing huge."

"How so?"

"Not so much the part about Glenn doing the shooting,
but the gun. The gun used to kill Myron Simpson is a very
rare and unique gun. They call it a Bren Ten. I won't bore
you with the details, but the bullet recovered from Myron's
body is also a unique bullet made for that gun. You've just
told me where the murder weapon is, and who has it. Do
you know how Masters got hold of it?"

"Yeah, he said he bought it from Glenn twelve years ago
when Glenn's father died. Guess he inherited it and sold it to
Chip."

"So, one of the guys involved in the robbery and murder
of Myron Simpson, just threatened your life with the murder
weapon."

"I guess that's right," Ray said. "Pretty much."

"Ray, because of this new development, if you agree to
testify, not just to what you know about the original case but
to everything you just told me about the gun and how Chip
threatened your life, I can have him arrested — today — and
make sure he stays locked up until the trial."

"Really?" Ray said.

"Really. That's witness intimidation and tampering, what
Chip did to you after we left. And a few other charges I can
think of. And now that I have the location of the murder
weapon and can trace it directly to Glenn and Chip, with

your testimony, we're pretty much at the open and shut stage."

"Well Lieutenant, if you're sure about that. Especially about the part where you can lock Chip up until I testify in court, then you have a deal. What do we need to do from here?"

"Give me your attorney's contact info, and I'll send the deal over to him. The DA's gonna want to videotape your testimony since you're out-of-state, to make sure you have enough good stuff to make such an immunity deal legit. No worries there. He hears what you've told me, and you'll have no problem. Make sure you include the part about Chip threatening you with the Bren Ten, and that it's the same gun used to shoot Myron. I'll call you back and let you know when we have Chip Masters safely behind bars."

45

After getting off the phone with Ray Dodson, Joe had met with Captain Pendleton, briefed him on this explosive news. Even before Joe was done explaining, Pendleton completely understood its significance. When Joe had finished, Pendleton said, "I'll set up a chat between you and the DA. You get with Hank, get him to head over to the courthouse for a search warrant on Chip Masters. And Joe, you might as well get in the car and start driving. I can't see the DA turning this down."

Joe headed down the hall, stopped in to see Hank. "Sorry to do this to you, my friend. But I need you to stop everything and head back to the courthouse for a warrant."

Hank stopped typing the report he'd been working on and looked up. "A warrant? What for this time?" Joe explained everything from his phone call with Ray Dodson and, just like Pendleton, Hank immediately got it. "So, what are we talking about... his person, his car, his house... what?"

"All of it, if needed. We know he has this gun. And we

know it's the murder weapon, and we know he's threatened to use it. Make sure the judge knows we need to be able to find it... quickly. I'm heading to the DA's now to convince him to let us arrest Masters, get this sick pup off the street."

Hank stood. "All right then. Let's do this."

"Call me as soon as you get it. We'll go after Masters together. Joe headed out into the hall toward the front door, on his way to Dunedin, the county seat.

Just as Joe pulled into the downtown parking lot of the District Attorney's Office, his phone rang. It was Pendleton. He hoped he hadn't just made this drive for nothing. "What's up, Captain?"

"You're all set, Joe. The DA will be waiting for you. I didn't go into the details but told him enough to wet his whistle. Fact is, when I told him it was urgent enough for you to head over there personally, that pretty much did it. Pretty obvious, he likes you better than he likes me. So, go in there and make this happen."

"Will do. Thanks, Captain."

JOE KNEW the way through the halls and walls of this upscale office building. The DA, Todd Rucker, was a fellow about Joe's same age, but he carried himself like someone ten years older. It was pretty evident by things he'd said over the last several cases Joe had worked on with him, Rucker had ambitions for bigger and better things. But he seemed to be going after them the right way, through hard work and straight dealing. But you really had to have your ducks lined up in a row. He'd only take a case when he was sure he could get a conviction.

Joe stepped off the elevator and across the marble floor toward the glass doors leading into Rucker's office. A young blonde with a pleasant smile greeted him at a reception desk. "Here to see DA Rucker. Lieutenant Joe Boyd."

"I was told to expect you, Lieutenant. You're his last appointment for the day. Do you know which office he's in?"

"I do." Joe headed straight for it, knocked twice and entered the same moment Rucker invited him in.

"Lieutenant Boyd, good to see you again. Your boss briefed me — very briefly — on the purpose of your visit. Sounds like you've had some big break on the Myron Simpson case. Lots of interest on this one for some reason. Come on in, have a seat and talk to me about it. I didn't live here when the boy was killed, but those who did are really wanting us to get whoever did it."

Joe sat on his office chair close to the edge. "That's exactly why I'm here, sir. We not only know who did it, but after talking to a key witness today, we can prove it. But I'm going to need your help to do this thing right."

"Tell me how."

"Did the Captain mention to you who our prime suspects are?"

"Just that they were prominent citizens in Culpepper."

"Yeah," Joe said. "One of them anyway. He's the pastor of one of the largest and fastest-growing churches in town, named Glenn Burton."

"Can't say I've heard of him."

"Well, he's kind of all over the place in town. When we arrest him, it's gonna be quite the shocker. But we're not ready for him just yet. I'm here about a fellow that works on his staff, Chip Masters. This guy is dangerous, sir." Joe told him everything he'd learned about Chip from his talks with Ray Dodson.

"You say this guy's on staff at a church?"

"Afraid so. People in the church call him Pastor Chip. But this guy's no pastor. And here's the thing...the gun he used to threaten Ray Dodson's life with is the very same gun that was used to kill Myron Simpson in 1988."

"How can you be sure?"

Joe told Rucker all about the Bren Ten, even the part about it being the gun used on Miami Vice. "It's a very unique gun, sir. Ray recognized it instantly when Masters showed it to him. I'm sure you're familiar with Dr. Hargrove."

"Very much so."

"Feel free to call him about this gun. He'll tell you how rare it is, even the ammo for it. I'd stake my reputation on this...when we do ballistics on that gun, it will be proved to be the same gun used against Simpson."

"So, how can I help you Lieutenant, specifically?"

"I need to get this guy, Chip Masters, off the street...like right now. Not only because he's a danger to society, but because until he's locked up, our primary witness is too afraid to come here to testify against him."

"That's understandable," Rucker said.

"Glad to hear you say that, because I need to ask you if we can file charges against him for witness tampering and intimidation. Like right now, based on what he's already done. And we need to ask the judge to hold him without bail till the trial. We do that, we will not only have proof positive of their guilt with the murder weapon but an eyewitness testimony who can put both of these men away for good."

Rucker sat back in his chair. "I'll want to talk to this fellow, Dodson, myself. Not that I don't trust you, Joe, because I do. It's just —"

"No need to explain, sir. I've already talked to Dodson. He'll talk to you on video anytime you want. And once we get this guy Masters locked away, we can get Ray Dodson here pronto. Probably tomorrow, if you want."

Rucker smiled. "Guess for something this pressing, I can come in on a Saturday. Okay then. I'm sold. Let's make this happen. And if Dodson confirms everything you said about this influential pastor, Burton. We'll go after him next."

46

Joe pulled into the parking lot of Victorious Life Church. On the drive here from his meeting with DA Rucker, Hank called and said he'd already gotten the warrants for Chip Masters and had confirmed that Masters was still at the church office. He said he'd wait there in the parking lot near Masters' car and detain him if he came out and tried to leave before Joe arrived.

Joe found Hank's car with him still in it, pulled in the parking space beside him. He got out, and so did Hank. "So, he still inside?"

"Yeah, looks like it. That's his blue Jaguar over there."

Joe looked at Hank. "I'm guessing when he drove that thing in here today, he wasn't thinking it was his last ride ever in that fancy car."

"The DA's onboard to take him in now?"

"Yep. Told him about Masters threatening Dodson's life

with that gun. I could tell after that he didn't need to hear anything else."

"So," Hank said, "let's go get Masters and the gun." They started walking toward the office door. "Feel kinda bad for these church folk."

"Me, too," Joe said. "I called Tom Hazelton at the Gazette on the way here. Was half tempted to tell him to meet us here, maybe call the local TV news folks, too."

"Get Masters' perp walk on video," Hank said.

"Yeah, but I changed my mind. Thinking about all the folks that go here. No reason to humiliate them because of what their leaders do. I did update him on everything else, though. Told him I'd fill in the blanks about who we're charging in the morning."

"Let me guess," Hank said. "He wasn't too happy about that."

Joe opened the glass front door. "No, he wasn't. But he's got plenty to write about even without the best part." He walked up to the receptionist, who greeted them warmly. "We need to see Pastor Chip Masters. I understand he's still in the office."

"He is. Do you gentlemen have an appointment?"

"No, we don't," Hank said. "But we don't need one this time." He took out his ID badge, showed it to her. So did Joe.

"Oh, I see. Okay, officers." She was clearly startled but stayed professional. "You just go right down the hall and you'll see the sign for the church offices on the right. Inside, you'll see a section of cubicles and desks, although most of the staff has already left for the day. Just go past those and you'll see all the pastors' offices against the far wall. Turn right down that hallway. Chip's office is the last one."

"Thanks," Joe said. He leaned over and said calmly, "Real sorry for what you're about to see."

They headed down the hall. Her directions were spot on. Once they got past the cubicles, they saw a couple of men dressed nice, chatting down at the other end. Maybe some of the other pastors. They turned right, walked straight to the last door. Hank opened it without knocking and they went inside.

Chip Masters was sitting at his desk typing into a laptop. He looked up, confusion on his face. "Can I help you, gentlemen?"

Both men identified themselves, showed him their ID badges. Hank took out the search warrant, handed it to him. "Mr. Masters, this warrant gives us the authority to search you and your property, including your desk, car and home if needed."

"What? What are you talking about? A search warrant, for what?"

"Could you please stand up?" Hank said.

"The gun," Joe said. "You know, the one you used to threaten Ray Dodson's life in Charleston on Thursday if he continued to cooperate with us."

Chip stood. Hank patted him down. "I don't have a gun on me. And I never threatened Ray Dodson's life. Is that what he told you? He's lying. I wasn't even in Charleston on Thursday."

"Sorry," Joe said. "I believe him, not you. Are any of the drawers in your desk locked?"

"A couple of them."

"Unlock them please," Hank said.

He complied. "There's no gun in any of these drawers."

"Good," Hank said, "then you won't mind us searching them."

"Go right ahead." He took a few steps back.

Hank searched them. "Not in here. We could search every nook and cranny of this office, make a real mess of it. Or, you can tell us where the gun is."

"What gun?"

Joe shook his head. "You're really something, you know that? You lie as good as anyone I've ever questioned. Your face stays the same. You look right at us while you're telling the lie. How do you do that... and still feel okay calling yourself a pastor? How do you threaten to kill somebody just for telling the truth, then lie to us about it, like you did just now, without skipping a beat?"

"I don't know what you're talking about, Detective," Chip said.

"See? You just did it again. We're talking about the Bren Ten, Mr. Masters. Where is it?"

Chip's face completely fell apart on that one.

"There's the look I've been waiting to see," Joe said. "You probably thought you got some sweet deal buying that rare gun from your pal, Glenn. He was probably happy to get rid of it, what with all the bad memories. Him using it to shoot poor Myron Simpson at that convenience store. But that didn't bother you, Chip. Did it? Your soul would have to be alive for something like that to get you upset. You probably thought, I've got me the same gun used by Sonny Crockett on Miami Vice. You probably felt like a real bad dude threatening your old friend Ray with it, along with that custom silencer you bought."

The look on Chip's face was priceless. Joe could see his

eyes trying to find someplace to focus. Some way to regain his composure.

"I say, let's skip searching the office and go right for the Jaguar," Hank said. "I'm guessing that's where we'll find it."

Chip's head snapped toward Hank.

"Bingo," Joe said. "He all but said so just now. Turn around, Mr. Masters. Put your hands behind your back."

"What for?"

"Chip Masters, I'm placing you under arrest for witness intimidation and tampering." Chip turned around, did as he was told. Joe handcuffed him, read him his Miranda rights. Then he reached in Chip's pocket, pulled out his keys to the Jaguar.

"And I'm guessing," Hank said, "once we get that Bren Ten out of its hiding place and down to ballistics, it'll be a perfect match for the bullet the ME pulled out of Myron Simpson's body."

"Then," Joe said, "as you can imagine, additional charges will be filed."

Joe handed Chip off to Hank, who led him out the door, down the little hall, past the cubical section and out into the main hallway. Joe really felt bad for all the church people they saw on the way out to Chip's car. They couldn't believe the scene unfolding before their eyes.

Joe held onto Chip while Hank searched the car. Didn't take long. Hank found the gun at the second location he checked...under the front seat, passenger side. And right there with it, Chip's custom-made silencer.

What Hank found in the first place he checked — the glove compartment — was like icing on the cake. "Lookee here," he said, unfolding a small slip of paper. "A receipt for gasoline in Charleston, South Carolina, dated on Thursday."

Joe looked at Chip straight in the eyes. "Now how do you suppose that got there?"

Chip said nothing, just looked down on the ground.

47

Back at the station, Hank was processing Chip Masters. Joe was headed toward Pendleton's office to update him, help him start to prepare for the inevitable press conference he'd probably want to call over the weekend. Halfway there, his cell phone rang. It was Tom Hazelton of the Gazette. Joe figured he might as well take it, save him from calling Hazelton himself, which was the next thing on his list.

"Hello, Tom. Great timing," Joe said. "I was about to call you in fifteen minutes."

"Hey, Joe. Hope it's gonna be about these pics that just went up on Facebook twenty minutes ago."

"What pics?"

"I'm looking at you and Hank, standing by a blue Jaguar next to Pastor Chip Masters, who's in handcuffs."

Joe wondered if he'd ever get used to social media. "Must be some of the staff over at the church. Yeah, I was going to call you about that. What are people saying about the photos?"

"There's already thirty comments, and they're all over the road. The one getting the most likes is a guess that it's for embezzlement, since Masters managers the money."

"What do you think it's about?"

"The cold case you and Hank are working on. Is Masters one of the murder suspects? That'd be my guess."

"And you'd be right. Can't tell you everything yet, but I can give you enough to write the story everyone will be talking about tomorrow."

"Tomorrow and tonight," Hazelton said. "I'm going to get this article uploaded to our online paper within the hour. So, fire away. Give me everything you can."

"For starters, we've arrested Masters for witness intimidation, but we'll be adding the murder charge before the weekend is out. We have a cooperating witness – who we're not going to name just yet — who was present the evening Myron Simpson was killed, and he will testify that both Chip Masters and Pastor Glenn Burton were the ones who shot Simpson and buried his body in the woods that night back in 1988. In fact, this witness said the convenience store robbery was Burton's idea, and he was actually the one who shot Simpson. In addition, when we arrested Masters he was found in possession of the gun used to threaten this witness's life. The same gun we believe ballistics will prove was used to murder Myron Simpson."

"Oh. My. Goodness," Hazelton said. "That's just crazy. People are literally going to lose their minds when this gets out, especially the church community. Mind if I ask, why you're so confident about the gun being the murder weapon before you've done the tests?"

"Because, a very rare and unique pistol was used. Well, that's probably all I can say right now. We'll be interviewing Masters in a few minutes. If anything comes out of that fit to print, I'll let you know. Oh, and you can be sure Captain Pendleton will be calling a press conference at some point this weekend."

"Great," Hazelton said. "This is really good stuff. Sad stuff. But what a great story. Thanks, Joe."

After briefing Pendleton, Joe got with Hank to conduct their first official interview with Chip Masters. When they sat down from him across the table, his face had managed to find its standard, upbeat, pastoral look.

Joe was certain it wouldn't last long.

"I don't know what you men are hoping to accomplish here," he said, "but I've got nothing to worry about. You're accusing me of...intimidating a witness. So, Ray says that I did. That's not evidence. I'm saying I didn't. His word against mine."

"You're forgetting the receipt for gas in Charleston," Hank said. "On the day Ray says this happened. Before we found it, you lied to us, saying you were never there. Joe and I both heard you lie about that."

"And beyond the receipt," Joe added, "I'm sure we'll be able to find you on video talking with Ray in that park."

"And I'm sure you won't," Chip said. "There were no cameras. I checked."

Joe smiled. "I knew there were no cameras in the park, because I checked. But you just admitted — and this interview's on video — that you were at the park, making sure there were no cameras, so no one could prove you were there threatening him." Masters' face fell. "But guess what, Mr. Masters? Something else I checked. Charleston's got cameras, for security purposes, all over the place. And so do a lot of businesses for the same reason. And you made the mistake of driving your blue Jaguar to do this dirty deed. A car very easy to pick out on these videos. As we prepare our case, we'll be collecting all those video clips showing you driving to the vicinity of the park and back at the precise time Ray Dodson will testify that you threatened his life."

"And that gun we got from you earlier," Hank said, "the Bren Ten? Ray recognized it at the park. But of course that was your intention, wasn't it? To intensify the intimidation. But it backfired on you, Masters. Because it's such a rare gun, Ray will have no trouble identifying it as the gun you used. If you weren't there in Charleston Thursday and hadn't flashed that gun in his face, how would Ray have any idea you own and carry such a unique weapon?"

"You couple all that info," Joe said, "with you being caught in all these lies...who do you think a jury's gonna believe? You or Ray? And when the ballistics comes back on that gun very soon — and I know you know this — it will confirm without a doubt it was the gun used to kill Myron Simpson. So, do yourself a favor, Masters. Make yourself a deal. We know Glenn Burton planned this robbery, and he was the one who shot Myron Simpson."

Masters looked like he was going to be sick. "I want a lawyer," he said.

Since Masters had lawyered up, there wasn't much left to be done with him. So Joe headed back to his office to complete one last task before heading home for the day. He closed the door, took a seat and called Ray Dodson. This time he didn't have to use any gimmicks. Ray answered on the third ring.

"Lieutenant Boyd, I was hoping you'd call," Ray said. "Didn't want this thing hanging over my head all weekend."

"Well, you'll be happy to know Chip Masters has been arrested and charged with witness intimidation. He's in a holding cell right now."

"You're not charging him with murder?"

"We definitely are, but the DA wants to hear your statement first. Obviously, you're going to be our star witness on this case. But when the ballistics comes back on the gun, we'll be in great shape. How soon can you get here? The DA would like to meet with you tomorrow, if possible. And he normally doesn't work on Saturdays."

"Will Chip be staying behind bars?"

"Oh, yeah. Not just for the weekend," Joe said. "When the DA heard he threatened your life with a gun, he agreed to ask for no bail until the trial. But if you'd feel more comfortable with an armed escort, I can arrange that."

"No, that won't be necessary. With Chip locked up, I'm fine driving myself. I can be there tomorrow by noon."

"Good," Joe said. "And so far, I've kept your name out of the media info. So, keep a low profile while you're here and it should stay that way. Eventually, when we get closer to the trial, it'll come out. But might as well enjoy some privacy while you can."

"Okay, thanks. See you tomorrow."

48

It was Saturday morning, so Joe decided to take it off. He made omelets and pancakes for Kate and the kids then sat down with his coffee and tablet to read over Tom Hazelton's article on Chip Master's arrest. Kate had already read it while Joe cooked. Her review was brief. "Wow, this is gonna shake things up pretty good I'd say."

He had barely started reading the first few paragraphs, when Tom Hazelton called. "Hey, Tom, I was just reading your article, as we speak."

"Look forward to hearing what you think. Listen, wanted to give you a head's up. This thing is really getting some legs. It's all over social media, locally anyway. And the local news station has been talking about it all morning. And I just found out, Glenn Burton's announced he'll be holding a press conference at the church office at eleven."

Joe looked at the clock on the wall. "That's in ten minutes."

"Right, I'm on my way there now. That's why I'm calling. Figured you'd want to see it."

"Yeah, definitely. Thanks."

Joe got up, headed to the kitchen and told Kate.

"Well, this should be interesting," she said. She grabbed her coffee and followed Joe into the family room.

He turned on the TV, navigated to the local news station, hit the mute button and called Hank to let him know.

"I was just gonna call you," Hank said. "I'm down here at my office. Pendleton just told me about it. Let's talk after."

Kate sipped her coffee. "I wonder what he's gonna say."

"Something tells me," Joe said, "it won't be anything close to an act of contrition."

A few minutes later, Joe noticed a familiar scene appear on the screen. An attractive black reporter was standing amidst a small crowd in front of the Victorious Life Church office building. Joe turned up the volume to catch what she said.

"As you can see, I'm standing in front of the church office. Just off to my left someone from the church has set up a temporary podium and sound system. We understand, Glenn Burton, the senior pastor of the church, will be coming out shortly to make some kind of statement. We don't know if he'll be taking any questions." She looked around. "More and more people are gathering to hear what he has to say. Most we've talked to are church members, all of them clearly shocked by the arrest of Pastor Chip Masters yesterday afternoon, and by the story written by Tom Hazelton in the Gazette. We'll share some of those comments after we hear the pastor speak. But it seems, the congregation is having quite a mixed reaction. While many are still showing support, some were quite angry by these developments. Especially by the notion that their senior pastor is alleged to be the one who planned the robbery of that convenience store in 1988, as well as the one who took the life of young Myron Simpson."

A commotion seemed to be happening on the reporter's left. The camera panned to capture Glenn Burton surrounded by several staff pastors, as he walked up to the mic. "Let's listen now to the pastor's remarks," the reporter said.

Burton looked pretty polished to Joe, not like someone whose entire world was crashing down around him.

"Good morning everyone," he said then cleared his throat. "Thank you for coming. Although this is not the kind of gathering any pastor would ever hope to address. I see a good number of reporters and journalists are here, which is good, since this scandalous and libelous report has come out last night and this morning about me. Hopefully, you'll not show people an edited version of my remarks, so they'll be able to make their own judgments when they hear both sides. I can also see many members of our church this morning. I'm sure those who aren't here will be hearing about these unfortunate developments soon enough. I'm sorry you're having to go through this with me, but it seems as though we have no choice. And we have prayerfully decided it would be best to address these unfounded accusations head-on."

Unfounded accusations? Good grief. Joe could already see where this was going.

Burton continued. "Let me say at the outset, that these accusations against me are completely false. As you know, someone I had considered a friend and a pastor on our staff, Chip Masters, was arrested yesterday afternoon. And, I understand, found to be in possession of a gun police are saying was, most certainly, used to kill poor Myron Simpson many years ago. The story in the Gazette also reported that an as-of-yet-unnamed, key witness to this murder claims that I was the mastermind of that crime so many years ago, and the one who shot and killed Mr. Simpson. The charge is false and completely untrue. I can only assume the identity of this so-called key witness has to be a former friend of both Chip Masters and I back in high school, named Ray Dodson."

Several people in the crowd gasped when they heard this.

Joe almost did.

"Will you listen to this guy?" Kate said. "He just outed your witness, Joe."

"It saddens me," Burton said, "to think someone you considered to be a friend would betray you this way. I can only guess at his reasons, but I'm sure it has something to do with the fact that Myron Simpson's body was discovered recently in the woods, as many of you know. I have one more very important thing to say before I conclude my statement. And I'm not proud of this, but back in the days before I started serving God, I engaged in all kinds of activities I came to regret later. But they don't include robbery and murder. Sadly though, they do include hanging around with some friends who did. The truth is, Ray Dodson actually committed the very things he is accusing me of. And unfortunately, I have strong reasons to believe, my friend Chip Masters may have helped him commit these crimes. Around that time, my father's gun went missing. A few weeks after Myron disappeared, I saw Chip putting that gun back in my father's safe. When I asked him why he'd taken it, he gave me some reason that I decided to believe. I never knew that gun was connected to the murder of Myron Simpson until Chip was arrested with it yesterday. Of course, like you all, we were shocked to learn about this connection. Please join with all of us here on staff to pray for Chip and his family as they go through this ordeal in the days ahead. And we should even pray for Ray Dodson, as well. That's all I have to say. Thank you."

He stepped away from the mic and headed back into the church office, followed by his entourage.

Joe looked at Kate, who was already looking at him. "Can you believe this guy?" he said.

She just shook her head in disbelief. "Does he really think this is gonna work?"

"Of course, he does. He's been hatching this plan all morning. Maybe started on it last night. But it doesn't matter."

"Why?" Kate said.

"Because, this whole scheme is about to blow up in his face." He stood up. "Sorry, Kate. But I've gotta go down to the station. Take care of something.

"Go ahead. I'll be here when you're done."

Before Joe got the police station, he'd called Hank. After listening to Hank rant a while about what a snake Glenn Burton was, Joe shared with him his idea. Hank liked it and agreed to meet Joe in their interview room with Chip Masters.

When Joe walked into the room, Chip was sitting there

on one side of the table, Hank on the other. In between them, a laptop. Joe came in, closed the door. "So, Mr. Masters, can I assume you being locked up and all, you haven't had a chance to watch the local news."

"You assume correctly."

"Well, as you can imagine, the story of your arrest hasn't gone viral or anything, but it is making quite a splash in the local news and online media."

Chip made a face.

"In fact, your good friend, Glenn Burton, just got done doing a widely covered press conference where he made a statement about your arrest. Would you care to watch it?"

"I definitely would."

"Hank, could you oblige our guest?"

Hank refreshed the screen, already set to the link of Glenn Burton's press statement. Made sure the volume was way up. He and Joe watched and listened, more at Chip than what at Glenn had to say. Chip's face went from passive indifference, to slight concern, to grave concern, then something very close to fury and hatred.

"I can't believe it. I can't believe he'd do this to me."

"Talk about throwing a guy under the bus," Hank said.

"What a jerk," Chip said. "What a total jerk. After all I've done for the guy. Seriously, he'd be nowhere without me. He'd have nothing."

"You realize, Chip," Joe said, "he's leaving you hanging out there, high and dry. He's pinning it all on you and Ray and thinking he's gonna get off scot-free, while you guys spend the rest of your lives in prison."

"Well, I'm not putting up with it. This whole situation — I'm talkin', the robbery and murder — wouldn't even have happened if it weren't for Glenn. I would've never thought of it, and neither Ray or I even owned a gun. The whole thing was Glenn. What kind of things did Ray tell you?"

Joe spent the next ten minutes telling him.

"Well, listen. I'm not gonna say too much here till I talk with my attorney. But you guys get him in here and tell him what kind of a deal you're willing to make me, and I'll give you Glenn Burton's head on a silver platter. Because everything Ray told you is exactly how it went down."

49

Yesterday was a crazy day. Started off eating omelets and pancakes with Kate and the kids, ended up with everything on the case hitting the fan at one time.

After Glenn Burton's surprise press conference and Chip Masters' decision to fully cooperate after watching it, Joe and Hank had met with Ray Dodson at the DAs office. Before interviewing Ray, they'd showed him and DA Rucker the YouTube video of Glenn Burton's Oscar-worthy performance. Of course, Ray was just as angry at what he saw as Chip, and it only reinforced his commitment to do whatever it took to clear his name and get Glenn Burton behind bars, where he belonged.

Ray had been pleasantly surprised to learn Chip was now willing to plead guilty to the charges against him and, along with Ray, to testify against Glenn. Because of this, the danger for Ray had passed. Since Chip was willing to cooperate, he had no motivation to harm Ray for doing the same.

Beyond this, the DA assured Ray neither Chip nor Glenn Burton would be granted bail before the trial. Since Chip's testimony was that Glenn was the instigator in the plot to threaten Ray's life to get him to keep quiet.

After hearing Ray's testimony in full, the DA followed Hank and Joe back to Culpepper and met with Chip Masters to get his statement and negotiate his plea deal. Just as they were finishing up, Joe got a phone call from ballistics. Pendleton had called them the day before insisting they test the Bren Ten with the bullet recovered from Simpson's body ASAP.

No surprise here. It was a match.

The Bren Ten, which Glenn Burton had sold to Chip Masters twelve years ago, was the gun used to kill Myron Simpson back in December 1988. Joe was able to catch DA Rucker in the parking lot before he headed back to his office in Dunedin and give him the news.

"Okay, Joe," he'd said. "I've heard enough. Go get him." Referring to Glenn Burton.

But Joe knew he'd have to run all this by Captain Pendleton. Joe's preference would've been to arrest Burton right then, discreetly on Saturday night. Just him and Hank. But as expected, Pendleton wanted to take full advantage of the moment and, as he'd said, "prove to all the fine people here in Culpepper my very wise choice in establishing this top-notch Cold Case squad."

The last thing Joe had done that evening before heading home to cold leftovers was to phone Tom Hazelton at the Gazette and share all this with him. Hazelton was properly impressed with how the case had come together and Joe following through on his commitment to give him first dibs.

Joe told him he could print as much as he'd like, except the part about them arresting Glenn Burton the following morning. They didn't want to take the chance that Glenn would flee when he realized what was coming.

Of course, if Tom wanted to write the whole story up and be ready to upload it a few seconds after they took Burton into custody, Joe was fine with that.

The next morning, Joe and Hank met at the station, as agreed, at 9 AM to drive together to Victorious Life Church and arrest the Rev. Glenn Burton. When they got to the church parking lot, it was kind of a madhouse. The first service was letting out as the folks wanting to get a good seat for the second were coming in. Then on the edges of the parking lot, Hank and Joe saw vans from every local news group between there and Atlanta. Reporters and cameras had already lined up close to the church office building, where Joe had told Tom Hazelton they'd be arresting Glenn.

"Looks like Tom got the word out," Joe said.

"He sure did," Hank said. "Checked the usual social media sites this morning at breakfast. He posted his article about yesterday's events last night and promised big news would be announced at the church facility this morning. Tons of people were talking it up."

Seeing the scene unfold through his windshield mostly saddened Joe. Not a good day for the church. This church — and by association — many other churches, too. But it had to be done. In the long run, the cause of Christ would be better served with one less wolf in sheep's clothing preying on the flock. As they neared the front, someone was backing out just in time.

"Let's do this," Hank said.

They got out of the car and headed for the front doors. Some of the local news people recognized Joe and started hammering him with questions.

"Any comment on Chip Masters changing his plea to guilty?"

"Is it true, Lieutenant, that you have the murder weapon? That the gun once belonged to Pastor Burton?"

"Are you here to arrest Glenn Burton?"

"We'll be holding a press conference back at the station two hours from now," Joe said. "No other comments until then. Now please excuse us. We have a job to do."

They reached the front door of the office building. A confused-looking young man in a suit let them in, identified himself as a youth pastor. "Can I help you gentlemen? Do you know what's going on out there? I'm getting all kinds of crazy questions."

Joe showed the young man his ID. "I'm Lieutenant Boyd. This is Detective Hank Jensen. Know where we can find your senior pastor, Glenn Burton?"

"Uh...yeah, I guess. It's in between services, so he's probably in the Green Room, praying or resting."

"We need to see him now," Hank said. "Can you take us to him?"

"Sure, follow me."

They wandered through some back hallways. There were plenty of young people and musicians standing or walking around, who all seemed to know their guide. They'd smile and greet him then look perplexed when they saw Joe and Hank behind him.

"You sending out negative vibes, Hank?" Joe said.

"Must be."

"The Green Room's right here," the young man said. He opened the door.

It was like a large, plush living room with big comfy chairs and couches placed around the perimeter. At the far end, was a stainless steel fridge next to a row of cabinets. Only a handful of people were in the room and all but one of them stopped whatever they were doing or saying and looked at Joe and Hank.

The one man who didn't look their way was sitting in an over-stuffed recliner, fully extended, his eyes closed.

Seeing this, the young man said, "Could we come back in a few minutes? That might be better."

"No, we can't," Hank said. He and Joe walked right up to Glenn Burton in the recliner.

Joe noticed it was electric. He bent over and pressed the down button. The recliner began contracting, startling Burton.

He sat up. "What's going on here?" He looked up at Joe and Hank.

"Get up, sir," Joe said. "Glenn Burton, you're under arrest for the robbery and murder of Myron Simpson, as well as a number of other charges."

"What? This is outrageous!" He looked around to catch the look on the faces of his staff. "You can't come in here like this."

"Uh...afraid we can, and we did," Joe said. "Now, get up and turn around."

He sat up straight but didn't leave the recliner. "I'm no murderer. I'm a man of God. This is a house of worship, for crying out loud."

Joe read him his Miranda rights, then said, "I get you

wanna make a good show for your folks, but you might wanna reconsider that right to remain silent."

"I will not remain silent. I haven't done anything wrong."

"We beg to differ," Joe said. "You going to stand up, or do you want Hank and I to make a scene here?"

He sighed, shook his head in resignation and got up. He turned around and allowed Hank to put him in cuffs, muttering, "This is totally ridiculous."

"Pastor," a guy in a suit said, "we're totally with you. This attack on our church won't stand."

"No one's attacking your church," Hank said.

Joe looked at the man. "The truth is, we're actually sorry to be coming here like this. But you'll find out very soon, he's not the man you think he is."

"Don't listen to him, Jed," Burton said to the man. "This whole thing will get sorted out very soon. Just keep praying."

As they led Burton out of the room and down the hall, Hank said, "I don't get it. I didn't see a single green thing in that room."

As they walked through the halls, they were met by a regular barrage of stares and either angry or fearful expressions. Half the people said nothing. The other half shouted out words of support and allegiance to Glenn. He responded with things like, "Pray for me, folks. Everything's going to be just fine. Don't worry."

When they got outside, the chaos began. Everyone was filming the scene. The journalists with their cameras, everyone else with their phones. The questions started coming at them, and at Burton, at a relentless pace. Joe and Hank just walked in silence until they reached the car. Burton kept repeating various phrases declaring his innocence.

Hank put him in the backseat. Joe got in, turned on the car and down the road they went. A few blocks away, he glanced at Burton in the rearview mirror. His entire expression had changed, now that there was no one left to impress. He stared out the window, a blank look on his face.

What a shame, Joe thought. He could be sitting in church right now with Kate hearing a great message from a real man of God. Instead, he was stuck in the car with this guy; a real shyster, clueless about all the lives he'd ruined with his lifetime of schemes.

Joe said a short, silent prayer for all the poor souls taken in by these two men at that church all these years. Prayed they wouldn't get so bitter they'd give up on church altogether but let the Good Shepherd heal their hearts and lead them to greener pastures. To a real church. A legit church.

The kind that would pass his pastor Ed's smell test.

EPILOGUE

Over the Next 5 Days

Although some of the excitement generated by the events last week had begun to ease, a number of significant things were still underway. The biggest ones weren't just surrounding the arrest of Glenn Burton and Chip Masters, but the even more shocking news that occurred two days later.

Glenn Burton committed suicide in his cell.

On the second morning of his incarceration, a guard found him hanging from a makeshift noose made from his bedsheets. Nothing he had said after his arrest gave any hint to indicate he might harm himself, so he wasn't ever put on any suicide watch. Even his attorney said Glenn seemed fully prepared to fight these charges and do whatever it took to clear his name.

Joe and Hank talked about it and figured once he'd heard

how solid the case against him was, including both Ray and Chip testifying against him, and coupled with the notion of being publicly recast as a complete hypocrite, he simply couldn't face it.

Oddly enough, because Burton was no longer around to contest the charges, and Chip had already agreed to plead guilty, they wouldn't need Ray Dodson to testify at a trial. He was a free man, released to return to his wife and family and his restoration business in Charleston.

But before he left town, he asked for Joe's help in facing up to one thing he still felt totally responsible for making things right with Myron Simpson's mother. Joe had mentioned in a conversation with Ray that he had spoken to her recently. Ray was planning on driving to wherever she lived to apologize and ask her forgiveness in person. Joe suggested, and later confirmed, that she would actually prefer talking to him through a video chat.

So, Joe set it up and sat next to Ray during his exchange with Myron's mother. Before Ray spoke, now that Joe fully understood the scenario of events on the night Myron died, Joe went over those with her. He was happy to confirm, based on the things that both Ray and Chip had said, her son was killed instantly when the gun went off, and that the shooting itself was never part of the plan. The boys brought what they thought was an empty gun to the store, never realizing a lethal bullet was still lodged in the chamber. Myron's mother seemed to take comfort learning that her son was not shot by ruthless killers.

After talking about these things, Joe moved the phone so that Ray could speak with her, face-to-face. Seeing her like that — even though it was only on video — overwhelmed Ray. He could barely get through his apology through all his tears. But he pressed on, expressing not only his regret for having anything to do with the events of that terrible night, but even more importantly, for his cowardice in not coming forward right after it happened, so that she and her family wouldn't have spent all those torturous years never knowing what had happened to their son and brother.

Joe was not at all surprised when Myron's mother — through her own set of tears — completely forgave Ray. She even thanked him for the courage it took to finally come forward to tell the truth. Joe got choked up later that night when he related this experience to Kate over coffee after dinner.

Another interesting thing happened the day after this, when Joe called Lisa and Melissa — the two women from the writers' group — to thank them for their help solving this thirty-year-old case. Melissa was especially helpful, so his conversation with her went a little longer. He also wanted to know how she and her husband, Cliff, were doing, considering their senior pastor and his associate turned out to be criminals. "I hope you guys don't give up on church altogether, because of this," he'd said to Melissa.

"Oh, no," was her reply. "There's no chance of that. In fact, Cliff said last night we should go back to our old church, the one we were attending for years before we joined Glenn's church. Cliff said their old pastor wasn't as flashy a speaker as Glenn, but that he was pretty sure Ed had never killed anyone." Turned out, their old pastor was Ed, Joe's pastor now, and their old church the church he, Kate, and the kids were going to now. Joe told

Melissa to tell Cliff he knew for a fact that Ed had never been a killer.

That same day, Joe had also decided to drive by Andrew Tubbs' mobile home, check in on him. They'd been a little hard on him, trying to force him to cooperate with their investigation. And Joe realized, Tubbs' main reason for not helping him was fear of retaliation from Chip Masters. As Joe walked up to Tubbs' trailer, he heard Tubbs talking with Percy, his parrot. "Okay, Percy. Today's a new day. Nothing can stop me now. Gonna start working on my new true crime book today. I've had a front row seat to the whole thing. And I even got this brand-new Mac laptop out of the deal." Joe was half-tempted to just get back in his car and leave. Clearly, Tubbs was doing fine. But he still knocked, chatted with him a few moments, made sure he knew they understood why he wasn't more helpful. They shook hands, then Joe left.

The last big thing that happened — well, sort of big thing — was a chat he and Hank had with Captain Pendleton, after Pendleton's press conference. During that event, Pendleton spent a good deal of time highlighting the magnificent skill and expertise displayed by his "crack cold case squad," in bringing these killers to justice and solving this long-standing mystery. The best part was, he didn't just talk about Joe. He mentioned Hank, too, then later said, from here on out he would consider Hank to be almost on equal footing with Joe.

Just before Joe left that meeting, Pendleton had pulled him aside and told him: "I know I almost ruined your camping trip with Kate and the kids when this murder case turned up, but since you and Hank have handled this so well, and put another feather in my cap, how about you take the next five days off on me. Leave your phone home. Anything comes up, Hank'll handle it."

Joe couldn't believe it. On the way home, he knew exactly how he would spend this unexpected surprise.

THE NEXT DAY, after confirming Jack and Rachel could watch the kids, Joe had Kate pack them a couple of bags with instructions for everything to be casual, except for one fancy dress for her, and one decent suit for him. He went online, made the reservations, then drove the four hours to their destination without telling Kate where they were going.

She started figuring it out when she saw the highway signs to Charleston. But he told her, "You aren't gonna believe how nice a place we'll be staying in, and when you see it, don't ask how much money I spent. It's a historic bed-and-breakfast right in the heart of town. We'll be touring historic old houses, taking slow walks through a crazy-nice shopping and Market area—"

"Did you say a *slow* walk?"

"Yes, a slow walk...let me finish...riding in horse-drawn carriages, wandering around beautiful plantations, eating some amazing southern cuisine —"

"Wait, did you just use the word *cuisine* in a sentence?"

"Yes, I did. That's the word they used on the website."

"And to what do I owe all this fancy, romantic treatment? I'm not complaining. I'm just curious."

"I'm making up for the fact that I was working during our fifteenth anniversary a few months ago. That's not the kind of anniversary a wife should get a card and a box of chocolates. When Hank and I came here last week, I knew I had to bring you back first chance I got."

She leaned over and kissed him on the cheek, then said, "You worked through our fifteenth, our twelfth, and our ninth anniversaries. Not that I'm counting. But I have a feeling...with this trip, you might just wipe the slate clean."

WANT TO READ MORE?

If you haven't read any of Dan's other suspense novels, you'll be happy to learn *An Inconvenient Death* is actually Book 2 of the Joe Boyd Suspense series. The first book is, *If These Walls Could Talk*. We're sure you'd enjoy it, even if read them out of order. Here's the Link:

https://amzn.to/2XDJfOi

If you have read Book 1, maybe you weren't aware the Joe Boyd series is a "**Sequel Series**" to Dan's bestselling 4-Book *Jack Turner Suspense Series*. The events and mysteries unfolding in those 4 books take place a few years prior to this book and include many of the same characters and places.

All of Dan's 21 other novels are similar in genre and style to *An Inconvenient Death*. Except half of them (including his 5 Christmas novels) feature more heart-impacting, spiritual themes, and some have a stronger romantic thread.

As of now, Dan's novels combined have received over 9,000 Amazon reviews (maintaining a 4.6 Star average). They've won multiple national awards and received rave reviews from publications like USA Today, Publisher's Weekly, Library Journal and RT Book Reviews magazine.

Here are some quick links to a few of *Dan's other novels*:

The Jack Turner Suspense Series (*over 1,800 Amazon Reviews, 4.6 Star Avg***)**

- When Night Comes - http://amzn.to/1xNat4G
- Remembering Dresden - http://amzn.to/1RO7WvN
- Unintended Consequences - http://amzn.to/2pvSvmG
- Perilous Treasure - https://amzn.to/2HOgpl7

The Forever Home Series (*Dog Rescue Series - over 1,800 Amazon Reviews, 4.8 Star avg***)**

- Rescuing Finley – http://amzn.to/1Hnovrg
- Finding Riley - http://amzn.to/2c7xdWY
- Saving Parker - http://amzn.to/2g9vKkA

You can check out all of Dan's other novels by going to his Author Book Page on Amazon. Here's the link:

http://amzn.to/2cG5I9o

WANT TO HELP THE AUTHOR?

If you enjoyed reading *An Inconvenient Death*, the best thing you can do to help Dan is very simple—*tell others about it.* Word-of-mouth "advertising" is the most powerful marketing tool there is. Better than expensive TV commercials or full-page magazine ads.

Leaving good reviews is the best way to insure Dan will be able to keep writing novels full time. He'd greatly appreciate it if you'd consider leaving a rating for the book and writing a brief review. Doesn't have to be long (even a sentence or two will help).

Here's the Amazon link for the book. Scroll down a little to the area that says "**Customer Reviews**," right beside the graphic that shows the number of stars is a box and says: "**Write a Customer Review.**"

https://amzn.to/2PfRZaJ

If you'd like to contact Dan, feel free to email him at dan@danwalshbooks.com. He loves to get reader emails and reads all of them himself.

SIGN UP TO RECEIVE DAN'S NEWSLETTER

If you'd like to get an email alert whenever Dan has a new book coming out or when a special deal is being offered on any of Dan's existing books, click on his website link below and sign up for his newsletter (it's right below the Welcome paragraph). Also, **every first-time member can choose to receive one of Dan's bestselling novels for FREE** (see the Tab for the Free Book in the Menu).

From his homepage, you can also contact Dan or follow him on Facebook, Twitter or Goodreads.

www.danwalshbooks.com

AUTHOR'S NOTE

I want to thank Eva Marie Everson, the president of Word Weavers International, for her permission to feature this excellent writers' critique group in my novel. You may recall the characters Lisa and Melissa, the two women who attend this writer's group and actually wind up helping Joe Boyd solve this murder.

Although the Culpepper Group I wrote about is fictional, there are REAL Word Weaver chapters all over the US (I belong to one). Go to this link to find out more about them:

https://word-weavers.com

ACKNOWLEDGMENTS

There is really just one person I absolutely must thank for helping to get *An Inconvenient Death* into print. That's my wife, Cindi. Her editorial advice and input on this book was indispensable.

I also want to thank my proofreading team: Patricia Keough-Wilson, Debbie Mahle, Jann Martin, Terri Smith and Rachel Savage for catching so many things we missed.

Dan Walsh

ABOUT THE AUTHOR

Dan was born in Philadelphia in 1957. His family moved down to Daytona Beach, Florida in 1965, when his father began to work with GE on the Apollo space program. That's where Dan grew up.

He married Cindi, the love of his life in 1976. They have 2 grown children and 4 grandchildren. Dan served as a pastor for 25 years then began writing fiction full-time in 2010. His bestselling novels have won numerous awards, including 3 ACFW Carol Awards (he was a finalist 6 times) and 4 Selah Awards. Four of Dan's novels were finalists for RT Reviews' Inspirational Book of the Year. One of his novels, *The Reunion*, is being made into a major full-length feature film (written and directed by Oscar-winning screenwriter, Nick Vallelonga).